X.I.A.

X.I.A.

Book Three
Xenofreak Nation

by Melissa Conway

This is a work of fiction. Names, characters, businesses, organizations,
places, events and incidents are the product of the author's imagination
or are used fictitiously. Any resemblance to actual persons, living or
dead, is coincidental.

Chapter One

Wailing sirens and mysterious booming, banging and popping noises woke Bryn throughout the night, but only briefly. The frightening sounds of unrest spreading across New York City were too far away to fully jolt her from her much-needed slumber.

Until a woman screamed.

Bryn bolted upright in Scott's bed and looked to the window as shrieks echoed up from the street. The blinds were closed, but a faint orange glow flickered along the wall between the top of the window and the ceiling.

She reached for Scott, but he was gone. It was still dark, but something told her morning was near. After struggling from under the tangled bedcovers, she went to the window, pinching one of the slats and lifting it to peer into the night. Outside Scott's fourth-floor apartment, across the gap provided by a narrow two-lane road, was the beige brick façade of another apartment building. It would have been an unremarkable view if it weren't for the black smoke pouring from two shattered windows on the second floor, and the flames that boiled out in great rolling waves.

The screaming had stopped, and Bryn listened for sirens that didn't come. It was chilly by the window, and there were droplets on the glass. She looked down at the wet black street and saw a group of people gathered near the intersection under a streetlamp. Someone had climbed one of the bare-branched old trees lining the sidewalk and was straddling the thickest branch. At first, she thought they were merely bystanders watching the conflagration grow, but then, quite inexplicably, one of them rose up into the air directly beneath the tree, his legs kicking out spasmodically.

The screaming began again, accompanied by shouts. Horrified, Bryn's breath caught in her throat. She could see them now, six men hauling on the length of rope strung over the tree branch, like tug of war contestants at a picnic. A woman, probably the one doing the screaming, was punching and kicking at them ineffectually. The crowd was an old-fashioned lynch

1

mob, and the man whose neck was in the noose was slowly strangling to death.

With no warning, a shot rang out, and the hanging man dropped to the ground, somehow landing on his feet. Bryn couldn't see well enough from her vantage point to tell whether the rope had been severed by the bullet or if the men had released it. The woman shoved her way through the crowd, and no one stopped her. Bryn realized why when Scott appeared from the shadows, bearing down on the crowd, gun arm extended out in front of him.

"Oh, no..." she murmured.

There were at least twenty riled up people out there, all facing one man with a gun. Bryn heard raised voices but couldn't make out what anyone was saying.

Her attention was briefly pulled back to the fire as a dull concussive blast rained glass onto the empty street below. The flames had spread to another apartment and several more windows had blown out from the explosion.

Was that a siren? She hoped so. Maybe the mob would disperse if they thought reinforcements were coming.

But they didn't look like they were leaving, and in a flash, it occurred to her why. The man they'd tried to hang was a xenofreak - but so was Scott. He would tell them he was a cop, but they would see his xenoalterations and wouldn't believe him. They were functioning under the influence of a powerful cocktail of fear and anger, and as Scott continued to hold them off without firing, they were gaining confidence. He couldn't possibly shoot them all.

Bryn stepped back from the window and looked desperately around the room. Her holophone was long gone, and Scott's was missing from the bedside table. She ran into the living room, switched on the overhead light, and went straight for the closet by the door. Earlier, he'd removed his bulletproof vest and hung it there, and she'd watched while he emptied his pockets of bullet clips and miscellaneous gear. He'd hung his gun in its holster on a hook. That was no longer there, but she'd also seen him unfasten an ankle holster and place it on the top shelf.

She stood on her tiptoes and felt around for it, encountering an object with her fingers. She nudged it off the shelf and caught it as it fell. It was a small caliber pistol, much like the one Carla had owned and Bryn had never learned to shoot. She knew enough to tell that the little gun was loaded, though, and she took a few precious seconds to hold the gun up to the light to check that the safety wasn't on.

2

Without pausing to look for a jacket, she left the apartment and ran barefoot to the stairwell, wearing only sweatpants and a baggy t-shirt. Her feet were nearly numb from contact with the cold concrete steps by the time she reached the bottom. She opened the door and ran through the lobby; but she was neither frightened nor foolish enough to burst out onto the street brandishing the gun. Instead, she slipped outside and walked quickly towards the commotion.

The crowd had swelled as people evacuated the burning building. It looked to Bryn like some of the lynch mob were trying to blend in with the newcomers in an attempt to disassociate themselves. But there were still several trying to intimidate Scott into backing down.

The man Scott had saved was standing next to him in the middle of the street, holding the rope coiled in one hand. The woman who'd been screaming clung to the man's arm, trying to pull him away. But whoever he was, he apparently wasn't going to abandon Scott, who spoke to the crowd in a calm tone.

As Bryn got closer, she made out his words. "There are cameras everywhere these days," he said. "You may think you can get away with committing a crime when everyone around you is doing the same, but you will eventually be identified and prosecuted."

The closest person, a tall bearded man whose hair looked red in the light from the fire, spat on the ground at Scott's feet. "My cousin *died* from the disease scum like you are spreading!"

Another man stepped forward, gesticulating wildly. "My sister's family had to abandon their home to the xenofreaks on Coney Island. They burned it to the ground! Just like that!" He pointed to the burning building, which radiated warmth that kept Bryn from freezing in the cold air.

"We had nothing to do with any of that!" the woman yelled. The man who'd been hanged looked like he wanted to say something, too, but he held a hand to his throat as if he couldn't talk.

Several people from the crowd began shouting, trying to talk over each other. Bryn stayed back, standing on a discarded piece of cardboard to protect her feet from the frozen sidewalk. She concealed the gun under the front of her t-shirt, deciding if she was going to shoot anyone, it would be the bearded man, who seemed to be lynch mob's ringleader. Without their leader inciting them, maybe Scott would get out of this alive.

Just when she thought the entire block might break out into violence, red and white flashing lights from down the street heralded a police vehicle. The bearded man sneered and turned, quickly disappearing into the crowd. Bryn exhaled in relief as several more men decided retreat would be prudent. She expected the man who'd been attacked to welcome the police, but he, too, made a hasty retreat, dragging the woman along with him.

Scott tucked his weapon into the pocket of his leather jacket and walked back across the street. He was still wearing the eye patch and almost passed by without seeing her.

"Hey," she said.

His head jerked around. "What are you doing out here?" He looked her up and down and shrugged out of his jacket to lay it over her shoulders. "It's dangerous."

"No kidding," she replied, falling into step next to him. The police car pulled over to let a fire truck through, and two firemen immediately began unrolling a hose from the side of the truck.

"Are you barefoot?" Scott asked. Without waiting for her response, he swept her up into his arms.

"I can walk." It was a weak protest because she was secretly glad to get her frozen feet off the ground.

When he saw the little gun in her hand, he rolled his eyes and muttered, "What am I going to do with you?"

He carried her all the way to the entrance of his building before she convinced him to let her walk the rest of the way. When they left the stairwell and entered the fourth-floor hallway, he held out an arm to stop her. Beyond his shoulder, she saw a dark-clothed figure sitting cross-legged in front of his door.

Bryn squinted in the dim light of the hallway. "Is that...Mia?"

Hearing her name, Mia turned towards them, and then scrambled to her feet as they approached.

Scott looked into her pale face. "Is it Alton?"

She closed her eyes briefly. "No. Can I come in?"

Scott shrugged and glanced at Bryn. "Sure."

When they were all inside, Mia said, "I apologize for showing up here like this, but I didn't really know what else to do." Her voice cracked on the last few words, as if she was fighting back tears.

Mia was petite, but Bryn knew she was tough as nails. Even though her erratic behavior seemed to be fueled by something more than exhaustion, Bryn asked, "Have you slept at all?"

"No. I've been running back and forth between the hospital, the morgue and the lab."

"You want something to drink?" Scott made a move for the kitchen, but she grabbed his arm, another unusual move for the germophobic doctor.

"I need your help. And I need it fast."

"Yeah, okay. What is it?"

4

Then she said quite possibly the last thing Bryn expected. "I need to get a xenograft."

Chapter Two

Scott tried to enter his apartment quietly, but he'd overloaded himself. In order to balance the cardboard drink carrier and open the door, he had to set the paper bag of bagels on the ground, which made the backpack he'd slung over his shoulder swing forward and bang into the doorknob. The keys rattled and he sucked air through his teeth as the weight of the backpack stretched the wounds on his back.

The door creaked open and Bryn appeared with her finger to her lips. She snatched up the paper bag and took the backpack from him, whispering, "What are you doing? You should have made two trips or called me to help you."

He had no logical excuse other than not wanting to bother her. "I picked up some clothes and shoes for you from Carla's and got breakfast from the corner deli."

"They're open?" she asked, shooting a glance over at the couch, where Mia still slept.

He set the drinks on the kitchen counter. "Yeah, I was surprised, too. They didn't have very many customers, but some of these small business owners can't afford to shut down for even one day."

She looked inside the paper bag and helped herself to a bagel. "Real food! Thank you. How is it out there? And how come you don't have a holovision?"

He leaned a hip against the cupboard and sipped from one of the coffee cups, relishing the hot liquid even as it burned his tongue. "I'm not home often enough to watch anything. And it's quiet so far today. Rioters gotta sleep, too, I guess. If you want to look at the news, you can use my holophone."

He handed it to her. It was a replacement phone just issued to him last night when they'd stopped by headquarters to pick up his motorcycle. The supply clerk had been snippy with him, as if the cost of all the phones Scott had gone through lately had come out of the clerk's own pocket. The munitions clerk, though, had been cool about assigning him a new gun. She'd only said, "You must be pretty special to get authorization without having to do the screenwork."

"I only dodged that bullet temporarily," he'd replied. Once the riots were over and things settled down, he expected to be buried in reports.

Bryn took the phone from him but didn't turn it on. She looked over at Mia, an unmoving lump under Scott's one and only spare blanket. "Did you find a place?"

He shrugged and then winced at the resulting twinge of pain. "Of course." If anyone could find a clean, safe place for a person to get a xenograft, it was an XIA agent. He'd simply used his new holophone to access the agency's database of all known xenosurgeons in the New York area.

She put a hand to his face and gently adjusted his eye patch. "So, did you have to make an appointment, or...?"

"Oh, yeah, the receptionist was very nice."

"You're mocking me, aren't you?"

He grinned. "A little."

"Well, what do I tell her when she wakes up? You've got to go to work, right? I mean, this isn't exactly XIA business and she's going to need someone to help her."

"I already sent the location of the xenograft den to her new phone." Mia's phone had been confiscated when Maddy Singh kidnapped her, but she'd managed to replace it. "Let her sleep 'til ten or so. The place doesn't open until eleven anyway. She can get a small graft with a local anesthetic and be out of there in a couple hours. *You* are going to stay in this apartment where it's safe, got that?"

Bryn's eyebrows lifted. "Uh, care to rephrase that?"

He sighed and grabbed her around the waist, careful not to prick her with his claws. "Bryn...babycakes..."

Her face lit up and she giggled but sobered all too quickly. "Don't worry. The last thing I want to do is go anywhere."

He felt a pang of guilt when the light in her eyes dimmed. She been through hell the last few days and he wished he could hole up in the apartment with her for a week and make her feel safe again.

The holophone in her hand buzzed, startling them both. She passed it back to him and he wasn't surprised to see Shasta's stern face.

"Good morning, Agent Harding. I trust you slept well?"

He laughed a little, thinking of the many times he'd been jolted awake the night before. "Sure. Let's go with that."

"Silicon earplugs," she said.

7

"What?"

"Like the kind you wear for target practice. Blocks out the sirens."

"Oh, right. Well, if I'd been wearing them, I wouldn't have noticed the building across the street burning down or that attempted lynching on the corner."

Shasta frowned. "Unfortunately, that's par for the course for the five boroughs at the moment, not to mention several other major cities – and not just in the US."

"It seems to have calmed down some," he said.

"They'll get their second wind. In the meantime, I've partnered you with Lo while Alton and Boardman are recuperating." Her eyes narrowed as she studied his holo from her end. "Are you up to it? Field work, I mean."

Scott had gone AWOL from the hospital and she knew it, so he figured her display of concern was a formality. His doctor had advised him to take two weeks off, but the XIA needed him now, even if he wasn't exactly hale and hearty. The hospital had given him a bottle of a strong enough painkiller to take the edge off his injuries without making him loopy, though, so he said, "Yes, ma'am."

"Good. The riots are being fueled by interweb speculation and our analysts detected a disturbing pattern in the socialnet – someone named 'Savvy' has been jacking Orbweaver accounts and sending inflammatory messages to everyone in the victims' contact lists. Now, that wouldn't tend to get our guys' attention except the content of the messages suggest they're originating from someone with specific inside knowledge of Fournier's involvement."

"Padme?" he asked.

"Not likely. Maddy Singh won't want to aggravate Fournier at this point. We do have the jacker's general location – he's using a public wifi holospot, so it shouldn't be too hard to identify him. I sent you the info. You and Lo go check it out."

"Got it."

"I'm with Unger all day, we just landed in DC. I won't be able to answer my holophone, but I expect you to text me any updates."

"Is he still testifying?" A congressional subcommittee had been formed not long after Bryn's father had her kidnapped and xenografted by Dr. Nicolas Fournier. Ironically, the reason her father had colluded with Fournier in the first place was to force the government to regulate the practice of xenoalteration. Unger, the Deputy Director of the XIA, had been testifying at a policy hearing for days.

"Yes, and it's not going well." Shasta didn't elaborate. "Be careful out there, Agent Harding."

"Yes, ma'am."

Shasta disconnected, and Scott accessed his messages, clicking on the holomap link she'd sent him. When the map popped up, he and Bryn looked at each other in surprise.

The holospot was located in a café on the first floor of an office building two blocks north of where the Warehouse once stood.

Chapter Three

"Hey, wake up."

Bryn gently shook Mia's shoulder. It was nine o'clock in the morning, but even though Scott wanted Bryn to let her sleep in, Mia had cried out in her sleep and was clearly having a nightmare.

Mia's eyelids opened and when her unfocused gaze took in Bryn's form hovering over her, she recoiled against the cushions in fear, no recognition in her dark brown eyes.

"It's me, Bryn. You're having a bad dream."

The terror slowly faded from Mia's face. She let out a shuddering breath and closed her eyes again. Bryn started to back away, but Mia said, "Where's Scott?"

"He had to work, but he sent you the info."

Mia pushed the blanket aside and sat up. The scrunchie holding her long black hair back had slipped down, so she pulled it off and redid the ponytail. Bryn felt a pang of envy when the silky strands fell into place without so much as a combing. Even before the quills, Bryn's hair had looked like a bird's nest in the morning.

"He brought bagels and coffee, but it's cold now," she said. "I can wave it for you."

"Cold's fine." Mia reached for her purse and took her holophone out of a side pocket.

Bryn brought her the bag of bagels and a cup of coffee and watched in silence as Mia wolfed down her breakfast while reading whatever Scott had sent her.

She heard a low rumble coming from outside that increased in volume, like long, rolling thunder. She went to the window and peeked out the blinds. Below, a military tank was lumbering up the center of the street. In the light of day, she saw the building across from them had scorch marks trailing up the facade, and one corner of the second floor had been gutted.

"The city's locked down," Mia muttered, shaking her head at her phone. "How am I supposed to come up with ten thousand dollars cash?"

Bryn dropped the slat and suggested, "Leave the city?"

Mia didn't respond. She tapped at her holophone and set it on the cushion next to her while she pulled on her boots. The holo of an automaton dressed as a nurse appeared and said, "The patient you are attempting to reach is unavailable right now. Please leave a message-"

Mia grabbed the phone and disconnected. "Have you heard anything about Jason?"

Bryn shrugged. The last she'd heard, he was recovering from an arthroscopic operation to repair a broken rib that had collapsed his lung. "Not today."

A loud thud came from the hallway beyond the front door, followed by running footsteps. Whoever it was began to bang on something, presumably another door, calling out, "Craig! It's me, open the door!"

Bryn exchanged a glance with Mia and went to the door to look out the peephole.

A guy in a black hoodie stood across the hall, his hands flat against the neighbor's door.

"Lemme in, man!" He looked down the hallway and even through the fisheye distortion of the peephole, she saw the panic on his face. He shot off in the opposite direction and a moment later she heard multiple footfalls. Several figures ran past. One of them held a baseball bat.

Bryn backed away from the door. "They're chasing him. Should we call 911?"

"And tell them what?" Mia asked. "Probably get a busy signal anyways."

Bryn knew she was right, but the response seemed wrong coming from the woman who'd defiantly told Maddy Singh, "I'm a doctor; I can't walk away from someone who needs help."

From the hallway, a man yelled, "Come out, come out, wherever you are!" The menacing glee in his voice gave Bryn the chills. She went to the closet to search for Scott's backup gun, but he must have taken it with him.

She was afraid to look through the peephole in case the men in the hallway could see her eye, but she also couldn't just stand around doing nothing. With trepidation, she tiptoed back to the door just in time to see a large man slam his shoulder against the neighbor's door. He was joined by another man and together they kicked and kicked until the doorframe splintered.

Mia whispered, "What's happening?"

Bryn shot her a warning look and shook her head. The men rushed into the apartment and from the sound of it, began tossing things around. No one cried out for help, so she hoped whoever lived there wasn't home.

She relaxed a bit, thinking since the men didn't find their quarry, they would move on, but then the big man came back out into the hallway and turned his determined gaze towards Scott's door.

"Oh, no," she breathed, backing away.

"I know you're in there, xenoscum!" the man called.

Bryn swallowed spasmodically. Scott had a sturdy bolt lock, but the neighbor's doorframe had buckled with only a few kicks.

Mia got off the couch and rushed over. She stood in front of the door and began coughing loudly, like she was hacking up a lung. In the current climate of paranoia, the implication was clear: this was a sick house.

Then in a voice that shook querulously like an old woman, Mia asked, "Who is it?"

Bryn heard the men arguing amongst themselves in furious whispers. She took a chance and peeked out. Two of the men were walking away, not willing to take the chance, but the big man and his friend with the baseball bat stood facing Scott's door stubbornly.

The first kick took her by surprise, and she sprang back from the door. Mia darted into the kitchen after the second kick and opened a drawer, pulling out a steak knife. Bryn ran to the couch as the men continued their assault on the door. She picked up Mia's holophone and whispered, "What's the passcode?" Mia told her, and she entered it before accessing the camera feature. When the doorframe finally buckled and the men shoved their way inside, Bryn held up the holophone in a desperate gambit and took their picture with a bright flash. She tapped at the screen and said, "There! Sent! You won't get away with this!"

The men were dressed alike in heavy plaid shirts, dirty jeans and scuffed work boots as if they'd come straight from a construction site. Even from ten feet away, Bryn smelled the stale alcohol wafting off them.

The younger one pointed at Bryn with the baseball bat. "I know you."

"You know who I am, but you don't know me," she replied. "Now get out."

The older man swung his head around to look at Mia. "I knew you was fakin' it. You ain't no sick old lady."

"I'm also not a xeno," Mia said.

A spark of interest appeared in the man's eyes. "Prove it."

Bryn knew what he meant. He might as well have said, "Strip."

12

While the men were distracted watching Mia to see how she would react, Bryn took a chance and dialed 911. To her chagrin, the holo of an automaton dressed in a police uniform popped up and said, "Emergency Services are overwhelmed with calls at the moment. Please leave a detailed message with your location and the nature of the emergency…"

As the message feature activated with a beep, the younger man stomped over and lifted the bat. Bryn pressed 'end' before he could smash it out of her hands. He held the bat suspended over his shoulder, rotating it like he was debating whether to hit her anyway.

"Why didn't you get it taken off?" He looked at her quills, upper lip lifted in disgust.

Bryn didn't think there was anything she could say to save herself, but she tried honesty. "The surgeons couldn't remove it because of the nanoneurons. They were afraid it would kill me."

He snorted. "So? I'd rather be dead."

For a moment, it looked like he was going to swing the bat and 'solve' Bryn's problem for her, but Mia stopped him by saying, "The man you're looking for is in the bedroom. He asked us to hide him, but we don't want any trouble."

Mia may not have convinced the big man with her sick old lady routine, but this time he smiled and started for the bedroom door. "That's more like it."

The last thing Bryn expected was for the man with the bat to follow his friend into the bedroom, but he did, leaving Bryn and Mia alone. They didn't stand around waiting to see what would happen – Bryn grabbed Mia's purse from the coffee table, and they bolted out the front door.

Chapter Four

Scott found Tina Lo waiting for him at headquarters.

"How you feeling?" she asked.

"I'm good. You?"

"Still sore, but the doc cleared me for duty, which doesn't necessarily mean I'm *fit* for duty."

Scott nodded in understanding. The XIA had been forced to test all of its employees to ensure none of them were carriers of the super typhoid. Calling in sick for anything else was not an option.

They geared up and took Lo's assigned car. She wanted to stake out the café where the messages from the jacker named 'Savvy' had come from, but Scott convinced her the proximity to the Warehouse was too much of a coincidence to be ignored.

He hadn't been to the neighborhood since the day the Warehouse burned to the ground. Whatever remained of the structure after the fire had been bulldozed into a big jagged pile, and the old chain link fence had been replaced. Despite the new fence and the off-putting heap of jagged refuse, it seemed the homeless had not been entirely discouraged from inhabiting the place. A few tents had been set up on the dirt-covered concrete slab, but it was apparent the bulk of the Warehouse's formerly bustling xenofreak presence had moved on.

Lo parked by an opening someone had cut in the fence and they got out of the sedan. It was another clear day, a bit warmer than yesterday, but still chilly.

"What's that smell?" she asked, putting a hand to her nose.

He smiled, remembering when Bryn had asked him the same thing and he'd told her, "That's just us xenofreaks."

"They used to manufacture chemicals here," he said. Then he ducked through the opening in the fence and walked to where the front of the building had been, watching his step. The ground was littered with broken glass, chunks of crumbling cement and bits of rusty metal. "This was the entrance to the parking garage." The bulldozer had been busy here, too, filling the underground tunnel with debris.

"It's completely blocked off," Lo said.

Cautiously, they approached the nearest tent. He called, "Hey there! Anyone home?"

No one responded. The front flap was zipped closed, but it was a sheer screen, and a quick glance inside told them it was unoccupied. They went to the next tent, which was also empty, as was the next.

"They must be out scavenging or panhandling or something," Lo said.

"Maybe, but the tents are exactly alike and there's nothing inside them." He touched the dark material of the third tent. He'd seen the same stuff strung between the rebar poles at Edgemere. "I think this is solar fabric."

"Not in the average homeless person's budget."

He examined the ground around the tent. The concrete slab that made up the floor of the former Warehouse was covered with a layer of dirt a couple inches deep in some places. He nudged the dirt with the toe of his boot. "Look at that."

There was a wire attached to one corner of the tent. Someone had made an attempt to bury it, but he bent down, gave it a good tug and it popped out of the ground. That wire and the wires coming off the other tents were connected to a thicker wire. He pulled the thick wire out of the ground and followed it to the central pile of rubble, Lo trailing behind him. The wire disappeared into a seemingly impenetrable wall of debris. "Fournier's facility was directly below us," he said. "This pile is situated right over the elevator shaft."

At its center, the pile was twice as high as Scott was tall, and it covered maybe as much ground as an Olympic-sized swimming pool. He took out his holophone and walked all around it, getting a good holo to send to the techs back at headquarters. After he fired that off, he and Lo got closer, inspecting the rubble for any openings. Most of it was broken brick and concrete interspersed with battered panels of aluminum roofing, but he also recognized bits of tile from the showers and the tortured remains of the fence that had separated him from the crowd during grease fights.

His holophone buzzed. It was one of the techs. Scott had never managed to remember their names, but the phone said this one was 'Bob.'

"That was fast," Scott said.

"Your op's got priority. If you look up at the top of that heap, you'll see there's a satellite dish pointed in the direction of the café. Looks like the perp converted it into an antenna to extend his range and tap into the wifi holospot. It's old school, but effective."

"Yeah, but where is he?" Lo asked. "No way he's inside that mountain of concrete."

Scott said, "Not inside, but maybe under. There were four ways in and out. The parking garage and elevator shaft are out, but Fournier had two escape tunnels. Bob, can you check the report to see what happened to them?"

"Yeah, hold on...it looks like the short tunnel collapsed on its own and the other was sealed off with an explosive charge," the tech replied.

When Fournier's underground facility had been torched, Scott and the others escaped through the longer of the two tunnels, which had exited inside an office building about a quarter of a mile away.

He stepped back from the mound to look across the empty lot towards the office building, then began to walk in that direction. "Just one charge? Can you confirm the tunnel was not only sealed off, but collapsed all along its length?"

When he got about halfway to the chain link fence around the perimeter of the Warehouse property, he found a large panel of corrugated sheet metal lying on the ground.

"Uh, that's a negative on the confirmation," Bob said. "They didn't bother to collapse it."

"Alright. Thanks." Scott disconnected and waved Lo over. "Look at this."

When she joined him, she frowned down at the oxidized sheet of metal. "Edges look sharp. Am I gonna need a tetanus booster after this?"

"Maybe."

She started to bend down, but he said, "Hold on. Our guy is smart and probably paranoid. Let's check for booby-traps first."

He took the flashlight off his belt and got down on the ground, lying on one side. "All right, lift up slowly."

Lo carefully curled her fingers around the edges and lifted the sheet with a little grunt, saying, "Ah, it's kind of heavy, can you hurry this up?"

Scott shone the light all around but didn't see any wires. He *did* see that his hunch paid off, though. The sheet metal concealed a hole in the ground.

Chapter Five

Bryn ran ahead of Mia down the hallway and yanked open the stairwell door. Just as it closed behind them, one of the men bellowed, "Git back here!"

"Faster!" Bryn said. "We don't have much of a lead." With one hand on the rail, she took the steps two at a time, quickly outpacing the smaller woman. They were both wearing boots, but Mia's heels were too high to be practical and Bryn had to slow down for her. They'd only made it to the bottom of one of the three flights they needed to descend before she heard the stairwell door crash open.

Mia swung around to the top of the next flight, lifted one leg and hopped up onto the rail. With her arms held out for balance, she slid rapidly down, allowing Bryn to move at full speed again. They beat their pursuers to the bottom and burst out into the empty lobby.

"How far away is your car?" Bryn asked as she opened the main door, one eye watching for the thugs on their tail.

"Six blocks. We should split up. I'll just slow you down."

"Shut up." Bryn grabbed Mia's hand and pulled her along.

The street was deserted, but even if it weren't, she doubted anyone would help them. They made it to the end of the second block when the men caught up to them.

Bryn was scared and angry, but she felt the quills on her head lift defensively and knew she wasn't helpless. Her quills had saved her before, and she was ready and willing to use them again. Panting from exertion, she spun around to face the men. Her voice pitched high from fear, she yelled, "Leave us alone!"

The younger man was closest. He skidded to a stop several feet away, while the larger, older man bent over and put his hands on his knees, clearly winded.

The younger man grinned and set the tip of the bat on the ground, leaning on it casually. "I'm not afraid of you. Savvy says only one in a hundred xenofreaks are actually contagious."

Savvy. The jacker Scott was out looking for.

Bryn doubted she could reason with these men, but her instinct was to stall. "Then why attack us? We never did anything to hurt you."

"Savvy says all xenofreaks are immune," he said. "And once the contagious ones kill off the rest of us, the world will one big xenofreak show."

"Why don't you get a graft to protect yourself then?" Mia asked.

He burst out laughing and turned to his friend, who straightened up and stuck out a sausage-like finger. "One, because there's a big-ass demand right now. Every xenosurgeon in town's charging ten times what they usually do, and we don't got that kinda cash lying around. Two, because it's a sin against nature. There's a reason you're called xeno*freaks*."

"I told you I'm not a xeno." Mia's tone conveyed both reasonableness and scorn. "In fact, I'm a doctor, and I've been working to determine the actual cause of this outbreak."

The smaller man chuckled. "Yeah, right. Nice try. Now why don't we all head back to your apartment so we can talk some more?"

"Here," Mia took her purse from Bryn and reached inside. Bryn thought she was going to show him her identification, but instead, she pulled out a slim, clear bottle and sprayed him in the face with an antiseptic-smelling mist. Bryn didn't wait to see what effect it had; she charged the larger man, slamming her head into his chin and neck before he could react.

Both men cried out, but Mia's victim was clearly in pain, while the man Bryn had stuck full of quills sounded infuriated. She tried to duck away, but his hand shot out and he clamped down on her upper arm. His grip was like a vise, but she struggled against it anyway, shouting, "Let go or I'll poke your eyes out!"

"I'm gonna *kill* you!" he shouted back.

The man Mia sprayed had dropped the bat to cover his face with his hands. While he was busy gouging at his eyes with his thumbs, Mia grabbed the bat and whacked the man holding Bryn's arm across his lower back. He ignored the hit, ignored the quills sticking out of his neck, too enraged to feel pain. He twisted Bryn's arm until she thought it would break, while grabbing for Mia with his free hand. Bryn tried to knee him in the groin, but his grip forced her to bend nearly double.

Mia danced away and sidestepped around behind him. This time, she aimed for his head, cracking the bat across the back of his skull. He let Bryn go and roared, staggering around in a half circle to bring Mia into view. She let out a surprisingly primal yell for someone so petite, and swung the bat again, bashing him in the jaw. He toppled to his knees.

Without a word, Bryn and Mia began to run again. After three blocks with no sign of pursuit, Mia tossed the bat into an alley and they slowed to a fast walk. Mia's car was a high-end, mid-sized rental. As soon as they got inside, Mia reached out and depressed the pump of a bottle of hand-sanitizer that was resting in the cup holder. As she rubbed her hands together vigorously, the same antiseptic scent Bryn smelled earlier filled the car.

"Kills germs and doubles as pepper spray," Mia said. Then she started the engine and drove off, squealing the tires.

Bryn sat catching her breath and rubbing her arm. It was several minutes before either of them spoke, and then they both started talking at once. Mia said, "What is *wrong* with…" at the same moment Bryn said, "What the *heck* is…"

They laughed, and neither one bothered to finish their sentence because it was clear they'd both been about to go off on a rant about crazy people. After a moment, Bryn said, "I should call Scott."

She'd tucked Mia's holophone into her purse as soon as they'd vacated the apartment, and took it out now. "I doubt those jerks bothered to even shut his front door. I hope no one steals anything."

"He didn't have much to steal. Not even a holovision."

Bryn stared at the holoscreen and sighed. "I don't remember his number. It was floating in my holocloud. Do you have it?"

"No, but Shasta's is there."

Bryn found Shasta's name in Mia's cloud, but when she went to dial it, Mia said, "Wait. Don't. She'll want me to come in, but I have to get the graft first."

"Why don't you just tell her you need some personal time?"

Mia let out a short, scoffing laugh. "I doubt that's even in her vocabulary. Besides, now is definitely not the time for me to flake, but I just can't…" she trailed off, a shadow crossing over her face, shades of the devastated woman who'd been sitting in front of Scott's door last night.

Bryn had been through a lot with Mia, but she was essentially a stranger and Bryn didn't have a clue what to say to make her feel better, if that was even possible. Instead of trying, she asked, "Can you drop me off at my godmother's house?"

The resulting silence spurred her to look at Mia's profile. It was hard to make out her expression from this angle, but Bryn thought she seemed disappointed. "What's wrong?"

The corner of Mia's mouth drooped a bit. "I don't know. I guess I thought you were coming with me."

19

"I don't think that's a very good idea."

"I could pay you."

"Are you serious? Look, I'm scared, okay? We just got chased out of Scott's apartment!"

"So it's safe at your godmother's house?"

Bryn looked out the windshield. Up ahead, a burnt-out car squatted at the side of the road.

"No, it's probably *not* safe," she replied. "Carla lives in a bad neighborhood. Where are you planning on getting the money?"

Mia flashed her an inscrutable look. "My parents. They live here in New York on the Upper East Side. After what those men said, I doubt ten thousand will be enough to bump me to the head of the xenograft line."

Bryn sighed. As they drove past the husk of the still steaming car, she imagined she saw the charcoal remains of a body in the front seat. Mia reached out and pushed the recirc button on the dash, but not before a barbecue-like smell filled the car. Mia grabbed a tissue from a box on the floor by Bryn's feet and held it to her nose.

Bryn thought about Jason, recovering in the hospital. He'd been assigned to protect her, had taken her to a safe house, but they'd been attacked. It occurred to her that there was no such thing as a safe place for a xeno, not now, not ever.

"All right," she said. "They'll probably have to give you pain-killers and you won't be able to drive. I'll come with you."

"Thank you. I owe you one."

Bryn looked back down at Mia's holophone. She couldn't call Scott, but he'd sent Mia the xenosurgeon information, so she settled for replying back to that text. It took a while to compose a message that covered the basics of the attack, but that hopefully wouldn't freak him out too much. By the time she hit 'send,' Mia had pulled up in front of a brick apartment building with a long green canopy over the front entrance. Two men in uniform stood waiting as they got out of the car.

Mia said, "Good morning, Brunson."

"Nice to see you again, Miss Padilla," one of the men replied, eyes skimming over Bryn's quills with no change in the pleasant expression on his face. "Your parents didn't mention you were coming."

The other uniformed man took Mia's car keys and the twenty-dollar bill she slipped him. Bryn figured he must be the valet, since he got into Mia's car and drove off. Brunson, who had spotless white gloves and shiny black shoes, had to be the doorman. Outside of holovision, she'd never experienced this kind of service.

"I wasn't expected," Mia said. "Are they home?"

"I believe Mrs. Padilla is in."

"Would you be so kind as to let her know we're on our way up?"

"Certainly." He opened one of the double doors and held it as a blast of warm air swirled out. Neither Bryn nor Mia had stopped to grab a coat when they vacated Scott's apartment, so the warmth was welcome.

Inside, a crystal chandelier hung from the center of a high, arched ceiling, its soft light reflecting off the veined marble flooring. As they waited for the elevator, Bryn couldn't help but compare this ostentatious lobby with the utilitarian one in Scott's building.

The Padillas' suite took up the entire fourth floor. When the elevator doors opened onto the apartment's luxurious entryway, a plump Asian woman in a brightly patterned silk kimono hurried to greet them, exclaiming, "Mia! What a pleasant surprise."

Mrs. Padilla placed her hands lightly on Mia's shoulders and kissed the air on either side of her head. Then she pulled back and beamed at Bryn. "And you brought a celebrity with you! How marvelous."

Chapter Six

Between them, Scott and Lo managed to shove the sheet of corrugated metal roofing along the ground until the roughly three-foot diameter hole was revealed. The aluminum sheet was heavier than Scott expected and the process of moving it produced scraping and screeching noises galore.

"If there's anyone down there, they know we're coming," he said.

Lo squatted next to the rim and ran her fingers over the broken concrete. "I'm no demolition expert, but does that look like a chisel mark? Like from a jackhammer?"

"Yep. Someone made this hole because they wanted in."

"Why? I thought Fournier's facility was destroyed and any evidence removed."

Scott shrugged. "Why don't we go ask?"

She made a face. "After you."

He took the flashlight off his belt, switched it on, and straddled the hole to get a better look. There wasn't much to see, just a packed dirt floor at the bottom, maybe six feet down. Several months ago, he'd walked the entire length of the crudely constructed tunnel, but it had been dark, and he and Kareem Williams had been carrying a panda at the time, so he couldn't say what else might be down there.

He sat at the edge of the hole with his feet dangling inside. "Cover me."

Lo shifted so one knee rested on the ground and drew her weapon. When Scott dropped into the hole, he halfway expected someone to rush him, but nothing happened. He stepped out of the circle of light and shone his flashlight around. No surprises, just support beams and dirt walls. He couldn't see to the end of the tunnel but hadn't expected to.

"All clear," he called.

Lo responded cheerfully, "Incoming!" and landed behind him with a grunt of effort. She switched on her flashlight and said, "What a pleasant place."

Scott led the way. The air was cold, damp, and in addition to the fetid chemical odor permeating the place, smelled of smoke. At the end of the tunnel, what had once been a closet with a false back wall was now a gaping hole. Lo took up a defensive position against one wall as Scott stuck the flashlight through the opening and briefly poked his head around. There wasn't much left of Fournier's facility. The drop ceiling was mostly gone, although the scorched and twisted infrastructure hung precariously from the bottom of the slab above them. The majority of the walls that had once neatly partitioned the former parking garage had either burned away to ash in the fire or been knocked down during the search for evidence afterward. The flooring seemed to have mostly survived, but it was covered with burnt and broken refuse.

He pulled back for a moment and then stuck his head in again to look in the other direction. His flashlight was strong but didn't reach the furthest walls. Someone had cleared a path through the refuse, however, and he thought whoever it was might as well have put up a neon sign saying, 'This way.'

He shone the flashlight in his own face so Lo could see him jerk his head to indicate he was going in. He heard her follow him; their footsteps echoed in the cavernous space. It didn't take long for him to lose his bearings as the cleared path turned this way and that, finally coming to an end at another tent. This one didn't appear to be made from solar fabric, which made sense down here in the dark. The tent opening was zipped shut, but a faint glow from inside indicated that someone was either home or had left a light on.

"Tent occupant!" Scott called, for lack of a better descriptive term. "We're with the XIA. Come out where we can see you."

A muffled male voice replied sullenly, "Leave me alone!"

"We just want to talk," Lo said.

"I've *said* everything that needs saying," the man replied.

"Not to us."

"Then you weren't paying attention."

"Are you Savvy?" Scott asked.

"Obviously." Savvy's voice hadn't lost any of its petulance. If it weren't for the deep timbre, Scott would swear they were talking to a child.

"You've been stirring things up out there," Lo said.

"I haven't done anything wrong."

"Uh, I beg to differ. Hate speech with the intent to incite violence."

"Hate? More like truth, and good luck proving my intent."

Lo took a deep breath and let it out slowly. "Whatever your intent, there are a lot of scared people out there."

"They're not scared enough."

Scott decided he'd had enough. "Come on out. Don't make us come in after you."

"You said you just wanted to talk. We're talking."

"You know, Savvy," Lo said in an exaggeratedly patient tone, "We've been tasked with identifying you. My partner doesn't care whether we get that ID pre or postmortem, but since I just killed a man yesterday, I don't have the heart for it today."

If Lo had intended to intimidate him, it didn't work.

"If you killed someone, shouldn't you be on administrative leave?"

Scott was beginning to see where Savvy got his nickname. He was smart *and* a smart aleck. Scott couldn't see Lo's face very well in the dim light from their flashlights, but he thought she rolled her eyes.

"Usually, yes," she replied. "But everyone's on high alert, in part because of the nonsense you've been posting."

"It's not nonsense," Savvy said, but the light inside the tent went out and Scott heard him rustling around. The zipper on the tent slowly rose and he stepped out, holding a hand over his eyes when they both spotlighted him.

As soon as Scott got a good look at the man's high forehead and heavy-lidded eyes, he revised his assumption that Savvy's nickname came from his smarts. Savvy was thin, middle-aged, and stood before them with shoulders hunched, head hanging so low his chin nearly touched his concave chest. Even with the scraggly beard hiding his lower face, he was familiar to Scott because he'd recently described Savvy's face to an XIA agent trained in recovering latent memories. Scott had met Savvy once, only briefly, but he hadn't been given his name – just that he was a 'savant' and a valued member of Dr. Fournier's team.

Scott and Lo had just stumbled upon one of the XIA's most wanted criminals.

Chapter Seven

Bryn didn't often find herself overwhelmed by a personality, but Mrs. Padilla, from her perfume to her opinions, could only be described as 'strong.' Mia indulged her mother for maybe ten minutes as the older woman prattled on, bouncing from one inane subject to another with hardly a segue, and then Mia said baldly, "I need money."

"Oh." Mrs. Padilla looked affronted. "For goodness sake, Mia, what a crass thing to interrupt me with. And in front of our guest, too."

"Well, I apologize, Mother. I realize you've insulated yourself from the world, but even you couldn't have failed to notice the riots."

"Of course I noticed. You don't need to be insulting. However, I'm at a loss as to what the state of the world has to do with your needing money."

Mia inhaled deeply and let it out in a slow sigh. Bryn knew that tactic well; it was always best to pause and regroup after a parent pushed your buttons, especially if you wanted something from them.

"You've heard about the super typhoid?" Mia asked.

Mrs. Padilla's head went back. "That's why you're here. I should have known you wouldn't come to New York just to see me."

Mia flinched a little but let her mother's dig slide. "Yes, my team was called in to identify the pathogen, which we have, but my job isn't done. We need to find a way to stop it, and until we do, I have to protect myself. That's why I need the money."

"Protect yourself how?"

"Xenos are immune."

"Xenos...? You're not thinking about getting a xenograft, are you? Because *that's* out of the question."

Mia clasped her hands together, bowed her head, and pressed her knuckles to her lips. In a tightly controlled voice, she said, "Mom. Every single solitary non-xeno who gets this thing dies, but not xenos. Whatever it is that affords them immunity has got to come from their grafts. Getting a graft after you catch it doesn't help – I know, because I watched a man who'd gotten it done die."

She lifted her head. "This is not just for me. You and Dad need to do it, too, and you need to do it fast. There aren't enough bioengineered animals for everyone in the world to get grafted. Demand is high right now, and as far as the public knows, the super typhoid is still only just a rumor. Imagine what will happen when the government is forced to admit the truth."

Mrs. Padilla didn't respond right away. Bryn watched her face as she processed Mia's words. A wrinkle of worry between her eyebrows smoothed out as doubt gave way to stubbornness in a brief thinning of the lips.

"I suppose you can confirm which rumors are true, then, right?" Mrs. Padilla asked. "For instance, the news reported that a xenofreak knew he had it and was spreading it on purpose, but that he was dead now, and the likelihood of getting infected was really low."

"The risk is low now," Mia said, "because not all xenos are infected and the majority who are, aren't contagious. But like I said, everyone's rushing out to get grafted. That may reduce *their* risk, but it increases the xeno population in general as well as the odds that someone you pass on the street might be a carrier."

Mrs. Padilla sighed dramatically. "I don't speak for your father, but I'm certain he'll agree that he and I are not in danger. However, given your profession, I will concede that you should probably protect yourself. How much money do you need?"

Mia looked at Bryn, who shrugged. Scott told Mia ten thousand would get her a small graft, but that was before they knew everyone was trying to get one. Plus, she'd have to bribe her way to the front of the line now.

"A hundred thousand?" Mia said.

Mrs. Padilla's jaw dropped open. "What? Isn't that a bit steep? I assume you need cash. I don't think your father keeps that much in the safe."

"Whatever you have then, and I'll have to hope it's enough."

Mrs. Padilla shook her head but bustled over to a painting on the wall. Within a short amount of time, she'd opened the safe behind the painting and removed a thick envelope. She took a moment to thumb through the bills inside before handing it to her daughter. "Fifty thousand. Best I can do on short notice."

Mia gave her a quick hug. "Thanks, Mom. It'll have to do."

"Honey…are you sure you've thought this out? I mean, is it going to bother you, having something foreign permanently attached to your body?"

Bryn had wondered the same thing given Mia's germophobia.

Mia's lips twisted wryly. "I hope not, because I'll be stuck with it."

Xenografts were meant to be permanent, but technically, they could be removed. Bryn flashed on the horrific memory of seeing Carla's bloody xenograft after it had been ripped from her body.

She and Mia started to leave, but Mrs. Padilla stopped them before they called the elevator. She opened a nearby door and stepped into a walk-in closet. After a minute or two of rustling around, she reappeared with two garments draped over her arm. She handed a classic wool overcoat in a sedate navy blue to Mia and turned to Bryn with a shorter coat in a heavy black fabric with an attached hood.

"This was in fashion for about two seconds a decade ago," she said. "But it might come in handy in case you need to be discreet."

Bryn and Mia put the coats on, murmuring their thanks. The hood on the black coat was so wide Bryn was able to lift it over her quills easily, and it was lined with something silky, yet tough enough that it slid right over her quills without getting stuck on them. She looked at herself in the entryway mirror, pleased. The sides of the hood draped elegantly on either side of her face like a cloak.

"One more thing, darling girl," Mrs. Padilla said as Mia held her finger out to press the elevator call button. "Don't, um…don't get anything obvious, okay?" Her eyes shifted to Bryn before her gaze dropped quickly to the floor. "Just…get something small that you can hide under your clothing. They're killing each other out there. I'd never forgive myself if you got hurt because someone saw your graft and thought you were…"

Mia laughed. "A xenofreak?"

Mrs. Padilla's answering smile was strained. "Just be careful."

"I will."

Chapter Eight

Scott knew nothing about savants other than that they were uncommon. At least, that was what Shasta told him after he'd mentioned that the programmer who'd helped Padme create Fournier's nanoneuron program was supposedly a savant. And now here that savant was, refusing to come along quietly; refusing, in fact, to come along with them *at all*. Scott was all for just forcing the squirrelly guy to cooperate, but Lo seemed to think she could reason with him, so he stood back and let her try.

Savvy's main complaint was that he didn't want to leave his 'stuff.'

"Your stuff'll be fine," Lo assured him. "Has anyone but us been down here?"

"That's irrelevant," Savvy said. He didn't look at her when he spoke, just like he hadn't looked at Scott when they'd first met.

"How is it irrelevant?" Lo asked.

"I'm not worried about someone stealing anything."

"What *are* you worried about?" Scott asked. It was clear that with Savvy you had to ask specific questions.

A furtive look crossed the savant's face. "I can't tell you."

"Okay," Lo said, the patience in her tone sounding thinner. "Maybe we can bring your stuff with us."

"It's not, um, portable."

Scott suspected Savvy was not only lying but was hiding something.

Lo gestured to the tent. "We've got a big car. I'm sure we can accommodate whatever you've got in there."

Savvy gave an abrupt shake of his head, but he also glanced involuntarily somewhere to the left of Scott. Scott shone his flashlight in that direction and was surprised to find an intact wall. Another path had been cleared, and it led straight to a closed door in that wall.

"What's in there?" Scott asked.

Savvy wrung his hands and shifted his weight from foot to foot like a child in desperate need of a restroom.

"Nothing," he said, but Scott already knew – there'd only been one heavy wooden door in the facility. Behind that wall was whatever was left of Fournier's personal suite. Months ago, Scott had waited for Fournier in the reception area behind that door. He'd also been inside his office and the large bedroom that belonged to Fournier's 'daughter,' Nicola. He'd been told by Bryn that Fournier's bedroom was back there, too, not to mention the entrance to the second tunnel.

Scott took a step towards the door, but Savvy lunged for him with an agitated, "No!"

Scott dropped his flashlight and turned, claws fully extended. "I *don't* advise it."

Lo had spotlighted them, and Scott saw from Savvy's astonishment that the savant hadn't known who he was talking to.

"Oh…oh!" Savvy said, relief suffusing his face. "You're Cougar. You're…" He blinked, and the relief changed to confusion. "XIA?"

"Yes, to both," Scott said. "And I'm going to find out what you're hiding behind that door, so I suggest you make it easy on us all by just telling me."

Savvy lifted clenched fists to his face and his shoulders rounded as if he was trying to disappear. When he began to mutter to himself, Scott picked up his flashlight, writing the savant off as no threat. But as soon as he took another step towards the door, Savvy shouted, "Nickie! *Run!*"

Lo leapt forward to restrain the savant as Scott pulled his gun from its holster with his free hand. The door to Fournier's suite opened and someone rushed out, right for him. He almost fired but caught a glimpse of a mussed blonde head and realized the 'stuff' Savvy was protecting was really a young woman.

Nicola Fournier ran up to Savvy and put her hand on his arm. "It's okay, Felson. We can trust them."

Chapter Nine

The address Scott had given them was in New Rochelle, a small shop in a nondescript strip mall. The neon sign in the window wasn't on, but the name of the place was Koo Koo Bamboo Tattoo. Bryn and Mia hovered on the fringes of a crowd of about thirty people gathered outside the front door. Most of the waiting patrons were watching a woman moving around inside as the clock ticked closer to opening time.

Mia looked worried. "There're too many people."

"Scott said it wouldn't take very long," Bryn replied. "We might have to wait awhile, but you'll get in."

"I hope you're right. I have to get back to work." Mia's holophone had rung several times on the drive until she'd asked Bryn to mute it. None of the calls had been from Scott.

Bryn was grateful for the coat Mrs. Padilla had lent her, not only for the warmth, but because the hood completely hid her quills, and no one paid her any attention. She looked around at the faces of the people waiting, some of whom were bundled up like they'd been here for hours. None of them had ink showing and based on their attire and the vehicles in the parking lot, most looked belonged to the middle class. She picked up on the desperation in their faces and imagined the majority had emptied their savings accounts to be here. One woman clasped the hands of her mittened children, and another had a baby strapped to her back. Bryn thought about the children and old folks at Edgemere who'd been exposed to the virus. All had died.

Four more people showed up, all men, and much tougher looking than the rest of the crowd. She didn't need to see their grafts to peg them as xenofreaks. Bryn's quills lifted of their own accord, and for a moment she almost ignored the sense of danger that prompted it. The newcomers had arrived in the same vehicle, but had split up, casually boxing the crowd in.

She grabbed Mia's hand and tugged on it, saying rather loudly, "I guess it's not a good day to get a tat after all." Mia gave her a strange look but allowed Bryn to pull her past the nearest of the men. He ran cold brown eyes over them like he was assessing their worth, and Bryn suddenly wished she wasn't wearing the expensive coat.

She and Mia wove around the vehicles in the full parking lot and got into Mia's rental. After she shut the door, Bryn said urgently, "Drive away like everything's fine."

"Is it those men?" Mia asked, starting the car but not backing out. "One of them had a xenograft, Bryn. I'm sure they aren't going to attack those people just because they want to become xenos."

"I don't think they're going to attack them for that. I think they're going to rob them. Every one of those people is carrying cash. A lot of cash."

Mia's face fell. "Oh, jeez, you're right. Those poor people."

Bryn used Mia's phone to dial 911 as Mia drove to the far exit so she wouldn't have to go past the doomed crowd. This time when the automaton came up and told them Emergency Services was overwhelmed, Bryn left a detailed message, doubting as she did so that the police would take her seriously. She was reporting a crime that hadn't yet happened, and they didn't have the resources to investigate based on her suspicion.

They drove aimlessly down the nearly deserted main boulevard for about five minutes before Bryn spotted an open bistro and suggested they stop for lunch. They went inside and agreed to get their sandwiches to go. Neither of them felt like lingering in a public place, especially not a place with a cash register.

When they were back in the car, Mia handed Bryn her phone and said, "Look up some other tattoo parlors, would you?"

"Why?" Bryn knew from her father's lectures that a person could legally *have* a xenograft, but the surgeons who provided the service weren't licensed to do so, therefore all of the facilities were underground. "They're not going to admit it if they have a xenosurgeon on staff."

"I know. We're not going to call them, just drive by and if there's a bunch of people there, we'll know, right?"

It seemed like a good enough plan, if only to kill time until Scott called and gave them another location, so Bryn did a search. They drove past three of the tattoo places she found but opted not to go near the rest. As soon as they entered those neighborhoods, they hightailed it right back out again. The unrest was sporadic, but seemed to be gearing up again, just like Shasta had predicted. After an hour it became clear they weren't going to find another tattoo parlor slash xenograft den, so Mia headed back to the highway.

31

Bryn was just about to ask where they were going, but then they drove past a store that seemed to have an awful lot of customers. She read the sign on the building, 'Scaly Companion Pet Store,' and jabbed a finger toward the sidewalk. "Pull over, right there!"

Mia slammed on the brakes and managed to grab a parking spot on the street. "Why exactly are we stopping here?"

"Did you see that pet store? It had a ton of people inside. It makes sense, doesn't it? Regular pets for sale out front, bioengineered animals in the back." Just saying it made Bryn cringe a little inside, despite the fact that animals had been slaughtered, eaten, and used as clothing by humans and their ancestors for well over a hundred thousand years.

Mia opened her door. "Let's check it out."

As they walked back down the block, Bryn adjusted the hood of her coat so it covered the quills around her face. She'd lost quite a few when she'd head-butted that man, but her lopsided head wasn't her concern. She didn't want anyone to recognize her and possibly bring unwanted attention to Mia, who just wanted to get in, get out, and get on with finding a cure for the super typhoid.

A bell jingled when they opened the door and several people looked around to see who'd come in. It was oppressively warm inside the store and a heavy animal stink made Mia pull a tissue from her purse and hold it over her nose. There were at least two dozen people milling about, not even looking at the glass terrariums housing snakes and lizards and tiny, brightly colored frogs. The people all appeared to be waiting.

"Do you see any mice?" Mia asked quietly as they walked down the wide central aisle. An indoor pond with rocks and water plants housed several dozen turtles.

"They probably have them in the back," Bryn replied. "Regular ones for the snakes and bioengineered ones for…us."

Mia nodded, but didn't seem reassured. A mouse xenograft was cheap, and generally didn't spur as much outrage in the general public as some of the more exotic ones. The lack of furry creatures in this store had probably spooked her. Mia was definitely not the sort to get a snakeskin graft.

They made their way to the counter and waited as the man in front of them concluded his business. Bryn nudged Mia and nodded in the direction of the man's head. A white gauze bandage on the back of his neck peeked out from under his shirt. When the man left, they stepped up to the counter.

The clerk was thin and balding, with a narrow face. His nametag identified him as "Turk."

"How can I help you, ladies?"

Still holding the tissue to her face, Mia said, "I'd like an, um, uh…"

"You lookin' for a xenograft?" he asked dryly.

The ends of the tissue fluttered as she exhaled in relief. "Yes."

"No can do. Not today, not tomorrow. Probably not even next week. We got customers out the ying-yang."

"I can pay."

Turk's eyebrows rose. "So can a lot of people."

"I can pay more than them."

"Yeah? You got thirty thousand bucks? Cash?"

Bryn and Mia looked at each other. Mia said, "Will that bump me to the head of the line?"

Turk made a 'tch' sound, and drawled, "Sure will."

Mia smiled again. "Then yes. I have thirty thousand 'bucks.'"

Chapter Ten

Nicola Fournier. The Bestia Butcher's most successful experiment, and most treasured possession.

Scott couldn't help but stare. Fournier's 'daughter' was an older version of Scott's adopted sister May. May and Nicola had been cloned from the same genetic material, but May hadn't lived long enough to discover her origins. He wondered briefly if Nicola knew, but mostly, he felt like Christmas had come again. They'd captured Lupus, Fournier's top lieutenant, removed Padme from Fournier's control, and now Nicola was standing here in all her innocence, like a present with a shiny bow on top of her head.

He still wasn't sure how old she was. She looked like a pre-teen, but her manner made her seem a little older. Her calm demeanor had a pacifying effect on Savvy, or, as she'd referred to him, 'Felson.' His agitation subsided as soon as she appeared at his side, but the savant said glumly, "They're going to take you away."

"I know," she responded. "And it's all right. I can't stay here, even though you've done such a good job protecting me."

Savvy seemed pleased at the praise, but the worried crease between his brows remained.

Nicola looked at Scott. One of her eyebrows, both of which had been replaced with a fan of delicate grey feathers, lifted. "My dad has no idea you're with the XIA."

"Good," Scott replied. "You know he's not really your father, right?"

Her head went back as if he'd slapped her. "He is, too."

"But you know where you come from." It wasn't a question.

She looked around at the destruction and spread her hands. "I come from here. I was born in this facility. It's home, or was until the fire. But yeah, I know what you mean. I'm a clone. I found out two days ago."

"Why are you here?" Lo asked. "Where's your father?"

34

"I'm *here* because I found out I'm a clone." Nicola's voice was scornful. "I ran away. And I may be mad at my dad, but I'm not going to tell you where he is. No matter what you do to me."

For the first time, Savvy lifted his eyes and looked directly at Scott. The threat in his gaze was unmistakable. Scott said, "No one's going to hurt her. Our job is to protect people."

Savvy looked back down. He seemed like he was going to cry, and Scott felt sorry for him, but not enough to drop his guard. The guy obviously had strong feelings for Nicola.

"Alright. Let's go," he said. "You too, Savvy."

"I need my stuff," Savvy said.

"And I won't leave without Perky," Nicola put in.

Perky turned out to be her cockatiel. Scott remembered the bird well – or rather its obnoxious squawking. He'd been trying to get Nicola safely out of the facility while enemy soldiers crawled the corridors, and the bird wouldn't shut up.

Savvy's precious stuff turned out to be a newer hologame system, a portable 3D printer, and several smaller items that looked as if they'd been scrounged from the debris. He crammed it all into a worn backpack.

When everything and everyone had been loaded into the sedan, Nicola said, "Cougar?"

"Name's Scott."

"Oh…Scott?"

"Yeah."

"Do you still have my mother's books?"

The books were the other thing Nicola refused to leave when Scott was trying to get her to evacuate the facility. In actuality, the psychology textbooks had belonged to *Bryn's* mother, but he wasn't about to tell Nicola that. He understood why she insisted on calling Fournier her father – the man had raised her, after all – but now that she knew she was a clone, did she realize she didn't actually *have* a mother? Whoever had carried and given birth to her was merely a surrogate.

"They're around somewhere," he said.

"Good. I want them back, okay?"

"We'll see what we can do."

Bryn had them, of course. He'd given them to her after the XIA released them from evidence. She didn't consider the books to be all that special since she had photos and mementos of growing up with her mother. Nicola had treasured the books, though; they were the only thing she had that belonged to Miranda Vega. Not that she necessarily knew Miranda's married name. The books all had the same inscription on the inside of the front cover: 'This book belongs to Miranda McKim.' He and Bryn had discussed it once.

"Do you think Nicola knew about me?" she'd asked.

"I highly doubt it. I got the impression she doesn't know anything about where she comes from."

"I wonder if she knows how awful he is? You know, the—the body parts?"

Scott knew Bryn was thinking about her mother's heart, wondering if Nicola knew Fournier had kept it. Fournier was the most infamous of the xenosurgeons, and it was well known he had a nasty habit of collecting keepsakes from his patients in jars of formaldehyde. Bryn had seen the macabre display in his bedroom.

"Maybe. He kept her hidden away. For all we know, she's just as twisted as he is."

Bryn shook her head. "You said she seemed normal."

"I spent like ten minutes with her, mostly running from people who wanted to kill us. She's young, and she seemed…naïve."

It wasn't the first or the last time they'd talked about it, but that particular conversation stuck with him. Was it possible Fournier had managed to raise Nicola to be normal? He turned in his seat and caught her looking at him.

"Are we going to your headquarters?" she asked.

"Yeah."

"Do you have showers there? It's been two days and I'm gross."

"I'm sure we can hook you up."

"Awesome." She heaved a sigh and slipped down a little in her seat. "This is going to really spork Daddy off."

Chapter Eleven

Bryn was worried she wouldn't be allowed to go with Mia into the back of the store, but Turk, who was clearly more than a store clerk, said, "We're a little low on donors, so you might want your friend along to help you choose."

"Choose?"

Mia was still holding the tissue to her face, so her expression was hidden, but Bryn heard the dismay in her voice. It probably never occurred to her that she'd have to come face to face with her live donor before she doomed it.

Mia's discomfort went right over Turk's head. He led them through a door into a brightly lit hallway with white walls, ceiling and floors. The lack of color gave the impression of cleanliness, and Mia seemed to relax some. Bryn noted the presence of a dome security camera on the ceiling and turned her face away.

Turk locked the door behind him, chattering away. "We got garter, gopher, bull and corn snakes, bearded dragons, and about ten baby alligators. For you, though, I'd recommend a gecko. We got about seven left, all different colors."

"What about a—a mouse?" Mia asked. He stopped outside another door and gave her a strange look.

"We don't do furries. Did you not *see* the name of the store?"

"What do you feed the snakes?" she asked weakly.

"Mice." He said it like he was talking to a moron. "Non-bioengineered. I mean, we could totally graft one of 'em on to ya if you want us to, but it wouldn't stick."

Bryn put a hand on Mia's coat sleeve, but then took it away as she realized the gesture of reassurance would probably backfire.

"Take a deep breath," Bryn said, "and remember why we're here."

"Yeah, really," Turk said.

Mia shot him a look of defiance and pulled the tissue away, but gagged as soon as she inhaled, even though the stink was almost non-existent back here. The tissue went back over her nose as Turk laughed.

"Alright, looks like we should get this over with before you hurl," he said.

Behind the door were glass cages just like in the store. They were lit with purplish bulbs and most of the occupants were unmoving. Mia stood stock still in the middle of the room, her eyes moving from cage to cage. Bryn fully expected her to back out of it at this point, but then Mia's eyes narrowed, and she walked over to a cage in the corner.

"Oh, that one's not available," Turk said. "It's a special order."

Bryn went to Mia's side and looked down at the fat, orange and black lizard that had captured her attention. It was a Gila monster, like Jason's graft.

"Uh, yeah, you don't want that one anyway," Bryn said, glad the lighting in the room wouldn't give away her blush. "Jason's had, um, problems with his."

Jason's xenofreak name was 'Dragila,' after his Gila monster xenograft and tattoo. The graft was extremely sensitive, a fact Bryn knew because she'd touched it and got a response that was more than she'd bargained for.

Turk chuckled suggestively. "I'll bet. Rumor has it monsters are gonna be a *real* popular graft soon."

Mia was still staring at the Gila monster. "How much?"

"Like I said, that one's not available."

"Not even for fifty thousand?" Mia asked.

Bryn bit her lip. Mia clearly didn't understand what she and Turk had been alluding to. Turk said, "Be right back."

He left them in the room and Bryn did her best to entice Mia with some of the colorful little geckos, but she seemed fixated on the Gila monster. When Turk returned five minutes later, he said cheerfully, "You're in luck. The boss doesn't think the person who ordered that little guy can pay the new price, you know, since demand has gone up so much. Let's get you prepped." He held the door open.

In the hallway, Bryn swallowed her embarrassment and tried to warn Mia again. "Look, the thing is, Jason's graft is kind of tied into his, um, nervous system in a sort of special way…"

"Yeah," Turk interjected, "we're gonna put performance enhancing drug companies out of business."

Bryn saw Mia's chin lift as understanding dawned, but she lowered the hand with the tissue so she could open her purse. She took out the envelope of cash and handed it to Turk. Clutching her purse to her chest, she said, "I'm ready."

Chapter Twelve

On the drive back to XIA headquarters, they ran into a roadblock. Traffic was crawling, so Scott took the opportunity to check his messages. He must have had a scowl on his face when he read the one from Bryn, because Lo asked, "What's wrong?"

He shook his head and dialed Mia's number. A holo with the CDC's logo popped up and Mia's voice said, "I'm unavailable to take your call. Leave a message."

Scott didn't want to say anything personal, so he just said, "Call me back ASAP."

Next, he sent an email to Shasta letting her know who they had in custody.

Up ahead, there was a bend in the road, and from here he could see the roadblock was manned by two soldiers with automatic rifles. The soldiers waved several cars through, then stopped a Mercedes. One of the soldiers stood in front of the car with his rifle pointed almost casually at the windshield while the other walked around to the driver's side and made a gesture with his hand to roll down the window. Over the top of the car, Scott saw him duck down to converse with the driver.

"What do you 'spose they're looking for?" Lo asked.

"I don't know, but that soldier's hair is kinda long, isn't it?"

"Think he's National Guard and got called in before he could get a crew cut?"

Scott looked down the line of cars, pausing at a shiny red Audi Electrica. "Let's see who they stop next."

Lo's face fell. "Ya think?"

"Yeah, I'd bet on it."

"What are you guys talking about?" Nicola asked.

Savvy cleared his throat. "They aren't real soldiers. They're robbing people."

Scott gave Savvy a dirty look, which the savant seemed not to notice.

"Is that true?" Nicola asked. "Are you going to arrest them?"

Lo shook her head. "They've got too much firepower. I'm sure one of their victims already called the police."

"Who are obviously not responding." Nicola's voice was acerbic. "I thought you said you helped people."

"Right now we're a little busy trying to help *you*," Scott said. "If we take them on, you'll be in danger. Do you understand that?"

Nicola pressed her lips together but nodded.

The soldiers let the Mercedes go and waved several cars through, but as Scott predicted, they stopped the Audi.

"They won't stop us, will they?" Nicola asked.

"Unlikely," Scott replied, not taking his eyes off the soldiers. "We don't look rich."

They waited in tense silence as the 'soldier' spoke to the driver of the Audi. It was taking a long time; much longer than the Mercedes, which only meant one thing.

"Come *on*," Scott said under his breath, mentally urging the driver to cooperate and hand over his wallet. He couldn't see the driver, but the passenger was a woman. Her pale face was turned in his direction.

He took his eye patch off, pleased to find the swelling had gone down enough for him to see, then looked at Lo and jerked his head in Nicola and Savvy's direction. "They'll be okay here. There's like ten cars ahead of us."

"That's what I was thinking," she replied. She reached under her jacket for her weapon and turned to Nicola. "Stay in the car. Keep your heads *down*. And don't think about running for it. I'm going to lock you in."

Lo slipped out the driver's side door and Scott crawled across the console to exit that way, too, since the second soldier would have seen him from the passenger side. Lo beeped the locks.

He pulled his gun and let Lo take the lead. Bent down, they ran past several cars, finally stopping next to a pickup truck four cars back from the Audi.

"Dude," Scott heard. He looked up. The driver of the truck had his window rolled down and was shaking his head at him. "What are you doing?"

"We're cops. Those aren't soldiers. Get down."

The driver of the truck didn't wait to be told twice, sinking down below the bottom of the window, but Scott heard him say, "Don't shoot up my truck, man. It's almost paid off."

41

"Yeah, that's my main concern," Scott muttered, but his voice was drowned out by the soldier standing by the Audi, shouting at the driver, "I'm gonna *kill* you man! Don't you get that?"

Lo looked around at him. "You wearing a vest?"

Both of them had been shot two days ago, but her vest and his bullet-resistant clothing had saved them.

"Nope. Not today."

"Me neither. What's the plan?"

"We got to draw them away from these cars. Too many civilians."

She glanced over at the metal guardrail, which had a sturdy concrete barrier at its base. "I'll go."

They didn't have time to work out another plan, so he covered her from the front of the truck as she leapt the barrier and ran, hunched over. He halfway expected the second soldier to see her, but the guy was focused on his partner, who was counting down loudly.

"Six, five, four…"

Scott could tell Lo wasn't going to make it into position in time, so he ran back behind the pickup truck and burst out from behind it. From this angle, the soldiers wouldn't have to shoot over cars, potentially hitting someone. Scott ran into an overgrown field and threw himself down as he shouted, "Drop your weapons!"

As expected, the soldier counting down straightened up and aimed. The second soldier also turned in his direction, but then Lo yelled, "Lower your weapons, *now*!"

Maybe it would have worked, but the driver of the Audi inexplicably decided to gun the engine and run down the second soldier with a sickening thud. The first soldier opened fire on the Audi, and it came to a sudden stop. Lo shot the soldier in the back, twice.

As the soldier fell, it looked like the danger was over, but Scott didn't take anything for granted. Gun arm extended out in front of him, he ran towards the Audi. Lo had already arrived at the body of the man she'd shot. Her hand was at his throat, feeling for a pulse. She spotted Scott and shook her head. He rounded the front of the Audi and saw the top half of the second man. His bottom half was under the car. His eyes were open and so was his mouth, which was filled with blood. Scott knelt down as the blood spilled over and trailed down the side of his face. He was obviously dead, but Scott checked his pulse to be sure.

When he straightened up, he saw Lo checking the occupants of the Audi. The driver was dead, but the passenger had a non-life-threatening wound to the lower leg. She was crying hysterically. "We told them we didn't have any money. We *stole* this car! Why would we steal a car if we had money?"

Lo called it in, then went back to the sedan, got in, and drove off the road into the field. She parked it in an out of the way place, while Scott went to the first four vehicles behind the Audi and told the drivers they'd need to stay to give a statement to the police when they got here. One of the drivers was a nurse, and she offered to look at the Audi passenger's wound.

The driver of the pickup truck tried to argue when Scott told him he'd have to stay put. "Come on, man, I'm late for work."

"Well, you got a good excuse, don't you?"

"Am I gonna have to go to court?"

"Maybe," Scott replied irritably. "Why don't you shut your mouth and do your civic duty, okay?"

Lo left Nicola and Savvy sitting in the sedan and met up with Scott at the side of the road. "Dispatch says it's going to be hours before anyone responds. The city's a mess."

Scott flexed his claws and asked, "You okay?"

"What, the kill? Fine."

He nodded. "I guess we got a looong morning of directing traffic ahead of us."

She pointed to a car and waved to the driver that he should leave the road and go around the other cars. "Booya."

Chapter Thirteen

It wasn't until Bryn had been waiting for ten minutes or so before she realized she should have asked Mia for her holophone. She wandered around the pet store, looking at all the animals on display and trying to avoid the other customers. Their conversations told her that some of them had family or friends in the back room getting grafted, while others were waiting their turn. One disgruntled man made a point of commenting within Bryn's hearing that rich people were going to be the only ones to survive the super typhoid. It was a dig at Mia, who'd cut ahead of everyone.

Scott had said it would only take a few hours, but two hours came and went, and Mia had still not made an appearance. Turk had been coming and going between the back room and the front counter as people came and went. Currently, he was nowhere to be seen. It was so warm in the store Bryn was dying to take her coat off, but she couldn't, not without revealing her quills. Her lower back had begun to ache, and she wished she'd gotten Mia's keys so she could sit in the car. A few of the other customers had planted themselves on the ground and she was considering doing so as well, when the bell on the front door jingled.

Everyone looked up at the newcomers, including Bryn, who froze in place when she saw who it was. The same four men who'd been casing the crowd at the tattoo place strolled in nonchalantly.

Bryn didn't know for certain whether the men had robbed those people, since she and Mia had gotten out of there before it went down, but her first instinct was to head for the door. She did so, acting just as nonchalantly as the four thugs, but when she started to walk past one of them, he blocked her way and said loudly, "Nobody leaves. Everyone in the center aisle. Now!"

After a shocked moment, the customers hurried to comply. One of the men pulled a gun and in a voice like a carnie at the fair attempting to attract people to his booth, called out, "Purses, wallets, watches, and jewelry!"

The man who'd stopped her held out his hand. He had a heavy silver ring hanging from his nose and smelled like sauerkraut. "Empty your pockets."

She'd run out of Scott's apartment with nothing but knew better than to argue. She stuck her hands into her jean pockets and turned them inside out.

He grunted and reached out to thrust his hands into her coat pockets, then when he didn't find anything, reached both arms around her so he could shove his hands into the back pockets of her jeans. She managed to cross her arms over her chest, using her elbows to keep him from pressing up against her. Still, he took his time, chuckling lasciviously. She had to actively suppress the urge to knee him in the groin.

He finally let her go, just as a woman cried, "No! Please, I need this graft. I don't want to die."

"Everyone dies," one of the men replied. Bryn glanced around just as the man ripped the woman's wallet out of her hand and shoved her. She stumbled backwards until her calves hit the edge of the turtle pond, then her arms did a full rotation windmill before she lost her fight for balance and fell into it. Water sloshed out onto the linoleum as the men laughed.

Bryn thought the thug with the ring in his nose was done harassing her, but he suddenly grabbed the hood of her coat and yanked it down.

"Whoa," he said, taking a step back. "You're that porcupine chick."

"Yeah, and I'm broke, okay? I'm just waiting for my—my boyfriend. He's in the back getting a graft."

"Alright, sister. It's cool." He seemed about to say something else, but the man with the gun barked, "Hey Bull! Get behind the counter and check the register!"

The man named Bull gave Bryn one last creepy look, like he thought he'd bonded with her and didn't want to leave, before heading for the front desk.

Bryn wondered about Turk and the staff in the back. Did they know what was going on out here? She looked up and spied another camera dome. Was there a live feed in the back or was the camera just recording? Turk had been gone an awful long time. In the two hours she'd been here, he'd always responded to the bell on the front door, but when those men had come in, he didn't.

Just when she was thinking she didn't blame him, the bell over the front door jingled again. Her first thought was, *Oh, no, some poor customer stumbling in on all this*. But when she turned, she saw two men with shotguns. She didn't even have time to register surprise before the first man raised his gun to his shoulder and fired off a shot, hitting one of the thugs in the chest. Instinctively, she dropped into a crouch, then scooted behind a display of terrarium figurines.

More shots followed. A woman, Bryn thought it was the same one who'd gone into the turtle pond, screamed shrilly. There was a crash and the sound of broken glass like someone had smashed into a glass cage. Bryn lay flat, her cheek pressed into the cold floor, eyes wide open even though she couldn't see anything. The acrid scent of gunpowder overpowered the animal odor.

Through it all, one terrifying fact stood out: she'd recognized the man who'd come in first, gun blazing. He was wearing sunglasses, but his blonde hair and the crocodile xenograft on his face were unmistakable. She was already frightened, but now terror blossomed in her gut.

Had he seen her?

That question was answered far more quickly than she expected. The shooting stopped and other than some moans and whimpers, a relative silence fell. The next thing she heard was heavy footsteps coming closer. She felt a firm hand on her shoulder and was rolled onto her back. She saw her own frightened face reflected back at her in his mirrored sunglasses.

Dundee grinned, a feral show of teeth. "Look what the dingo dragged in."

Chapter Fourteen

A group of about fifty people was gathered on the sidewalk and steps outside the building housing XIA headquarters. It was a secure building, an unprepossessing nine stories tall, and had several government agencies ensconced within. The XIA took up the top two floors and was open for business, but because of the riots, the other agencies had closed up shop. A notice had been posted on the main glass doors that the building was closed to the public.

From the hastily cobbled-together signs some of the men and women in front of the building were holding, Scott figured the crowd was composed of xenos looking for protection – and answers. Then he saw a familiar xenograft, a Mohawk of ragged feathers down the middle of a bald head. It was Chief Joe, standing next to his girlfriend Liz. Both were members of the XBestia gang, and neither had any business being here if the crowd was indeed what it seemed.

When Lo drove past, several of the protesters broke from the pack and followed the car around the corner to the parking garage entrance. Scott was glad for the dark tint on the sedan's windows when he saw Chief Joe and Liz among them.

In order to gain entrance to the parking garage, Lo would have to roll down her window and hold her hand under a holoscanner, but the xenos were suddenly all around them. Lo inched the car forward to avoid running over anyone as they shouted, shook their fists and banged on the hood and windows. Scott kept his head down and his hands out of sight.

There was no police presence, of course, and the one security guard behind the gate was unprepared to handle the situation. He shook his head to indicate he wasn't opening the gate, then held a hand up to his head to show them he'd called for backup.

Several tense minutes later, two armed guards arrived, dressed in tactical gear. One of them shouted a warning before lobbing a tear gas grenade over the fence. The crowd scattered to a safe distance as Lo drove through the gate and checked in with the guard. She parked in the underground lot on the nearly empty first floor.

They still hadn't heard from Shasta, so Scott talked it over briefly with Lo and they decided to put Nicola and Savvy in separate interview rooms for the time being. Technically, Savvy was being detained for questioning and would have had a date with an interview room anyway, but Nicola was a juvenile runaway. They wouldn't be able to hold her long before they had to turn her over to Children's Services – unless, as he suspected would happen, Shasta made her a protected witness.

Scott got out of the car and let Savvy and Nicola out. They all headed for the elevator, but before they got there, it opened and three of the XIA techs, who normally never left the control room, hurried to intercept them.

"Hold on," one of them said, panting a little as if trotting across the parking lot was too much for him. He was pale and flabby with thinning brown hair. Scott caught a glimpse of his ID badge: Bob.

"We got a loud ping when you drove in," Bob said.

Scott didn't know what that meant exactly, but he looked at Savvy, who as usual wouldn't meet his eyes. "What's in the backpack?"

Savvy tightened his fingers around the straps. "My stuff."

"We're going to have to confiscate it," Bob said.

"No." Savvy took a step back, as if he was prepared to run away to keep them from taking it.

Nicola, who had her arms wrapped around the covered bird cage, said, "Felson, just let them have it, okay? You'll get it back."

"I highly doubt that," Savvy replied, but he removed the backpack from his narrow shoulders and handed it to Bob.

Bob gestured to the bird cage. "That, too."

Nicola gasped and turned to Scott with pleading eyes. "Don't take Perky."

"Nobody's going to hurt him," Scott said.

"Her." Nicola sniffed like she was about to cry, but reluctantly held the cage out to one of the techs. He took it by the handle and Nicola said, "Careful! Hold it level or you'll spill her water all over the paper."

Bob frowned at her, lifted the cover to look inside and was immediately rewarded with an indignant, ear-piercing chirp. He gave Nicola an unreadable look, then turned and waved for the other techs to follow him. As they headed for the elevator, he unzipped Savvy's backpack and looked inside, saying, "Test everything for everything. Standalone equipment only."

Nicola sniffed again and glowered at Scott. "Are you happy now?"

Scott wasn't, actually. He and Lo hadn't bothered to frisk Savvy back at the Warehouse, and there was a distinct possibility that whatever the tech guys thought had set off their alarms was still on him. He caught Lo's eye and jerked his head in the direction of the door that led to the main lobby. She lifted her eyebrows in silent inquiry, and he said simply, "Scanner." She nodded and waved for Nicola and Savvy to precede her.

Nicola turned to Savvy and asked, "What was that all about?"

"They want to scan us for weapons."

"Oh." Nicola pouted, but said nothing further.

There was only one guard in the main lobby, which made sense, since the other two had just dispersed the crowd so Lo could drive in. The guard greeted them with, "And I thought today was going to be boring with the building shut down."

Scott looked out at the crowd, which seemed to have grown significantly in the last few minutes alone. He saw Chief Joe and Liz again, but they couldn't see him – the windows and glass doors making up the entire exterior wall of the main floor were coated with a reflective surface.

After their guests went through the body scanner without raising any alarms, Scott and Lo took them upstairs. The receptionist buzzed them into a nearly deserted office. There were only a few administrative staff members in sight, and they were all on the phone, keeping the communication lines open. Scott assumed the other agents and handlers were either out in the field or unable to do their jobs due to the state of the city.

Lo went off to find Savvy and Nicola something to eat while Scott processed them, obtaining holoprints and running their DNA. By the time the two were settled in their respective interview rooms, it was after noon.

The minute Scott got back to his cubicle and sat down in his office chair, he texted Shasta again, letting her know they'd arrived and that the techs were going over Savvy's 'stuff.' Then he attempted to call Mia, grinding his teeth in frustration when she didn't answer. Finally, he called Carla.

Bryn's godmother answered on the first ring. She wasn't home, if the noisy crowd of people in the background of the holo was any indication.

"Where are you?" he asked.

"Poppy's Pier. How's Bryn?"

"I was hoping you'd heard from her. Why are you at Poppy's Pier? It's condemned, isn't it?"

"Don't you know? The National Guard is rounding us up. Xenos."

"You're kidding. How do they know who to round up?"

Carla's xeno name was 'Mouse,' after her old xenograft. After it had been forcibly removed by an ARA operative, she'd had another one grafted on. It was located in the same place, on the curve of her breast, but wasn't normally visible.

She wrinkled her nose. "They have a list of people who've gotten transplants, and they're sweeping xeno neighborhoods for the rest of us. One of my neighbors ratted me out. When the guardsmen showed up, I was given the choice of showing them my graft or being treated to a strip search. So I showed them."

"That's—"

"Barbaric? Just a sign of the times, sweetie. Besides, I'm actually kinda glad to be here. My neighborhood's a war zone and at least here I'm safe."

Scott had seen for himself how badly her neighborhood had been hit by the rioters when he'd picked up Bryn's clothes that morning. He'd invited Carla to stay at his place, but after what happened to Bryn and Mia, it was probably best that she'd refused. Not that being threatened with a strip search and detained by the National Guard sounded like a better option. And Poppy's Pier…what made them choose *that* place?

Back in 2020, an unprecedented storm surge from hurricane Poppy critically damaged the already deteriorated infrastructure of Pier 40 on the Hudson. The fifteen-acre pier, part of Hudson River Park, was shut down until a funding source to repair it could be identified. Unfortunately, by the time an amendment to the Hudson River Park Act had been agreed upon, the cost to repair the damage exceeded any potential returns on the investment, and a commercial source of revenue couldn't be found. The pier remained officially closed to the public for their safety.

Poppy's Pier, as it came to be known, was a huge, square structure jutting out over the Hudson River with a former soccer field at its center, surrounded by a multistory building and parking lot in various stages of collapse. Because of its proximity to Lower Manhattan, local law enforcement swept the pier regularly, preventing gangs from taking over like they had at Coney Island, but the pier was still a dangerous place.

"Do me a favor," he said. "Stay close to an exit. If things get dicey, I don't want you to get trampled."

"That's sweet of you to worry, but I can take of myself."

He believed her. Carla was a survivor. "Tell Bryn to call me if you hear from her, okay?"

"Shouldn't she be at your place?"

"Yeah, but it turned out my place wasn't safe either."

"Great. Now you got me worried. Will you call if you hear from her first?"

"If I get a chance. Lot going on."

"Tell me about it."

After he disconnected, he sat and stared unseeing at his cubicle walls, heightened anxiety and a sense of lingering regret burning a hole in his gut. He'd told Bryn he loved her last night…*after* she'd fallen asleep. He didn't regret saying it, he just wished he'd been brave enough to tell her when she could respond back one way or the other.

"Heard you caught a big fish."

It was Jason Alton's voice, and Scott reluctantly turned around in his chair. Alton had a white strip across his nose and both eyes were surrounded by colorful bruising.

"What are you doing out of the hospital?" Scott asked. "Aren't you missing a lung or something?"

The question came out sounding more antagonistic than he'd intended; not because he didn't harbor major hostility towards the guy, but because he usually hid that sort of thing better.

"Nope, all patched up," Alton said. "Amazing what they can do these days. You should know. What was it – four bullets in the back?"

Before Scott could point out he'd been wearing bullet-resistant clothing, Lo arrived and tossed him a plastic-wrapped sandwich. "Food court was closed, so I had to hit the machine."

He said, "Thanks," and used his claws to tear into the plastic wrap before shoving the turkey on wheat into his mouth. The cheese tasted funny, but hopefully the sandwich would help settle his stomach.

Lo turned to Alton. "You on duty already? I thought you were at death's door."

"Felt like it, but I'm alright."

"You don't look alright, but you know what? I have some cream that'll make you pretty again in no time." She took off for her cubicle.

Scott ate his sandwich in silence, happy to have a reason to ignore Alton. He wasn't jealous exactly – Bryn had very specifically told him she wasn't interested in him – but it rankled that Alton had gotten close to her. Just because Bryn didn't want *him*, didn't mean he didn't want *her*.

Lo came back with a tube of something that she proceeded to squeeze out onto her finger. Alton jerked his head back when she lifted her hand to his face.

"What's in it?"

"How would I know?" she responded. "It's for bruising, and trust me, it works miracles."

Alton let her smear the stuff around and under his eyes. "Smells terrible."

"Shut up."

51

When Lo was finished, she stepped up close to Scott and said, "Your turn."

Scott sighed, but tilted his head back obediently. The stuff did smell terrible, but he kept his opinion to himself.

When she finished, she asked, "You text Shasta?"

Scott had taken another bite of the sandwich, so he nodded.

"Heard back?"

He shook his head no.

She turned to Alton. "You?"

"Haven't heard from her since this morning when she was on the way to the airport with Unger. Have either of you, um, heard from Dr. Padilla?"

Scott didn't particularly want to tell Alton about Mia, but Bryn had sent that message telling him they'd been chased out of his apartment hours ago, and Mia should have been in and out of surgery by now.

"She's getting grafted," he said.

"*What*?" Alton had been leaning against the cubicle frame, but he jerked upright so quickly it must have hurt, because he winced and put a hand to his ribs. "Where?"

"New Rochelle. Why?"

"Gangs have been hitting rival dens all over the city, trashing surgeries and robbing customers. Haven't you been paying attention to the news?"

Scott clenched his jaw but didn't respond to Alton's implied criticism other than to say, "We've been working." He pulled his holophone out of his pocket and checked his messages for the text he'd sent Mia. "She went to a den called Koo Koo Bamboo Tattoo. You got a list of the places that have been hit?"

Alton made a move like he was going to go somewhere to find out, but Lo said, "Hold on." She'd also taken her holophone out, and lines of text flowed around her finger as she scrolled through information.

"Koo Koo was one of the first to get hit," she said. "Dr. Padilla's not on the list of victims, though."

"What about Bryn?" Scott asked.

Alton shot him a look of disbelief. "You let her go, too?"

"I didn't *let* her do anything," Scott snapped. "Have you *met* her?"

Alton backed off, muttering, "Yeah, alright."

"Bryn's not here, either," Lo said. "Maybe they didn't go after all."

Scott looked at Alton, then Lo. "So where the hell are they?"

Chapter Fifteen

All eyes were on Dundee and Bryn as they walked across the store to the front counter. He had a hand on her upper arm, but she wasn't resisting. There was no point. None of the shell-shocked customers would have interceded on her behalf.

The last time she'd seen Dundee, he'd forced himself on her and she fought back, using her quills much like she'd used them on that man earlier, but in Dundee's case, the quills had pierced his eyes. It had seemed to be a horrific injury and she'd been worried for months that she'd blinded him. That was obviously not the case, but he *was* still wearing his sunglasses, so maybe his eyes were light sensitive now or something. Either way, she'd made a mortal enemy that day, and here he was, almost casually claiming her – for payback? Bryn didn't doubt it for a moment.

His presence could only mean one thing: the Scaly Companion Pet Store and its xenografting den were owned by Dr. Fournier. Was the Bestia Butcher even now in the back operating on Mia?

As they approached the counter, Bryn avoided looking at the dead men, but was hyper-aware of their sprawled bodies. Turk was standing next to the cash register, a handgun resting within arms-reach, evidence that he'd been waiting for Dundee and friend to arrive before he came out shooting.

"Alright, everyone," Turk announced. "That sucked, but it's over now. Anyone who wants to avoid the police can go ahead and leave, but you'll lose your place in line."

Nobody moved.

The guy who'd come in with Dundee had a heavily freckled face and long red dreads. He hooked his hands under the arms of one of the dead men and started to drag the body away.

One of the customers said, "You're not supposed to move the bodies."

"Yeah?" the guy said. He pointed up at the ceiling. "See that camera? That's all the police need. And just for that, you can help me move this meat. Get his legs. Unless you want his dead eyes staring at you until the cops get here – which will probably be hours from now, if they bother to show up at all."

The customer who'd spoken up swallowed convulsively. Bryn didn't hear what he said, because Dundee pulled her with him to the door leading to the back room.

Turk held out a hand as they walked past. Dangling from one finger was a blue surgical mask.

"Oh, right," Dundee said. He set his shotgun down on the counter with a clunk and took the mask, fitting it over his nose and mouth without taking off his sunglasses, and hooking the elastic behind his ears.

It was a pointed reminder that Bryn was now in the company of patient zero, the first known case of the super typhoid. Dundee was Fournier's man through and through, a carrier who had deliberately infected people with it at Fournier's bidding, just like Junk had.

They went through the door and walked down the hallway, past the room with the bioengineered animals and through another door into a larger room. There were around fifteen people sitting on chairs or lying on cots, in various stages of prep or recovery. The air was cold and smelled of antiseptic.

A man in blue scrubs saw Dundee and said, "Hey, you can't be back here."

"Just leaving," he replied. He nodded towards Mia and told Bryn, "Get your friend, or I will."

She didn't ask how he knew she was with Mia. There were cameras in every room. Fournier installed them in all his facilities. Bryn had kept her quills hidden until that xeno thug had pulled her hood off. If he hadn't done that, would she be out there blending in with the other customers right now? Or had Fournier known she was here all along?

As soon as Mia saw Bryn she jumped up from her chair. She was clutching a white plastic bag, but her purse, which had been in her lap, slid to the floor. She started to bend down but stopped and looked up at Bryn.

"Can you get that for me?" She extended her hand towards the purse.

Bryn picked it up, but Dundee snapped his fingers and she handed it over. Mia didn't seem to notice. From the dull look on her face, Bryn figured they'd given her a hefty dose of something to kill the pain. Before she took Mia's elbow, she asked quietly, "Where did you get it? Your back?"

Mia nodded and then held up the plastic bag. "Post-op inshr...instructions."

Dundee loomed over them and Bryn gently took Mia's arm. "We have to go now."

Mia smiled up at Dundee. "Who's your friend?"

Bryn almost said, "He's not my friend," but didn't think it would be wise to aggravate him. "His name's Dundee. Come on." Bryn tugged on Mia's arm now.

"Okay, okay. Grumpy."

She wobbled the first few steps as Bryn helped her into the hallway. Dundee led them to the back door, which opened onto an alley. An older full-size truck was waiting, engine running.

"Where we goin'?" Mia asked.

"We're getting a ride," Bryn replied. The lie made her feel worse than lousy, but she didn't see any alternative. Bryn might be able to outrun Dundee, but Mia was in no shape to do more than walk unsteadily. Explaining the circumstances would only upset her.

Dundee put them both in the back, got into the driver's seat, and turned all the way around so he was facing them. He reached up to his face with both hands and for a moment, Bryn was afraid he was going to take the mask off and expose Mia to the typhoid. Instead, he removed his sunglasses with careful precision and just looked at them. It took her a minute to realize he was revealing his eyes, and there was no mistaking his pride.

There were no scars to speak of, even though Bryn had left at least half a dozen quills sticking out of his face. Fournier must have fixed them, just like he fixed Dundee's eyes. They were large and round, an inhuman golden green with slit pupils. No white showed around the iris at all.

He chuckled at the looks on their faces and turned back around to put the truck into gear.

"What are those?" Mia had already been leaning forward to avoid putting pressure on her back, but now she grasped the top of Dundee's seat. "Cat's eyes?"

Dundee snorted. "I got a croc graft on my face, lady. No, they're not cat eyes."

"*Crocodile* eyes? That's amazing." Mia seemed to have completely missed his sarcasm. "Do you see color? Is your vision sharper? Crocodiles have excellent night vision, you know."

"Yes, yes, and yes, they do."

Bryn knew Dundee to be a violent psychopath, but he answered Mia's questions almost indulgently.

"Have you got the nictitating membrane?" Mia asked. She stumbled over the word nictitating, but as soon as Dundee said no, she blithely barreled on. "How did they seat them in the socket properly? Crocodiles are huge. Surely their eyes are, too."

"Depends on the kind of croc," Dundee said.

"Oh," Mia said. Her questions stopped as she considered it. Bryn figured the new eyes had come from one of the smaller, probably endangered, crocodile species. Mia must have come to the same conclusion, because she said, "Right," and looked out the window.

She didn't dwell on it long, though, as if the topic was just too compelling to resist.

"I knew successful optic nerve transection between *mammals* was still eluding surgeons, but that it had been possible in cold-blooded vertebrates for some time," she said. Then with only a tiny pause, she turned to Bryn and explained, "What I mean is: you can't transplant a human eye, for instance, into another human. Not if you want them to see. Or a monkey into a monkey, or a mouse into a mouse. But you can put a frog eye into another frog, no problemo. Mammal to mammal, can't be done, but for reptiles and amphibians, they've been doing it for a long time.

"Now this…" Mia gestured to the back of Dundee's head. "Putting a reptile eye into a mammal, well, it's fascin – no, *more* than fascinating – it's a tremendous leap forward." She turned to Bryn. "Maddy would be very interested in this development. Her functioning eye is photosensitive."

Bryn scowled as soon as Mia brought up Maddy's name, but it was too late.

"Maddy…Singh?" Dundee asked.

Bryn put a hand on Mia's arm and squeezed, wordlessly telling her to shut up, but Mia was still under the influence of whatever painkiller they'd given her.

"Ow, stop it," she said, yanking her arm away. "What's wrong with you?"

"Yeah, Bryn," Dundee said. "What's wrong with you? I want to hear more about Maddy's eyes."

Bryn had had enough. "Where are you taking us?"

Dundee laughed. "If you must know, we're going to see an old friend who wants to thank you for attempting to save his life."

Bryn's blood went cold. He could only mean one person.

Fournier.

Chapter Sixteen

In a discussion that took less than ten minutes, Scott, Alton and Lo exhausted the possible places Bryn and Mia might have gone in the middle of riot-torn New York. Scott was thinking about who else he could call that might know where she was when he caught sight of Shasta's dark head over the top of the cubicle walls. Instead of going directly to her office as she usually did, she headed straight for them, still dressed in the grey pantsuit she must have worn to the subcommittee hearing.

"Damned protesters," were her first words, followed quickly by, "Where are they?"

"Interview rooms one and two," Scott said. He stood and handed her the holofile with Nicola and Savvy's information.

She waved a hand over it to open Savvy's folder and glanced at the identification page. His fingerprints told them his name was Felson Ostling, originally from Michigan. "Techs find anything?"

"No word yet."

"You heard from Dr. Padilla? Her team can't get hold of her."

"Not since this morning." Scott was about to expound upon that, tell her where Mia was *supposed* to be, but Shasta turned to Lo and said, "Gear up and go pick up the UAAV. I need you and Boardman on protection detail. Deputy Director Unger's flight will be arriving at 4:16 at JFK. Pick him up, escort him home and no matter what he tells you, keep an eye on his house."

Lo nodded. "Where's the threat coming from?"

"Fournier, apparently. Lupus – I mean Agent Quinones – isn't talking exactly, but he *has* made some cryptic comments about the Deputy Director. It's just a precaution."

Lo frowned. "I know Fournier's a whack job, but you really think he's going after Unger?"

"Word on the street is he's gearing up for something big. Quinones is a hot mess, but in case there's something to it, I don't want to take any chances."

"Where is he? Lupus," Scott asked.

She hesitated. "Here, actually."

"In the building?"

She dipped her head. "Rikers is on lockdown because of the riots, and frankly, we don't have the staffing resources to house him offsite. He's being kept mostly sedated. Yang's outside the door guarding him."

"Will sedation be enough to block out the fear if Fournier activates his nanoneurons?" Scott asked.

"Fournier can't get to him anymore – at least theoretically. The tech guys found something that's supposed to block cell signals, a special paint." At Scott's raised eyebrows, she said, "I know what you're thinking, but Unger *did* authorize me to requisition it for Bryn right after Padme attacked her. Stuff's expensive and hard to get hold of, though, and by the time it came in and the painters were finished, Bryn and Alton had already gone missing."

She turned to Lo. "Boardman picked me up from the airport. He's waiting in the parking garage for you. He's still on crutches, but you need backup and he's all we got."

Lo said, "Yes, ma'am," before striding off towards the weapons room.

"You know," Scott said, "I saw a couple of XBestia in that crowd down there. Seemed to be trying to blend in."

"Huh. Lying in wait for Unger, maybe?" Shasta shrugged. "Alton, I need you to relieve Yang. She's been there since last night. They're on the eighth floor, central."

"Got it." Alton started to walk away, but he looked over his shoulder at Scott and mouthed, "Call me," which Scott interpreted to mean: call if he heard from Mia and Bryn. He nodded but couldn't help but wonder why Alton seemed so concerned.

He opened his mouth to mention Mia's situation to Shasta, but she began to walk briskly towards the interview rooms, saying, "Have they said anything useful?"

"Not really. Savvy's socially awkward, but perceptive. Nicola found out she was a clone and ran away. She's not planning on betraying her father."

"We'll see," Shasta said.

She paused outside the door to interview room one, and accessed Nicola's information on the holofile. She scanned the page with the DNA results.

"So it's true."

Scott nodded. Nicola's DNA identified her as Miranda Vega, Bryn's mother, who'd been dead for some years.

Shasta tilted her head towards the door. "Has she bonded with you at all?"

"A little. She's not crushing on me, if that's what you mean."

Shasta made a wry face as she studied his black eye. "Not looking like that, she's not. Where's your eye patch?"

He pulled it out of his back pocket, and she helped him adjust it over his injured eye.

"There," she said. "That's more like it. Romantic instead of scary. Now let's see if we can get her to tell us where her father is."

When Scott had joined the XIA, the agency put him through intense training and then he'd gone immediately undercover. He'd never officially interviewed a suspect before but assumed Shasta would take the lead and he'd sit quietly, observe, and try to look 'romantic.'

Nicola was slouched at the table staring at a crushed soda bottle and the wad of plastic wrap from her sandwich. Crumbs were scattered across the surface of the table. She stood when they entered and demanded, "Where's Perky?"

Shasta turned to Scott with a look of inquiry.

"Her pet bird," he said. "Perky's hanging out with the tech guys."

"When are they gonna be done? And you said there were showers here. I've been sitting in this room forever."

It had been less than an hour, but he didn't contradict her. "This is Shasta Fox, my boss."

Nicola turned a distrustful gaze Shasta's way, not returning her smile.

Scott pulled a chair out and after Shasta sat, he settled in the chair next to her. Shasta crossed her legs and set the holofile on the table. By default, the text and holos in the file were only visible from one direction. She and Scott could see it, but Nicola would only see a blur that was difficult to look at.

Shasta invited Nicola to join them with a wave of her hand. "Have a seat, Miss Fournier."

"I'm sick of sitting." Nicola's voice had a distinct catch in it. She took one step back away from the table and crossed her arms sullenly.

"Then you'll want to cooperate so we can get you that shower and a nice room," Scott said.

"A room where?" Nicola asked.

"Somewhere safe."

"There's nowhere safe from my dad. Padme can find anyone and Lupus…"

She trailed off, more than a trace of apprehension on her face. Scott had wondered how much she knew about Fournier's activities, and her reaction seemed to indicate she knew quite a lot.

Shasta must have wanted to ease her concerns, because she said, "Lupus is in custody, and Padme has left your father's employ."

"Really?" Nicola looked astonished. "That must have been why she told me. Because she was leaving."

Scott tilted his head. "Told you…that you're a clone?"

Nicola decided to sit after all, sliding down in her chair, arms still crossed. "I didn't believe her, but then I talked to Dad and he admitted it. That he made me."

"Where is your father?" Shasta asked.

Nicola rolled her eyes. "Why? So you can arrest him? Like I'm gonna tell you."

"Are you aware of what he's been doing?" Shasta leaned her elbows on the table. "Dozens of innocent people have died."

"That's not his fault."

"No? And yet you've been with," she glanced down at the holofile, "Mr. Ostling for two days now, while he's been diligently using the socialnet to spread some very specific information about the outbreak. Information he had to get somewhere."

Nicola licked her lips. "Yeah, so what? Daddy tried to warn people, but they didn't listen. Savvy thought we could do a better job getting the word out. Besides, Daddy didn't *create* that bacteria. He's not responsible for that. He's just…using it."

"Well, I didn't invent guns," Shasta countered, "but if I use one to kill someone, I *am* responsible."

"Whatever." Nicola's gaze slid past Shasta towards the corner of the room.

Scott was pretty sure Shasta wasn't going to get Nicola to cooperate by attempting to undermine her loyalty to her father. In fact, she was only forcing the girl to vehemently defend the man. Maybe if they eased up on her, gave her the opportunity to plead her father's case, she'd relax again.

"Who did your father try to warn?" he asked.

Nicola made a sour face, like he'd asked a stupid question.

"You," she said, spreading her hands to indicate the room around them. "The XIA."

Chapter Seventeen

Bryn kept an eye out for road signs, all the while acting like she wasn't paying attention to where they were going. Not that it mattered, really. Since Dundee hadn't blindfolded them, he was either taking them to a meeting place other than Fournier's new hideout, or they just might not be getting out of this alive. She'd been anxious so often lately, she was beginning to feel as if the fight or flight response was a normal state of being.

The holoclock on the dash showed half an hour had passed. Mia talked a good portion of that time but had finally seemed to run out of steam. She was resting her forehead on the back of Dundee's seat, and Bryn thought maybe she'd dozed off until she said, "Where are we going again?"

Something told Bryn the effects of the painkiller were wearing off and Mia wouldn't appreciate another lie.

"Dundee is Fournier's man," she said. "We're, um, going to see him, apparently."

"What? Why?" Mia directed the questions to Dundee.

"How would I know? Do I look like his best friend? He wants to talk to you."

Mia's eyes slid to Bryn, who couldn't muster a reassuring return look. She lifted her shoulders a little to indicate she had no idea why Fournier wanted to speak with them.

Their surroundings gradually transitioned from residential to rustic as the houses got farther and farther away from each other. As the yards got bigger, the houses became smaller and more derelict. Dundee took a right turn onto a rutted road that didn't have a sign identifying it. Bryn felt sorry for Mia, who stiffened in pain each time they hit a pothole or bump. They travelled along for at least a mile past what looked like an abandoned manufacturing plant. Bryn saw two armed guards patrolling the place and fully expected Dundee to pull up to one of the corroded metal industrial buildings, but he drove on.

The road ended at a tall, gated chain link fence. Dundee pressed a button on the visor and the gate slowly pulled open. He drove onto a gravel track that went up a low, rocky hill. At the top, Bryn looked down upon a wide winter-brown field complete with a few cows and sheep, beyond which was a barn, a house and several outbuildings. She counted three men on horses riding the perimeter fence. Beyond the farm was a large body of water she assumed was the Hudson River. She glanced behind her at the abandoned plant, where the sun glinted off old-fashioned solar panels on the rooftops. The plant's grunge contrasted sharply with the charming scene ahead of them.

Dundee took them down the hill past the red, two-story barn with white trim. He stopped the truck in front of a ranch style brick house behind a low picket fence.

Bryn took it all in and thought about the XIA's efforts to track Fournier down after he'd narrowly escaped death in the Warehouse tunnel collapse. Scott hadn't told her much, but he had mentioned the XIA's focus was on a small detail Padme had let slip: that Fournier kept the larger bioengineered animals offsite. An innocent-looking farm like this would be the perfect place to hide in plain sight.

Dundee got out and opened Mia's door. "Let's go."

Mia complied, moving slowly. She seemed steadier now, but her lips were compressed into a thin line of pain.

Bryn slid across the seat and got out as well. Her stomach was tied in knots. She couldn't help but think of the one and only time she'd met the man who'd surgically removed her scalp and replaced it with a porcupine pelt. He'd been buried up to his chest in dirt from the collapsed escape tunnel and she'd forced him to tell her about the typhoid in exchange for helping him. Her efforts had been in vain, however – she'd watched in horror as he'd been buried alive – or so she thought.

The front door of the house opened, and he appeared on the front step. Other than a short, neatly trimmed beard, he looked the same as when she'd last seen him, except he wasn't covered in dirt and there was no scar across his forehead where the shattered support beam had gashed it.

There was a faint blue glow on his face, and she realized he was wearing a holopiece over his right ear. She heard him say, "Keep an eye on it," before he blinked twice to discontinue the call. He then beckoned to them to approach, calling out, "Welcome! Please come in."

When Bryn got closer, Fournier reached out and tipped her chin back with one finger, running his gaze over her quills. "Lovely," he murmured. "Except…you're missing a patch just there in the front. Have you been in an altercation?"

63

When Bryn didn't respond, he looked at Dundee, who said, "Not my doing."

"Well, then," Fournier said, smiling like a good host and gesturing them inside. As Bryn and Mia crossed the threshold into a dark living room with overstuffed brown leather couches, he said, "I apologize for detaining you this way, but I assure you it was necessary. Please have a seat."

He swept a hand to indicate the couches. Bryn and Mia sat with their backs to a large window that overlooked the river. Fournier strode into the kitchen and brought out a silver tray with a cobalt blue teapot and matching cups and saucers. He set it on a glass-topped coffee table fashioned from the tortuous stump of a tree, and then sat facing them on the smaller couch.

Dundee set Mia's purse on the couch next to Fournier and went to stand by the door. He was still wearing the surgical mask, his slitted green eyes staring out over Bryn's and Mia's heads at the river. Bryn imagined him floating there among the reeds growing along the bank, motionless, only the top half of his face visible as he waited for his unsuspecting prey.

"I hope you like tea," Fournier said as he poured.

"I like answers," Mia responded.

"Don't we all." He held out a cup brimming with amber liquid.

Mia took it, but didn't sip, choosing instead to balance it on one knee. Bryn curled her cold fingers around the cup he handed her almost gratefully, savoring its warmth.

"Alright," Mia said. "Enough with the pleasantries." She gave sarcastic emphasis to the word. "What do you want with us?"

"I'd like to know how the anti-xenofreak poster child," he nodded in Bryn's direction, "and an infectious disease specialist with the CDC became acquainted."

"How do you know who I am?" Mia asked. "I used a fake name."

He shrugged. "My staff looked through your purse. Normally, they wouldn't have bothered, but you arrived with Bryn. So tell me how you know each other."

Mia shook her head. "Maybe you should be asking why I took time off in the middle of a deadly outbreak to get a xenograft."

He laughed. "I don't need to ask why. It's obvious you've figured out what my colleagues have been trying to tell the mainstream scientific community for years: xenografts protect against certain pathogens. Is the CDC planning to tell the public?"

"I've informed my superiors of my team's findings."

"Have you?" He set his cup on its saucer with a hard clink. "Because I've been monitoring the official press releases, and they've mentioned nothing."

Mia smiled thinly. "We *are* a bureaucracy."

"How very true. Bloated and corrupt like all government. However, that's beside the point. I ask again: how did you meet Bryn?"

From the door, Dundee said, "Maybe we should ask Maddy Singh."

Chapter Eighteen

Once Scott and Shasta left Nicola in the interview room to stew in her newly outraged mood, he asked, "Was that true? Did Fournier warn the agency?"

"Warn? No. Threaten? Yes. I assume whatever he told Nicola was meant to pacify her."

She opened the door to interview room two, where Savvy was seated at the table.

Scott took his eye patch off and tucked it into his back pocket. "Savvy, this is Shasta Fox, my boss."

Savvy lifted his head but didn't look at them. He'd kept himself occupied by hanging bits of twisted plastic wrap around his empty soda bottle.

Shasta sat and glanced down at the holofile. Scott chose to stand behind her chair this time, arms folded across his chest.

"Your real name is Felson Ostling," she said. "Is that Swedish?"

"I'm American," Savvy replied.

"Yes, I see you were born in Michigan. Diagnosed with savant syndrome as a child. What specifically does that mean in your case?"

"I don't forget."

"Prodigious memory. Okay," Shasta said. "And how has that been useful for your employer?"

"I'm unemployed."

"I meant your former employer, Dr. Nicolas Fournier."

Savvy had been staring at a spot on the table, but now he looked down at his lap, where his hands were clasped. "I *can* lie, you know."

"I don't doubt that. The question is whether you can lie well enough to fool me."

Savvy glanced up at Shasta's face, but didn't respond.

She sighed. "What is Miss Fournier's relationship to you?"

"We're not related."

"How did she find you?" Scott asked abruptly. Maybe Savvy's evasive way of answering was part of his syndrome, but it was annoying.

"She was running away and wanted to see if her old room had survived the fire. I was hiding out at the Warehouse facility because I thought it was the last place Fournier would look for me."

It was the first time Scott had heard Savvy string more than a few phrases together, and the answer immediately struck him as coached.

"Who told you to say that?" he asked.

Savvy may have been able to lie, but he was terrible at it. He blinked several times and his upper body began rocking back and forth in small movements. "No one."

"Because Nicola said the exact same thing." The lie rolled easily off Scott's tongue. "I think maybe even word for word."

Savvy's rocking increased; a physical barometer of his agitation. It struck Scott that all they had to do was ask the right questions and Savvy's unconscious body movements would answer for him.

"Why were you hiding from Fournier?" Shasta asked.

"He scares me."

"If that's true, you should be willing to help us capture him."

"No." He stopped rocking.

"Why not?"

"He scares me."

She took a breath to ask another question, but a tone sounded from the holofile, indicating that new information had been added. Shasta accessed it, and Scott read over her shoulder. The tech guys had finished going over Savvy's stuff. The hologame system was clean, but the portable 3D printer had piqued their interest. It was state-of-the-art and very expensive, with the ability to construct complex objects out of multiple materials, including nanoscale electronics. They'd tried, but were unable to access the printer's hard drive.

The other items among Savvy's 'stuff' were a holophone without a battery and a mishmash of things apparently scrounged from the debris at the Warehouse facility. The birdcage was exactly what it appeared to be. The techs concluded that whatever had set the alarm off when Lo had driven in wasn't among the items Nicola and Savvy had on them.

Scott stepped out from behind Shasta's chair and leaned forward to rest his palms on the table, extending his claws to scratch its surface lightly. Savvy seemed to be trying not to look at the claws, but his eyes kept flicking back and forth from the floor to the table.

"Your 3D printer," Scott said in a severe tone. "Can it make nanoneurons?"

Savvy recoiled against the back of his chair. "I – I can't tell you."

"Do you have a copy of Fournier's nanoneuron program?" Shasta asked. Scott could sense her barely concealed excitement.

Savvy said, "No," but he began to rock again.

"What's the printer's password?" Scott asked.

"I can't tell you."

Shasta nudged Scott's forearm with her elbow and he backed off, stepping away from the table.

"Have you been conditioned like Lupus?" she asked. "Are you worried that Fournier will flood your nervous system with fear?"

Savvy shook his head. "I don't have nanoneurons."

"Why not?"

"He didn't want to risk damaging my brain."

Before Shasta could ask anything else, a light began flashing in the room. Scott squinted up at the overheads before locating the fire alarm unit on the wall behind him, where the white strobe light had been activated. A mechanical voice told them this was not a drill, that there was a fire in the building, and advised them that evacuation was mandatory.

Lips pressed together angrily, Shasta shoved back her chair and strode out of the room, pulling her holophone from her pocket. Scott was two steps behind her. At the end of the hallway, what little staff had been in the building were exiting the floor through the stairwell door. Shasta accessed a phone number, muttering, "I got a bad feeling about this."

The head of building security appeared on her phone. His hair was dripping wet. Shasta asked brusquely, "Where's the fire?"

"Parking garage. Car fire."

"What's the threat level?"

"Depends. Fire department didn't even answer when we called. Sprinklers went off and my men are trying to put it out with extinguishers, but if it explodes, things could get dicey fast."

"We have prisoners up here and severely limited staff!" Shasta sounded unusually rattled. "Can you spare anyone?"

"I got two guys on the fire and two waiting for your staff to get to the lobby. Building's surrounded by xenos and they won't be able to evacuate. Don't know how you're going to get your prisoners out."

Scott leaned over Shasta's shoulder and asked him, "Whose car was it?"

"Uh," the guard looked down at something, "It's one of yours. Assigned to Tina Lo."

Shasta growled in her throat and disconnected abruptly, glaring at Scott. "I presume our guests left an incendiary device in the back seat?"

"The tech guys said we set off some kind of alarm when we drove in. That's why they were checking Savvy's stuff. None of us thought he might have left something in the car."

She sighed and gestured to the interview rooms. "Get them. Alton and I will take care of Lupus. Meet us in the parking garage."

Scott didn't question her. The parking garage was the source of the fire, but they couldn't very well walk out the front door with Lupus. They would have to pack the staff and prisoners into cars and drive out – even if they had to mow the protesting xenos down.

It occurred to him that this might be the 'something big' Shasta had been expecting: an attack on the XIA itself. She'd sent Lo and Boardman off to guard Unger, but what if Fournier's plan had been to take advantage of the city's overwhelmed law enforcement and military and break Lupus out?

As Shasta disappeared down the hallway, he opened the door to interview room two.

Savvy didn't resist when Scott grabbed his upper arm and urged him to his feet. The savant's face was turned away as usual, but when Scott caught sight of his profile and realized he was hiding a smile, he jerked his arm roughly.

"You think this is funny?"

"Chaos is always funny," Savvy replied.

Scott shoved him towards the door with a little more force than necessary. In the hallway, he kept a close eye on him as he opened the door to interview room one. Nicola rushed out, saying, "It's about time! I thought you were going to leave me in there!"

Scott almost said, "Don't think it didn't cross my mind," but stopped himself. There was still a possibility she might open up to him, which wouldn't happen if he was a jerk to her.

He walked between and a little behind them as they headed for the exit. When he opened the door at the end of the hallway, Nicola balked at entering the stairwell.

"Do you smell that? Is that smoke?"

The air in the stairwell did smell faintly of smoke. Scott said, "It's the only way out. The elevators won't work in an emergency."

"Where's Perky?" she demanded.

Scott suffered through a moment of déjà vu, remembering the girl's stubborn refusal to abandon her bird and her 'mother's' books when the Warehouse facility was under attack.

"He'll be fine," he said.

"*She! She'll* be fine – but she *won't*."

With no warning, Nicola bolted in the opposite direction.

Chapter Nineteen

Bryn felt as if the temperature in Fournier's living room dropped about ten degrees when he asked, "Maddy Singh? What about him…or her, or whatever?"

Dundee took several steps closer, crocodile eyes narrowed like he was smiling under the surgical mask. "The chatty germ doctor let it slip on the ride. Said Maddy's one working eye was photosensitive."

Fournier looked at Mia with a shake of his head. "Is this true? You know Maddy Singh?"

"They both do," Dundee said helpfully.

Fournier turned his penetrating gaze on Bryn. "What *have* you been up to?"

She certainly couldn't tell the truth, but a lie would get complicated fast. She thought about keeping silent but was afraid of what Mia might blurt out. She settled on, "We met once. I don't know her."

"And you?" he asked Mia.

"She kidnapped me. Her people were dying of the typhoid and she thought I could help."

"So this happened recently."

"You should know," Mia replied, "since you're the one who sent the carrier to infect them."

Bryn closed her eyes briefly. Mia just couldn't resist goading him.

"Ah," Fournier said. "You must be referring to Junk."

"His cause of death was blunt force trauma, in case you're curious."

"Nothing less than what he deserved for getting caught."

"More like what he deserved for killing a bunch of innocent children." Mia was getting worked up, and Bryn laid a cautionary hand on her arm that she immediately shook off.

"Innocent?" Fournier asked. "Maybe. I won't get into a debate with you about the wisdom of preventing the children of one's enemies from growing up and becoming enemies themselves. Regardless, my intention wasn't to kill anyone, but simply to spread the infection among xenos."

"And create carriers."

Fournier sat back against the couch cushions. "You *are* well informed, aren't you? Is this your own insight or Maddy's? Oh, wait – the CDC is working with the XIA on this one, am I right?"

Even though it was a logical conclusion for him to make, Bryn began to silently panic. In Mia's agitated state, she might slip up and mention Scott. According to Padme, Fournier still didn't know he was an agent. Thankfully, rather than answer him, Mia looked up at Dundee and demanded, "Why is that man wearing a mask? Is *he* a carrier?"

"He is indeed. And in case *you're* curious, your graft won't begin to protect you until several weeks after it's fully healed."

Mia didn't respond other than to stare up at Dundee from beneath knitted brows. Bryn was frankly relieved that something had shut her up before she revealed anything that could get them killed – assuming she hadn't already.

A gentle tone sounded, and Fournier blinked to activate the holopiece over his ear. No one but the wearer could see who he was talking to, but she heard his side of the conversation. "Why not?" "Then use the truck!" Slowly, like he was speaking to a child, he said, "Drive it through the front entrance."

After he ended the call, Bryn tried her best to sound respectful. "When are you going to let us go?"

He leaned forward to take another sip of his tea, regarding them intently over his cup. "I really just brought you here out of curiosity, but I have serious reservations about turning you loose now that I know about your connection to the Mad Eye. My organization has suffered some severe setbacks thanks to their leader."

"But we *aren't* connected to them," Bryn protested. "We don't want anything to *do* with them."

Mia was still staring at Dundee as if his crocodile eyes had mesmerized her. She tilted her head to one side and murmured, "Junk had a crocodile graft, too."

The moment the words left her mouth, she gasped, and all the color leached from her cheeks. She turned to Fournier. "Is that it? Do all the carriers have reptile grafts?"

Fournier chuckled. "That would be ironic, since you just got one, wouldn't it? But no, it doesn't appear to be all reptiles, just crocodilians. And unfortunately, now that you've figured that out, I really must continue to detain you."

"Why?" Bryn exclaimed. "I thought you wanted the government to tell the public the truth."

"Did I say that?" He looked at her derisively. "It doesn't matter what the government tells them. Everyone gets their information from the interweb. Besides, I doubt anyone as young and attractive as Ms. Padilla has much sway within the CDC. Why do you think they sent someone so inexperienced on such an important mission? So she would fail."

Mia's cheeks turned pink again. "I'm hardly inexperienced, but I don't keep my résumé in my purse, so you wouldn't know."

For the first time, Fournier's mask of politeness slipped. "What I know is that as we speak, the legislature is hearing testimony in yet another futile effort to regulate xenoaugmentation, while at the same time, some very powerful people are determined get it outlawed entirely – people who have significant influence over the decision-makers in this country, including those at the CDC."

"You're suggesting the CDC is withholding information that could save lives?" Mia asked.

"I'm not suggesting it; I'm saying it. I'm sure they justified it by claiming they didn't want to panic the people, but it's too late now, isn't it? The riots changed everything. People aren't sitting on their hands waiting for answers; they're actively searching them out."

Bryn thought about the men who'd chased them out of Scott's apartment. One of them had referred to the jacker Scott was out tracking down, saying, "Savvy says all xenofreaks are immune, and once the contagious ones kill off the rest of us, the world will one big xenofreak show."

Shasta had said Savvy's messages seemed to be originating from someone with specific inside knowledge of Fournier's involvement.

"It was you," Bryn said, suddenly understanding. "You're Savvy, aren't you?"

"Oh, you've heard of him?" He looked pleased. "Savvy is what you might call my mouthpiece."

"I don't get it," she said. "You're turning people *against* xenos."

"I prefer the term 'polarizing.' For or against. A necessary first step to accomplish my short-term goals. I find that when things are particularly chaotic, the ones who don't panic can accomplish quite a lot."

"Like the men who tried to rob your den?" Bryn asked.

"Exactly. They saw an opportunity and went for it. To their detriment, as it turns out."

"But you're not just taking advantage of the riots, you're making them worse by fanning the flames." She took a breath as something occurred to her. "Because you need the police to stay overwhelmed. You're going to do something!"

"Clever girl." He looked thoughtful for a moment. "How much did your father tell you?"

"Not a lot. He said he asked you to do this," she gestured to her quills, "to protect me. And because he wanted to exploit what happened to me in order to turn people against xenos, which would then open the door for human cloning."

"What?" Mia sounded aghast. "That's ridiculous."

Bryn didn't feel the need to defend her father, but she thought Mia at least ought to understand. "He was the head of the Pure Human Society. He thought if we could clone human hearts, livers and kidneys instead of getting them from bioengineered animals, it wouldn't be such an…aberration, I guess."

"Your father's vision was limited," Fournier said. "There are hundreds of thousands of people whose lives have been saved with bioengineered organs – a process, as you know, that I pioneered. Coincidentally, every one of them is now protected against the typhoid."

"But they aren't protected against mobs of scared and angry people." Mia said.

Fournier got that same fervent look in his eye Bryn's father always used to get when he was gearing up for a lecture. "Transplant patients may be xenos, but they aren't so-called xeno*freaks*. It wasn't a lifestyle choice. No one will judge them for choosing to save their own lives. Just as you won't be judged for getting a graft to save yours."

"It cost me fifty-thousand dollars. Only the wealthy will survive this pandemic. Was that your intention?" Mia's full lips twisted in a sneer. "To get rich through genocide?"

Fournier sighed. "Believe it or not, I'm doing this to save lives. It may sound melodramatic, but 'sacrifice for the greater good' and all that. There are so many things you don't know."

He paused to gather his thoughts. "Were either of you aware that lawfully bioengineered animals cannot reproduce?"

Bryn nodded. In the dark days before she'd come to terms with her quills, she'd done her research. Around the turn of the twenty-first century, genetically modified crops had been introduced into America's food sources. The pros and cons were hotly debated, but it wasn't until a rapidly growing variety of cultivated grape resistant to pests, herbicides and harsh environmental conditions began to spread across the southern states that people began to really take notice. The grapevines invaded other crops and orchards, quickly killing them through strangulation and heavy shading.

Eradication of the plant took almost a decade. The entire debacle set the stage for heavy penalties for any corporation responsible for letting a genetically modified organism loose on the planet, including bioengineered animals.

"They make them sterile on purpose so they don't disrupt the ecosystem," Bryn said.

"Correct. Which means all animals provided to the *authorized* xenofarms in this country come from government-mandated bioengineering labs. The farms then raise the animals in as sterile an environment as possible and slaughter them on demand for transplant hospitals. Do you know what they do with the rest of the animal after they've removed the useable organs?"

"They incinerate it."

Fournier dipped his head. "Every xenofarm in the United States is contracted with a single company charged with disposing of the remains. Instead of doing so, that company has begun selling the skin and other parts on the black market."

"Okay, so you have competition," Mia said. "What's that got to do with you supposedly saving lives?"

"My 'competition,' as you call them, are utterly ruthless. They've been fighting xeno regulation for years, because regulation would make the practice officially accepted, which is the opposite of their goal, to make it illegal."

"Why make it illegal?" Mia asked. "It's a simple dermatological outpatient procedure."

"The majority of grafts are simple, as you say, but there are the more extreme forms of augmentation, those that require nanoneuron implantation."

"Your specialty," Bryn sent him a hard look.

"Who are these people?" Mia asked. "Animal rights activists?"

"No. They have a much more sinister goal than the ARA. On the surface, they're a faceless corporation that doesn't care who or what it hurts in its pursuit of money and power, but in reality, one man calls the shots. You might think the xeno black market would be small potatoes to him, but it's become essential that he control it. Can you guess why?"

"I'm sure you're going to tell us – eventually." Mia rolled her eyes.

"His corporation is huge, dealing not only in over-the-counter pharmaceuticals, but prescription medications and immunizations. He recently purchased both the xeno donor waste disposal company and the bioengineering labs I mentioned. With those acquisitions, the only thing preventing him from obtaining a stranglehold on this country's xenoaugmentation trade is entrepreneurs like me."

"And the saving of the people...?" Mia's reminder was unsubtly contemptuous.

"Let me put it this way: if you had gotten your graft from someone who buys their skins, you would eventually discover you were *not* immune to the typhoid."

That got Mia's attention. "That would mean..."

"Yes. His bioengineers finally figured out how xeno immunity works, and they eliminated it. The skin flooding the market now doesn't protect xenos. Nor do the transplants."

"Why would they do that?" Bryn asked.

Fournier smiled, a bleak stretching of the lips. "The definition of immunity is freedom from disease. Illness is big business."

"And this mystery man sells immunizations and drugs." Now that she understood his argument, Mia's contempt was less evident.

He raised his eyebrows, but then jerked his head around at a distant sound from outside. Bryn had heard it often enough to recognize it instantly.

Gunfire.

Chapter Twenty

Scott started after Nicola, but stopped, deciding of the two of them, Savvy was the one he needed to watch. He grasped the savant's arm and pulled him down the hallway.

Savvy had that creepily amused smile on his face again as Scott dragged him into the empty main workspace. Nicola was nowhere to be seen, but he heard the faint chirp of the bird and followed the sound towards the tech room.

He found her standing outside the locked tech room door. Her feather eyebrows looked like thunderclouds over angry green eyes that reminded him of Bryn.

"Perky's in there. I want her out, *now*."

"You should have thought about that before you set Lo's car on fire."

"It wasn't my idea."

Scott jerked Savvy's arm just enough to get his attention. "Why'd you do it?"

"Diversion," Savvy muttered.

Scott glanced around the empty office. "For what?"

"Chaos."

"Oh, not that again," Nicola said. "He's always going off about how chaos is what drives biology."

"It drives *change*," Savvy said. "Biology would be stagnant without chaos."

"Whatever." Nicola put a hand against the tech room door. "Can I have my bird back, please?"

"You want the bird? Answer me. Why'd you set fire to the car?"

"I told you I didn't have anything to do with that!" Nicola cried.

"You just admitted you knew what Savvy was doing, which makes you an accessory. What was the diversion for?"

Nicola set her jaw stubbornly, and Scott practically felt his patience snap. He took a fistful of Savvy's shirt and shoved him up against the nearest cubicle wall.

"Stop it!" Nicola said shrilly.

Scott looked over his shoulder at her and snarled, "I will rip his head off if the two of you don't tell me what the hell's going on!"

"I don't know," she wailed. Her eyes shone with unshed tears, but Scott wasn't fooled this time. Nicola wasn't as innocent as she seemed. He let Savvy go as something occurred to him.

"The holophone in Savvy's backpack. It didn't have a battery, but that's because he took it out and used it to power the incendiary device, is that right?"

Savvy turned his head away, and Scott took that as a 'yes.'

"But you made a call at the roadblock first, didn't you?" he asked.

"No." Savvy met Scott's gaze in a rare moment of eye contact, which Scott took as an indication he was telling the truth. He turned his attention to Nicola. "*You.* You called your father."

Her face fell into a look of belligerent denial, but before she could voice her protest, Scott's holophone rang. As soon as he answered it and saw Shasta, he knew something was wrong.

"We've got a situation down here," she said. Her normally tidy hair was mussed and her face tense. It didn't look like she was in the parking garage, but in the background, he saw what appeared to be the dented front end of a truck. A flash of light exploded somewhere above her, and sparks rained down all around. The view became a blur, and everything went dark.

Shasta's face came into view again as she lifted the holophone. She appeared to have ducked down behind something. In the dim glow emitted from the phone, Scott caught a glimpse of Lupus' wolf face in profile. His eyelids were at half-mast and his black lips hung slack.

"The xenos outside stormed the place," Shasta said.

Several loud gunshots rang out, followed by Alton's voice, "I'm almost out of ammo!"

Shasta held the holophone closer to her face. "I sent Bob up – get the printer! That's an order. Do you hear me, Agent Harding? Get the printer and *get out*!"

The call ended abruptly. Scott's first instinct was to ignore Shasta's orders and rush to help her, but Savvy was smiling again, and his second instinct took over. He threw a swift punch to the side of the savant's face, ignoring Nicola's gasp of protest. Savvy's knees buckled and he sagged to the floor just as Bob, cheeks red from exertion, rounded the corner.

Bob trotted over and immediately held his shaking hand under the holoscanner mounted next to the tech room door. He said his name for the voice recog-lock, but was breathing so hard it took him three tries to get the lock to respond. When the door swung inward, he hurried inside, saying over his shoulder, "I gotta initiate emergency protocols and shut the system down. Printer's over there."

Scott spotted a black container the size of a lunch box and strode over to the counter to retrieve it. When he turned, Nicola had entered the room. He started to chase her out, but she headed straight for the bird cage near the door. As if in greeting, Perky let out another of her jarring chirps.

It only took Bob thirty seconds to lock down the tech room. When he was done, and the secure door slammed shut behind them, Savvy was nowhere to be seen.

Chapter Twenty-one

Bryn sat next to Mia in frozen silence as Fournier and Dundee burst into action. Dundee ran out the front door while Fournier jumped up and crossed the living room. He opened a drawer in the bureau under his holovision unit and removed a pistol, which he tucked into the back of his waistband. Then he reached up to his ear, attempting to call out with the holopiece over his ear. Bryn saw the blue glow turn to red each time the other party didn't answer. As Fournier tried another number, the sound of gunfire stopped.

Whoever he called this time picked up, and again Bryn heard his side of the conversation. "How did they get past security?" He scratched the side of his face, looking disconcerted. "Could be the ARA."

The ARA, or Animal Rights Army, was defunct as far as Bryn knew, ever since its leader had been sent to prison. Why Fournier thought they might be responsible for the gunfire, she had no idea.

"No! Catch the dangerous ones first," Fournier snapped. He blinked to end the call, shaking his head. He didn't explain anything to them, but as if he was talking to himself, said, "Why would they do that?"

"I did it," a voice from the front door drawled, "to create a diversion. Should be a familiar tactic to you."

Fournier spun on his heel and reached for the small of his back, but Maddy made a sharp 'tch' sound and he stopped. She wore dark sunglasses and her long, white-blonde hair was hanging in a thick braid over one shoulder. She was dressed in a crisp black wool coat and slim jeans. Standing next to her were Dillo and two xenos Bryn hadn't seen before, a bald man holding a sawed-off shotgun, and a thick-necked female xeno with short dyed-red hair. Dillo's left arm was in a sling, but in his right he held a gun she suspected was the same one that used to belong to Scott. She doubted it was still loaded with plastic bullets.

Fournier's face went florid with anger, but his eyes remained strangely blank. He was a man used to having the upper hand with his enemies, not the other way around. "How did you find me?"

"A little birdie," Maddy said.

His lips thinned and his jaw clenched in enraged comprehension. "Padme."

Maddy smiled and removed her sunglasses, revealing her one brown eye and one red. "A very lucky discovery on my part. Her head is simply bursting with interesting facts about you and your business dealings. For instance, she mentioned most of your men would be out storming a certain castle this afternoon, and you'd be particularly vulnerable."

As an apparent afterthought, she tilted her head and said, "Hello Bryn. Dr. Padilla. Having tea, are we? The two of you do get around."

Mia stood. "We were just leaving."

Maddy rolled her strange eyes. "Sit down. I already know you aren't here willingly." She glanced up at the ceiling, at a domed security camera, and shook her head at Fournier. "You thought changing the passwords would keep Padme out? She *designed* your security system. We've eavesdropped on every boring thing you've said and done today."

Bryn turned to look out the picture window and saw Maddy's yacht anchored just offshore. Was Padme on deck right now, waiting for Maddy to bring Fournier's head to her mounted on a pike? Bryn didn't doubt Maddy intended to kill him, since he was indirectly responsible for the death of her brother, but what was she waiting for?

Fournier must have been thinking along the same lines, because he asked, "What do you want from me? You would have killed me by now if there wasn't something."

Maddy pointed at him and then touched her nose, like he'd won at charades. "I'd like the nanoneuron program, please. Apparently, it's the one thing Padme can't access remotely."

"I don't have it," Fournier said.

Maddy didn't give an order, merely glanced at Dillo, who raised his gun and nonchalantly shot Fournier in the upper arm. Fournier let out an agonized cry and dropped to his knees right in front of Bryn. Blood bloomed on his sleeve.

Definitely not plastic bullets, she thought. As horrified as she was, she still found she had to resist the urge to take advantage of his weakness and smash him over the head with the teapot.

Maddy waited until Fournier's moans subsided enough for him to hear her. "That was just a teaser. I assure you my friend is capable of much worse. Now take me to the control room and give me the program."

80

Fournier produced a series of sounds that Bryn thought at first was sobbing but turned out to be laughter. "I honestly don't have it." When Dillo raised the gun again, Fournier added hastily, "But I know where it is."

"Fine. I'll bite," Maddy said. "Where is it?"

"The XIA has it."

Chapter Twenty-two

Scott didn't have time to search for Savvy. He didn't think the little weasel would risk going down to the lobby, so he was either hiding on the floor or had taken the stairs to hide on another floor. If he'd attempted the latter, he was in for a disappointment, since the only door in the stairwell that wasn't secure was the one leading to the lobby. Even getting into the parking garage from the stairwell required a holoscan of an employee's palm.

Scott looked at Bob and asked, "You got access to the weapons room?"

Bob jerked his head to one side, producing an audible crack from his neck. "Heck, yeah."

Scott doubted Bob had ever held a real gun in his life, but if hologaming had given him enough self-confidence to at least attempt to protect himself, it was better than adding to Scott's burden.

"Let's go."

Inside the weapons room, he helped Bob into a vest and gave him a loaded handgun. "Safety's off. Only use it if you absolutely have to."

"We're not going to survive this, are we?" Bob's upper lip had beads of sweat on it, but his voice seemed calm enough.

"We will if I can help it." Scott shrugged into his own vest, quickly fastened it, and then strapped a utility belt around his waist. He tucked four grenades into the belt before slinging a semi-automatic rifle over his shoulder.

"How are we supposed to get out of the building?" Bob asked.

"Shasta said to meet her in the parking garage."

"When I was coming up, I heard her say the garage has been compromised."

"They we'll have to fight our way out. You up for it?"

Bob squared his jaw. "Alright."

Scott nodded approvingly before grabbing some extra clips. He and Bob shoved them into every available pocket.

Nicola was waiting for them, arms wrapped protectively around the birdcage. After Bob secured the weapons room, Scott began striding towards the stairwell, the black case with the 3D printer in his left hand and a weapon in his right.

"Where are we going?" Nicola asked.

"Your father sent some of his friends," he replied. "We're the welcoming party."

He made a quick detour past his cubicle to grab his leather jacket, putting it on over his vest. When he opened the door to the stairwell, he was greeted by darkness. He switched on the flashlight clipped to his utility belt to illuminate the steps and began to take them rapidly. Halfway down, he heard panicked voices echoing up the stairwell. When he reached the second floor, he saw why no one had come up – the first flight was gone. The moving-type truck he'd seen in the background of Shasta's holocall had smashed through the wall and torn the lightweight biopolycrete steps completely away from the second-floor platform.

Scott knelt on the unsteady platform and peered over the edge. The cab of the truck was directly below him and the back of it was blocking the hole it had created in the wall except for a chunk missing along the right side. Through that opening, he could see water from the fire sprinklers raining down in the lobby.

In the corner across from the truck, near the closed door to the parking garage, a cluster of people were hunkered down behind a hastily constructed barrier composed of the remains of the staircase. The low light coming in from the lobby made it hard to see exactly who was had taken refuge there, but he assumed it was people from the building.

Someone from the lobby fired a shot into the stairwell that ricocheted off something. The bullet thudded into the wall not far from Scott's head. He unslung his rifle and aimed, but from this angle, he could only see a patch of the lobby flooring beyond the hole.

To his relief, he heard Shasta's voice. "Is that you, Agent Harding?"

"Yes, ma'am."

"You got any ammo for a standard-issue weapon?" It was Alton.

"Plenty." Scott set the printer down, took four clips out of a pocket and called out, "Heads up!" before lobbing them one by one into the group of people.

Just then, Nicola and Bob arrived, hesitating on the lowest step above the platform.

"Doesn't look safe," Bob said at the same time Nicola asked, "How are we supposed to get down?"

Scott didn't answer. The cab of the truck was only maybe a five-foot drop, but at least one of the xenos in the lobby had a gun. Someone, Scott thought it sounded like Chief Joe, shouted, "We got you surrounded! All we want is Lupus and you can go."

"Yeah right," Scott muttered. He looked down as something occurred to him. He'd worked with Chief Joe on the job to recover the panda from the ARA. They'd used a ten-foot decommissioned U-Haul truck, and unless he was mistaken, that same truck was right below him. It was armored and had honeycomb bullet-proof tires. Chief Joe had been an ex-NASCAR mechanic, so Scott knew the truck would have been running fine before the crash. Whether it was running now was the question.

For the driver to have gotten the truck to its present location, he would have had to drive it up the wide, shallow cement steps in front of the building in order to crash through the aluminum-framed glass doors. The fact that he'd also curved to the left and smashed into the far wall indicated one of three things: he'd panicked and lost control, overestimated the speed required to get the job done, or the truck had been damaged.

Scott leaned over the far side of the platform. It creaked ominously, but from that vantage point, he could see the front of the truck, which looked banged up, but didn't appear to be totaled. The driver's side door was open, and the keys dangled from the ignition.

He turned to Bob and Nicola, who'd stepped out onto the platform but were hovering near the door leading to the second floor. "Wait here, but be prepared to jump when I say."

Bob looked terrified but nodded.

Nicola said, "I'm not jumping."

"Oh, really?" Scott strode across the platform and before she realized what he was doing, yanked the birdcage out of her hands.

"Hey!" she exclaimed.

He ignored her, walking back to the edge of the platform. With his free hand, he held up a concussion grenade. "Shasta?"

"I see it. We're ready," she replied.

He pulled the pin, bent down, and with his best high school baseball sidearm throw, sent the grenade flying through the hole in the wall. As soon as the blast went off, he stepped into thin air, one hand holding the birdcage and the other the printer.

Chapter Twenty-three

Maddy looked down her nose at Fournier, her lips twisted in a grim approximation of a smile. "Padme told me you would move the program, but even I didn't think you'd be so foolish as to let it fall into XIA hands."

"I'd rather they had it than you," Fournier replied. "Or your father."

Maddy frowned. "My father? How is he relevant? No, don't answer. I'm quite sick of everyone bringing him up." She paced to the kitchen and back, hands folded in the small of her back.

"Assuming for conversation's sake I believe you, who exactly in the XIA has it?"

"By now it's possible my people have gotten it back."

"Oh, that's right. Padme filled me in on the details of your little rescue attempt. Quite bold of you, I must say, but unfortunately for Lupus, I arranged to have a few of my people blend in with the mob as a favor to her. She'll rest easier knowing that sadistic bastard is dead."

Bryn wasn't entirely sure what she was saying, but it sounded like Fournier was attempting to rescue Lupus. She didn't know where he was being held, but assumed it was some place like Rikers. No matter where it was, arranging a prison break seemed ambitious even for Fournier.

Maddy clapped her hands, producing a sudden pop of sound that made Fournier jerk like he'd been shot again. She reached out and snatched the holopiece from his ear, and then removed the gun from his waistband. "I'll take those. We're going on a little field trip. That arm looks painful. I much prefer you take us to the control room under your own power, but if you try to run, Dillo will shoot you in the knee next time. Is that clear?"

Fournier nodded.

Maddy tucked the gun into the inside pocket of her jacket and turned her attention to Bryn and Mia. "You two present a bit of a problem, but for the time being, I'm going to take you with us. If what he says is true," she gestured to Fournier, "you might come in handy."

85

Bryn scowled. She knew exactly what Maddy meant: if the XIA did have the nanoneuron program, Bryn would once again be Maddy's leverage to force Scott into doing what she wanted. A crushing sense of helplessness swept over her. She was sick of being treated like a pawn on a chessboard.

Maddy put her sunglasses back on and said, "Shall we?"

She led the way towards the door, the female xeno a step behind. The bald xeno grasped Fournier's uninjured arm and jabbed the short barrel of the shotgun into his side before marching him down the hallway. Dillo waited to escort Mia and Bryn. Mia picked up her purse and wrapped her arms around it, daring Dillo with her eyes to take it away from her. He seemed unconcerned, however, and simply waved for them to precede him. Bryn stayed close to Mia's side as they left Fournier's quaint little farmhouse.

They traveled on foot, passing the motionless body of Dundee in the driveway. The surgical mask, still attached to one of his ears, fluttered in his face from the cold breeze off the Hudson. Bryn stared in revulsion at a blotch of half-congealed blood in the blonde hair at the back of his head. If he was dead, she certainly wouldn't mourn him, but despite the amount of violence she'd been exposed to lately, she wasn't immune to it. Her stomach clenched and she swallowed against a rise of bile.

She glanced over at Dillo's impassive face as they walked past Dundee's truck. When she'd met him, he'd seemed almost kind underneath the frightful surface – but since then he'd proven to be completely loyal to his queen. With a little shiver, she remembered what he'd told Maddy in yesterday's standoff: "I've got her in my sights. Just give the word." He'd been referring to Bryn and the fact that he was willing to kill her at Maddy's whim.

Near the barn, where earlier it had been quiet, now it seemed as if there were animals everywhere. A goat stood behind the picket fence, a clump of purple and white pansies hanging from its mouth. A pink sow with black spots on her rump suddenly ran squealing across the lane and disappeared into a box hedge.

Fournier walked resolutely along the drive next to the bald xeno, blood dripping from his knuckles into the gravel. His head turned this way and that as if he was looking for someone who wasn't there. *His soldiers, probably,* Bryn thought. Maddy had arranged for some kind of diversion. Had her men killed them?

They passed the barn, and the white doors that had been closed on their arrival were open and swinging slowly in the wind. The animals must have come from there.

At the top of the hill, Bryn looked around and realized what Maddy's diversion had been. She'd arranged to have all the animals on the farm released. The cows and sheep Bryn had seen earlier had been joined by several other species, some of them quite exotic, all running loose in the fields. A deer-like animal, she thought it was an impala, bounded along the fence line, chased by what could only be a cheetah. A man on horseback headed the cheetah off and attempted to shoot it.

It occurred to Bryn that Fournier's men weren't dead; they were out chasing down his livestock.

"If you're wondering how I did it," Maddy said, addressing Fournier, "it was pathetically simple. A few shots fired into the air, and while your brilliant soldiers went running to investigate, Padme remotely unlocked every door on the property."

"I didn't know she could do that," he mumbled.

"You severely underestimated her," Maddy said, finishing with an upbeat, "to my benefit!"

At the bottom of the hill, the tall chain link gate was wide open. They walked through it unchallenged and continued on down the road towards the abandoned manufacturing plant. Bryn hadn't seen any vehicles other than Dundee's truck, so she assumed Maddy and company had arrived on the yacht's outboard. Mia seemed winded, so Bryn offered to help her, but she shook her head, either from stubbornness or because she didn't want to be touched.

The men Bryn had seen patrolling the plant were still on the job. When the closest one caught sight of his boss he reached up to his head. A moment later, a tone sounded from Maddy's coat pocket. She pulled Fournier's holopiece out and held it up for the man to see.

"I suggest you tell them to stand down," she said.

Chapter Twenty-four

Scott landed on his feet on the cab and immediately dropped down behind the lip of the back of the truck. From there, through the sheets of sprinkler water, he saw a circular scorch mark surrounded by broken tiles, which told him his grenade had rolled into the middle of the lobby. There were no bodies nearby, but he spotted some of the xenos hiding behind the body scanners and x-ray belts, while others had taken refuge in the elevator alcove. He couldn't see much beyond the alcove, but he got the impression the food court had been trashed. He presumed the counters at the various establishments there were also providing cover for the xenos.

What had started as a mob appeared to have dwindled to maybe twenty determined men and women. Most, if not all, would be Xbestia. He set the birdcage and printer down and called, "Cover me!"

As the others responded with a hail of bullets, he jumped off the truck, retrieved the cage and printer and ducked inside the cab. He shoved the cage onto the passenger seat so he could shut the door. Perky screeched in protest at the rough treatment.

He grinned when the truck started right up, thinking, *something's finally going right.*

He backed up over the debris into the lobby. Water rained down over the windshield, so he turned on the wipers. Bullets began to hit the exterior of the truck with dull, metallic thunks, and broken glass crunched under the tires as he performed a three-point turn. When he backed the truck into the hole, Chief Joe appeared from behind the closest x-ray conveyor belt and, even though the xeno knew the truck was essentially bullet-proof, emptied his clip at the windshield. The Native American xeno's mouth worked as he shouted obscenities Scott couldn't hear in the cab. Chief Joe would undoubtedly recognize him, but there was nothing he could do about that now.

Once he'd angled the truck so it blocked most of the hole, he shifted into park, removed the keys and slipped between the seats into the back of the truck. As soon as he opened the back doors, he tossed the rifle to Alton, who said, "Yeah, that's what I'm talkin' about."

Alton dropped flat to the ground and army-crawled under the truck. Scott knew he'd been a sniper in the war, so from behind the front tire, he'd be able to target xenos as soon as they raised their heads to shoot. With Alton providing cover, Shasta shuttled the survivors into the truck.

Scott went around and looked up at Bob and Nicola. The back of the truck was higher than the cab, but the truck was no longer directly under the platform. Bob stood frozen with his hand on the handle of the second-floor door.

Nicola scowled and shoved past him. She made the jump easily, sat down, flipped onto her belly and dropped to the ground. She gave Scott a look that was both triumphant and filled with disdain. Then she started for the driver's door, clearly planning to get to Perky's cage. Scott grabbed her arm and said, "Get in the back."

She frowned, but he didn't hear what she said over the thud of Bob's feet hitting the top of the truck – only when Scott looked up, he saw it wasn't his feet. Bob was lying flat on his back, and at first, Scott thought he'd just slipped on the wet roof of the truck. He'd landed with one arm sticking out over Scott's head and it took a moment for Scott to realize he hadn't just botched the landing – he'd been shot.

Chief Joe would have known the instant Scott began backing the truck into the stairwell that Scott's intention was to rescue his trapped coworkers and escape in it. With the truck blocking the hole and Alton providing cover, any shots fired towards the stairwell were unlikely to hit anything. Unfortunately, one of the xenos had gotten lucky and hit Bob.

Scott swore, shoving Nicola out of the way before grasping Bob's arm and pulling the prone man down into his arms. Bob's eyes were shut tightly, his mouth open in shock. The bullet had missed the vest completely; his khakis had a hole in them not far below the beltline. There was blood, but not much.

Bob was heavy and didn't seem capable of standing.

"I need some help here!" Scott called.

Shasta glanced around the back door of the truck. "Alton! Let's go!"

Alton took another quick shot before rolling out from under the truck and springing to his feet. He took one look at Bob and said, "I'll get his legs."

Between them, they got Bob into the crowded truck. The XIA and security staff inside were quiet and hollow-eyed. Several were injured, with bloodstained, makeshift field dressings. Nicola was sitting cross-legged on the floor. When Scott backed in, she held her hands up, so he lowered Bob's torso in front of her. She pulled the tech's head and shoulders onto her lap, cradling him gently.

Shasta was waiting for them behind the protection of the rear tire. "Last one." She lifted her chin at a figure slumped in the corner behind the barrier. "I gave him an extra dose to keep him compliant, so moving him will be a challenge."

Bob had been heavy, but Lupus was much taller, a big man with dense muscles. He was dressed in a short-sleeved, prison-orange jumpsuit and was conscious, but barely responsive. He had no shoes, just white socks with dirty imprints of his feet on the bottom. He smelled awful, a combination of human body odor and wet dog. Scott thought at first he wasn't even aware of what was going on, but when Alton helped him haul Lupus to his feet, Lupus' shaggy head swung Scott's way. Eyes at half-mast in his hairy wolf face, he slurred, "Going to kill you."

Scott turned away in disgust. "What, with your breath?"

Lupus dragged his feet most of the way to the truck, making the short journey as difficult as possible. Not far from their goal he suddenly went limp, head lolling forward. The sudden weight of his body as he sagged to his knees jerked his wrist out of Scott's grasp. As Scott turned to prevent him from crashing to the floor, he felt a hand at his belt and knew the collapse had been a trick.

"Grenade!" he yelled as he clamped both hands around Lupus' forearm, digging in with his claws and forcing the arm backward. Almost simultaneously, Alton knelt and clasped Lupus to him, pinning his free arm and getting him into a headlock. Scott knew in a close fight Lupus had the advantage, but not against Scott and Alton both, and not while under the dulling influence of whatever drug Shasta had given him. The grenade itself was no threat as long as Lupus couldn't pull the pin.

"Let it go," Scott said through gritted teeth. His claws were deeply embedded in Lupus' flesh, but even as rivulets of blood began to trail down his arm, Lupus kept a death grip on the grenade.

A gun barrel appeared against the grey and black fur on his temple and Shasta said firmly, "I *will* do it, Agent Quinones. You are not worth risking my people."

Lupus abruptly relaxed, but before Scott could retract his claws and retrieve the grenade, it dropped, bouncing off Lupus' right calf and rolling a few inches away from his stockinged foot. Scott barely had time to register the danger when Lupus shifted his weight onto one knee and swept the other foot out, shooting the grenade on a trajectory that sent it under the truck and into the lobby.

"Present for you, Joe!" he howled.

Chief Joe now had a high-powered concussion grenade, courtesy of the man he'd come to rescue.

Chapter Twenty-five

Maddy left the female xeno, whose name was an unxeno-like 'Rose,' guarding Fournier's six soldiers. Those men watched warily as Maddy forced their leader to march towards the abandoned manufacturing plant. Other than the steady plod of their footsteps, the only sound was the wind whistling mournfully through sagging utility pole wires, and the clatter of dried leaves swirling in the space between two rusty smokestacks. To Bryn, the site seemed more than just neglected; it felt like a ghostly, sinister presence lurked here.

The stucco covering the walls of the main building had been beige at one time, but was now cracked and crumbling, spotted with hundreds of spider webs that held a multitude of insect corpses. The busted-out windows were boarded up and spray painted with the message, 'Danger. Keep out.' Everything from the walls to the concrete was covered in a thin layer of some filthy, greasy-looking substance.

The Warehouse had been deliberately uninviting on the outside, but underneath it, Fournier's facility had been clean and sterile. Bryn wasn't surprised to find the inside of this building had fresh paint and shiny black flooring. It was a huge open space with bare steel I-beams as columns. It was lit throughout by hanging fluorescent fixtures. Most of the floor was empty, but a strange structure had been set up at one end; a large geodesic dome with clear, flexible plastic walls. Connected to one of the structure's triangular frames was a loudly humming row of what looked like air conditioners, but which she figured was probably a hospital-grade air purification system. Inside, there were white cabinets and tables holding electronic and medical equipment. A woman in a lab coat looked up from a microscope, but none of the other seven or eight people seemed to notice as Fournier and company trooped past. This was Fournier's new bioengineering lab.

Just like the Warehouse, the back wall had been allocated for office space, but here it hadn't been built as part of the original structure. Fournier had brought in what looked to Bryn like a prefab school trailer, lifted on a raised platform. The bald xeno's shotgun never wavered as Fournier took them up a set of metal steps and walked along the platform to the only door.

"This is the control room," Fournier said.

Dillo opened the door to a small space so crowded with equipment it fairly hummed with electricity. A very thin man with a crooked nose looked up, his face the picture of surprise. He was sitting in one of two office chairs. On the desk in front of him was a holoscreen with two dozen camera views of the plant and Fournier's house. The views of the fields were peaceful – there wasn't an impala or cheetah in sight. One view showed Fournier sitting in his living room, apparently relaxing and watching a show on holovision. Padme had replaced the live feed with recordings.

"What the…?" the man started to say.

"Hands where I can see them." Dillo sounded amused.

The man slowly lifted his hands, staring in confusion at Fournier.

"You're fired," Fournier said.

Maddy pushed her sunglasses on top of her head and addressed the man. "You must be Curtis. Padme told me you were a wretched little man. I see she's described you well." She turned to Fournier. "Really, Nicolas, couldn't you have found someone a *little* closer to her level of intelligence?"

She reached into her coat pocket and pulled out a holophone. Seconds later, Padme's face appeared. There were hollows under her cheekbones and dark smudges under her eyes. Bryn knew from Scott that she was pregnant, but she looked thinner, in an unhealthy way. In the background of the holo, Bryn recognized the opulent salon on Maddy's yacht.

The Pakistani girl cringed when she caught sight of Fournier in the holo on her end, but Maddy was quick to reassure her. "He's well under control, don't worry."

Padme lifted a hand to rub the fur on one of her cow ears as if it soothed her. "Good."

"You heard?" Maddy asked.

Bryn raised her eyes and caught sight of another camera dome mounted to the ceiling, a reminder that Padme had been watching and listening the entire time.

"Yes," Padme said. "The nanoneuron program is kept on a standalone machine, a portable 3D printer. I installed a tracking device on it. Pull the bottom drawer of the desk all the way out."

Dillo nudged Curtis aside and did as she asked, dumping the contents on the floor. He held the drawer up; taped to the back was a tiny pinkynail drive, the kind that connected to a holophone.

"I told you where it is," Fournier said. "The XIA have it."

"Shut up." Maddy peeled the tape off the drive with her long fingernails and plugged it into her phone. Underneath the holo of Padme's head and shoulders, the words 'Globalocate 2020 installation in progress" appeared. A moment later, a window popped up in the lower right corner with a set of coordinates and an address.

Maddy read it and glared at Fournier. "How did they get it?"

"Tactical error on my part. With Padme in the wind, I decided to send it where I didn't think anyone – particularly her – would look."

"Lovely. Well, I suppose that's it then." Maddy nodded at the bald xeno and Bryn instinctively stepped back, bracing for a shotgun blast.

"Wait!" Fournier held up his good hand. "I can give you new eyes."

"What?" Maddy was obviously thrown by Fournier's out-of-the-blue declaration, but she rallied quickly. "I'm not letting you operate on me! You really are a nutter, aren't you?"

"I'm not offering to do it myself. Ask Padme. I've perfected a technique to implant crocodile eyes into a human and I'm willing to trade that information for my life."

Maddy, who was still holding her phone, turned to Padme's holo.

"I want him dead," Padme said, "but I owe you too much to lie. He can do what he says."

Fournier stood a little taller. "You're losing the sight in your one working eye, aren't you? I can give you better vision than you could even imagine."

Maddy stared at him, clearly torn, but after a moment, she gnashed her teeth and snapped, "I'd rather be blind. At least then I'd have the satisfaction of knowing you aren't tormenting some other innocent girl with your perversions."

She turned and started to walk away. With a wave of her hand, she said with finality, "Kill him."

The bald xeno raised the shotgun to his shoulder, but never fired. Instead, he made a choking sound and slowly keeled over, dropping to his knees and then flopping forward in the doorway. Dillo stepped behind Fournier, placing Scott's gun against his cheek and crying out, "Your Majesty! Get down!"

Bryn didn't wait to see what Maddy did, she pulled Mia backwards past the fallen xeno into the relative safety of the control room. The walls of a prefab certainly wouldn't stop a bullet, so she whispered, "We should get down, too."

As she and Mia squatted by the wall, Curtis the programmer began typing madly, probably in an effort to wrest control of the security system from Padme. Bryn looked up at Dillo's severe face as he stared upward, scanning the dark corners of the main building. She assumed he was looking for a sniper even though she hadn't heard a shot. Fournier, too, was looking around, a small smile on his face, eyes bright with hope. None of the men noticed as Bryn tugged the sawed-off shotgun out from under the lifeless hand of the bald xeno and fit her finger to the trigger.

Chapter Twenty-six

Scott didn't think for a minute Chief Joe would pull the pin and lob the grenade back at them. The best use of it would be to disable the truck somehow – take out the engine or axle to prevent them from escaping – but Chief Joe wouldn't attempt it as long as he might injure or kill Lupus, which was very much to Scott and the embattled XIA staff's advantage.

Lupus had gone limp again, like a two-hundred-and-fifty-pound sack of rotten potatoes. Scott grabbed two handfuls of his coverall and boosted his torso up enough for Alton to wrap his arms around his chest from behind. As Scott lifted Lupus' legs, he glanced into the truck, where Shasta was kneeling over Bob. Her body language and movements – one hand over the other in the middle of Bob's chest, elbows locked, arms pumping up and down – told Scott all he needed to know about Bob's condition.

He closed his eyes, just for an instant. Bob had asked if they would survive this and Scott had given him a pat answer: "We will if I can help it." There would be time for regret and sadness later, but for now, he focused on the job.

He and Alton had moved Lupus all of two feet when a muffled boom sounded somewhere in the building. It was obviously the grenade. There were two stairwells in the building, and he was pretty sure Chief Joe had sent someone into the other stairwell to blow the door and gain access to the second floor. From there it would be a simple matter of walking across to the stairwell where Scott and company were holed up. They were about to be boxed in.

He looked up the stairwell shaft. From this angle, he could only see bottom of the second-floor platform and the top portion of the door.

"They're coming," he said to Alton.

Lupus must have heard him, because he suddenly wrenched his leg out of Scott's hand and kicked upward, narrowly missing his chin. Alton let out a wordless snarl of frustration and released his hold on Lupus' upper body so he could reach for the rifle slung over his shoulder. With the butt facing downward, Alton jerked his arm back and smashed Lupus across the side of the head, shouting, "Hold *still*!"

Lupus finally stopped struggling, but it was too late. Scott heard the door bang open and figured from the sound of the shoes drumming across the platform that several xenos were taking position to ambush them.

The platform creaked alarmingly under their weight, and someone cried out, "Get down! Get down!"

The barrel of a gun appeared over the edge. Alton took aim at the same time Scott reached for a grenade, but it was unnecessary. With a loud groaning *snap*, the edge of the platform broke away from the bottom of the stairs. Still attached to the wall, it crashed down, folding up against the wall and dumping its cargo of men. Two were hurled to the floor, one clung to the now vertical platform like a gecko, and the fourth managed to jump on top of the truck. Scott saw the man jump, his arms shooting out for balance as he attempted to stay upright on the wet surface, but he slipped and went down, sliding across the roof until his feet hung off the edge.

The man clinging to the wall had dropped his gun and wasn't an immediate threat, and Alton was dealing with the men who'd hit the floor, so Scott ran over, leapt up onto the deck of the truck and grasped the fourth man's ankles. He stepped back off the deck and hung his full body weight from the man's lower legs, effectively pulling him from the roof.

Shasta was still giving Bob CPR, when one of the injured security guards stuck a pistol in the xeno's face and said, "Hands in the air."

Scott was fine letting the guard handle that one; there was still the matter of getting Lupus in the truck.

He started to go help Alton but saw there was no need: the other three xenos were laid out on the floor around him. Alton, flexing his hands in satisfaction, began heading back towards him just as another xeno kicked the second-floor door open again. The new xeno was armed with a rifle, and as the barrel lifted, Scott reached for his weapon. He opened his mouth to shout a warning, but the xeno behind the rifle fired twice in rapid succession. Alton stopped cold but didn't fall. Confused, Scott noticed the angle of the xeno's rifle barrel was off, as if he hadn't been aiming for Alton at all.

Scott turned towards Lupus in what seemed like slow motion. Two rapidly growing stains on the wolf-faced xeno's orange coverall revealed him as the target. When Scott spun back around, Alton had dropped flat to the ground and rolled to look up at the rifleman, who grinned and saluted before disappearing behind the door.

Chapter Twenty-seven

Bryn was still on her knees in the control room. The shotgun was much heavier than the other two guns she'd held. The first had been Carla's little handgun, which she'd used to bluff her way out of a tight situation. The second had been a few days ago when she'd taken Jason's gun and actually fired it at someone. On both of those occasions she'd used the guns as a last resort, aware each time that her impulsive decision to use them opened herself up to violent reprisal.

Dillo and Fournier had yet to notice she'd taken possession of the shotgun. It occurred to her that she still had time to set it back down, to relinquish the questionable control it gave her.

Her hand tightened on the cold barrel and she muttered, "I don't think so."

"What are you doing?" Mia whispered.

"Taking my life back."

"You're going to get us killed."

Bryn glared at Fournier's profile. "Not before I take someone with us."

She shifted her gaze to the shotgun. There was a little switch near the trigger that had already been flipped to reveal a red dot. From what Scott told her, the red dot meant the safety was off and the shotgun was ready to fire, which made sense, since the bald xeno had been about to kill Fournier. She thought about how he'd been holding it before he fell, and lifted it, placing the heel of the stock against her shoulder.

Curtis the programmer made a triumphant little sound, and Bryn stood up in order to peer over his shoulder at the holoscreen. It looked as if he'd managed to connect to the live camera feeds. He raised a hand and swept it through the holo, scrolling through camera views until he stopped at one inside the main building but outside the prefab control room. The camera he accessed must have been located nearby; the view looked down on Dillo and Fournier. Curtis spread his fingers, zooming out. Maddy was crouched about ten feet away from Dillo, who was subtly gesturing to her with the hand sticking out of his sling, urging her towards the control room.

Dillo, Fournier and Maddy were not the only people the camera picked up, however. A shadowy figure was walking stealthily across the roof of the control room, zeroing in on Dillo. Bryn heard tiny creaking sounds above her head. Whoever it was, he hadn't gotten close enough to the edge to see his targets – or to be seen by them.

Bryn was still watching the holoscreen when Maddy made a break for it, running the short distance to the control room door. As she burst into the room, Bryn swung her way, shotgun ready. Maddy skidded to a stop as soon as she saw the gun. If she was surprised that Bryn was armed, it didn't show.

"Oh, please," Maddy said, reaching for the barrel to push it away.

Bryn didn't let her touch it. Instead, she raised the shotgun, aiming for the ceiling. The blast put a fist-sized hole in the roof and slammed the stock back against her shoulder. Maddy slapped her hands over her ears and Dillo looked furious, but his face changed when he heard footfalls drumming across the aluminum roof. Whoever it was, Bryn must not have hit him.

She caught Maddy's eye and nodded towards Curtis' holoscreen. Maddy turned in time to see the shadowy figure disappear from view before Curtis waved a hand to shut the screen down.

Maddy's chin lifted as she gave Bryn an assessing look. "So you've chosen sides."

"You mean between bad and worse? I suppose."

Bryn looked around the control room. There were no other doors, even though the prefab structure seemed larger on the outside than the interior suggested. She swung the shotgun barrel so it was pointing at Curtis. "How do we get out of here?"

He shrugged and answered evasively, "The door."

She sighed, impatiently shifting her weight from one leg to the other. "I mean, where's the escape tunnel? Fournier has them in all his buildings."

Curtis' eyes slid to where Dillo was still standing in the doorway, holding the gun to Fournier's head. Curtis' expression told her there was no way he was going to answer honestly with Fournier looking on. Bryn briefly debated whether to ask Fournier himself, but decided it would be a waste of time.

"Call Padme again," she said to Maddy. "She'll know."

Maddy pulled her holophone from her pocket just as Bryn caught the sound of raised voices echoing from outside the prefab. Dillo forced

Fournier across the threshold into the control room and shut the door, leaving it open a crack so he could look out.

"We got company," he said.

Bryn figured either the rest of Fournier's men had returned, or the six soldiers being held by the female xeno had somehow overpowered her. Either way, they were trapped.

When Padme didn't answer her holophone, Maddy stomped over to Fournier and thrust a finger into his face. Shaking with anger, she said, "If your men hurt her, I will roast you over a slow fire. Do you understand?"

"You know she's as valuable to me as she is to you," he responded coldly.

"Oh, that's right. The clone you forced her to carry. Whose is it? Yours? Or some rich fool who thinks it will help him live forever? If that's the case, I'm sure you're disappointed you won't be able to deliver. Pun intended."

"Have you aborted it?"

"Padme would never do such a thing. It's not the child's fault you like to play God – for money."

"That…child…is worth more to humanity than money."

Maddy let out a short laugh. "Of course it is."

She continued to berate him, but Bryn tuned her out and looked around at the four walls. It struck her that this was the second time she'd been trapped in one of Padme's control rooms. She'd escaped from the last one, but the circumstances had been vastly different. Now she wasn't threatened by fire; she was caught between two opposing forces, neither of which considered her all that valuable.

Like Curtis said, there was only one door – one obvious way in and out. The control room didn't have so much as a closet. Even though she'd asked him about an escape tunnel, an actual tunnel wasn't possible because the prefab had been constructed on a raised platform. The sniper hadn't come up the platform steps, so how had he gotten onto the roof? After she'd fired the shotgun, he'd run out of view of the camera towards the right end of the prefab.

The desk took up the wall to the left, and metal shelving had been installed along the back wall, but nothing marred the smooth surface of the wall to the right. Unlike the rest of the space, which was crowded with equipment, the only thing along that wall was a narrow cot with a blanket and pillow.

She carefully removed her finger from the trigger and nudged Curtis in the shoulder with the shotgun. "There's a room on the other side of that wall, isn't there?"

"No," he said, but his voice was weak, and he looked like he was about to burst into tears. Bryn was pretty sure he was lying.

Dillo had been keeping an eye on the situation outside the prefab, but he shut the door with a distinct *click* and turned his full attention to Fournier. "You've got three seconds to tell us how to get out of here, or I begin shooting off important body parts."

Fournier waited until Dillo began counting before saying, "Bryn's right. The wall opens onto an escape route." He looked at Curtis and jerked his head towards the wall.

Curtis started to get up, but Bryn was suddenly not so sure. Fournier had to know Maddy would kill him as soon as she was free. He seemed almost eager for them to open the wall.

"Hold on," Bryn said. "I think it's a trap. They're waiting on the other side."

Maddy stared at her a moment and then nodded. "I agree. If it seems too good to be true, it generally is."

She turned to Curtis. "You are extraneous unless you can come up with a solution to get us out of here safely. No, don't look at your boss; he can't help you."

Bryn almost felt sorry for the man as he considered his options. He only had a few seconds to live if he didn't cooperate with Maddy, but if he did and Maddy failed to escape, Fournier would certainly kill him for his betrayal. It all depended on whether Curtis knew of a surefire way for them to escape.

From the look on his face, he didn't.

Maddy sighed, but before she gave Dillo the order to kill him, Bryn said, "Wait. I know what we can do."

Chapter Twenty-eight

Alton came up alongside Scott as he placed two fingers against the carotid artery in Lupus' throat. Under the blood-stained orange coverall, the big man's chest was still.

"Who was that?" Scott asked.

"Mad Eye soldier."

In the back of the truck, Shasta had finally given up on CPR efforts for Bob. She was still on her knees, looking exhausted and defeated. Scott met her eyes and shook his head.

"Leave him," she said. "Let's get out of here."

Scott had no compunctions about leaving Lupus where he lay, but there was the matter of the fourth xeno, who stood by the truck with his hands in the air.

Alton turned his rifle around and said, "I got this." Scott watched impassively as Alton brought the barrel down alongside the xeno's head. The man dropped like a stone. Scott wasn't sure the blow was enough to knock him unconscious, but either way, he was smart enough to stay down.

Scott and Alton jumped into the back of the truck. After slamming the doors, Scott stepped over Bob's legs and made his way through the people crowded inside until he reached the driver's seat. Water from the sprinklers still rained down over the windshield. It prevented him from seeing very far into the lobby, but also kept the xenos from seeing that he and the others were about to make a break for it.

Shasta lifted the bird cage from the passenger seat and passed it to someone before sitting next to Scott. He shifted into gear, turned on the headlights, and pulled forward. He expected the xenos to open fire again, but they didn't. When he flipped on the windshield wipers, he saw why they hadn't bothered and slammed on the brakes. The truck skidded a little on the wet tile but came to a stop about fifteen yards from the busted out front doors – and the human barrier there.

The xenos had lined up bodies from one end of the lobby to the other. To get the truck out of the building, Scott would have to drive over them.

"They're dead," Shasta said grimly. "Go!"

It was a deep moral outrage and the xenos must have been counting on it to at least slow them down, but Shasta had given him a direct order, so he grit his teeth and shifted into gear. Then Alton leaned between the seats, wearing Bob's discarded vest. He thrust a hand over her shoulder and pointed. "That one's not dead. She's tied up."

The woman in question lifted her head a little. She was gagged and her eye makeup was smeared, if not from the sprinklers then from her tears. It was the XIA receptionist. Scott found he couldn't remember her name, but she'd always smiled and greeted him cheerfully.

"That one's not dead either," Alton said, pointing farther down the line.

"Damn it!" Shasta reached into the front of her suit jacket and removed her pistol from its holster. "We'll to have to attempt a rescue. Harding, drive the truck up to the prisoners. Alton, you're with me."

"No, you drive," Scott said. "I have a vest and I'm stronger than you."

For a moment, it looked as if Shasta was going to rip into him for countermanding her order, but she said, "Go! Check all the bodies. I'll pull forward slowly."

She took the driver's seat as soon as he vacated it and waited until he and Alton were at the back doors. Then she drove close to the line of bodies and turned parallel to the first of them.

Alton cracked one of the doors so Scott could reach around it and blindly lob the third of his four grenades towards the elevator alcove. Immediately after the blast, the fire sprinklers shut off. Scott didn't stop to wonder why; he jumped out, and using the truck as cover, began to check the bodies for signs of life. After he and Alton verified the first two were dead, it occurred to him that the xenos hadn't fired so much as a shot.

"Something's wrong," he said. "They aren't doing anything."

Alton squatted down next to the receptionist. The xenos hadn't bothered to clear a space for her on the tile; she was soaking wet and lying on a thick layer of broken glass. She began making sounds like she wanted to say something. Scott tried to remove her gag, but it was too tight, and the wet fabric was impossible to untie. He made eye contact with her, but when she immediately looked away and made an urgent, "Mm!" sound, he followed her gaze outside the building.

When the truck had crashed through the doors, it ripped away the central section of framing, leaving a wide-open space and shattering the floor-to-ceiling windows. The empty window frames along the ceiling were intact, as were the frames closer to the walls on either side. Scott's view into the street was nearly unobstructed. It was getting dark and there were no cars on the road; nothing moved in the cold air.

Just as it occurred to him that the receptionist was trying to tell him the xenos had repositioned themselves, Chief Joe appeared from around the exterior corner of the building to his right. Scott started to lift his weapon, but knew it was too late – Chief Joe had used the human barrier to get the drop on them. Scott stiffened in expectation of a bullet, but when the shot came, it was Chief Joe whose body jerked backwards as a bullet tore into his chest. His gun skittered across the top step and he slammed up against the wall and then slid into a sitting position. More xenos appeared and more shots followed in rapid succession. One of the xenos ran down the steps instead of attacking – Scott recognized her as Chief Joe's girlfriend Liz. A few strides into her escape, she took a bullet in the leg that sent her rolling down the steps.

He looked around for the shooter. It wasn't Shasta; she was still in the driver's seat. Was it the same guy who'd taken out Lupus?

"There!" Alton pointed towards the street.

Scott squinted in that direction, seeing nothing at first. Then he caught a glimpse of something fluttering in the wind, but on second glance realized it was a hand waving, seemingly out of thin air.

He grinned. "It's the UAAV!"

Lo and Boardman had arrived in the Urban Amphibious Armored Vehicle, and its adaptive camouflage panels were activated. The vehicle was nearly invisible to the naked eye.

With Lo and Boardman covering them, Scott and Alton rescued the three living prisoners and loaded them onto the crowded truck. By then it was obvious any remaining xenos had abandoned the cause and retreated. Lo left Boardman in the UAAV and cautiously approached.

Shasta leaned over and opened the passenger side door. "Where's Unger?"

"Didn't you get my message?" Lo asked.

Shasta made a face that clearly said, "Are you serious?"

"He wasn't on the flight."

"Awesome." Shasta sounded anything but pleased. She climbed into the passenger seat and retrieved the 3D printer from the floor of the truck. Scott helped her out, but as soon as her delicate black pumps hit the glass-littered tile, she grimaced and lifted a foot. A shard was embedded in the sole. She scraped her shoe on the running board to dislodge it before gesturing irritably at the ground.

Scott swept his foot through the worst of it, using his boots to clear a path for her to the back of the truck. Once there, she pointed to Nicola. "You. Out. The rest of you, who can drive?"

The security guard who'd helped earlier raised a hand and Shasta told him, "I'll need you to get these people to the hospital."

Nicola, gripping the handle at the top of the bird cage, stepped gingerly over Bob's body. She climbed out of the truck and stood near Shasta in the spot Scott had cleared, staring into the dark stairwell at the vague orange lump that was Lupus' body.

Shasta nodded towards the xenos Lo and Boardman had taken out. "Get their firearms."

As the truck rumbled down the shallow concrete steps in front of the building, Lo and Alton went out to search the fallen xenos. Scott knelt next to Chief Joe, who was sitting propped against the lobby wall with a wet, black hole dead center of his chest. Each intake of breath rattled, and each exhale caused blood to bubble forth on his lower lip.

"The ringleader's alive," Scott called.

Shasta's shoes prevented her from coming any closer. "Is he conscious?"

At a subtle fluttering of Chief Joe's eyelashes, Scott replied, "I think so."

"Secure him."

Chief Joe opened his eyes as Scott pulled a zip tie from his utility belt. "Liz dead?"

"Nope." Last he'd seen, Liz had been shot in the leg and fallen down the steps, but when he'd looked for her a moment ago, she was gone.

Chief Joe smiled. "Give her…message…"

"Give it yourself." Scott's words sounded cold, but he wasn't unmoved. He took both of Chief Joe's limp wrists in one hand.

"Not gonna make it. My heart…"

Scott threaded the zip tie and tightened it. "You'll get a new one at the hospital."

Chief Joe laughed and then choked as blood dribbled down his chin. "Won't be any left…"

Scott started to tell him to save his energy, but Chief Joe closed his eyes and stopped breathing.

Chapter Twenty-nine

"Well?" Maddy said. "What's your brilliant idea to get us out of here?"

Technically, Bryn wasn't sure her idea would work, but she didn't want Maddy to shoot Curtis and it was the only thing she could think of that might stop her.

"Use the soldiers' nanoneurons against them," she said. "If Padme could do it, I'll bet Curtis can, too."

Maddy's mouth formed an "O" of surprise. "That's perfect! Send them a dose of fear! You," she pointed to Curtis. "Do it."

"Believe me," Curtis said fervently, "I would if I could, but I need the program."

Maddy's head rolled back on her neck as she directed her gaze to the ceiling. "Which the XIA has."

As soon as the words left her lips, her head snapped upright, and she jabbed a manicured finger at Bryn. "Call your boyfriend."

Bryn briefly debated whether it would be worth it to refuse. As the one holding the shotgun, *she* should be the one calling the shots, so to speak, but refusing to call Scott because she didn't want to blow his cover would be stupid. Scott just might be her only hope of getting out of this alive, and at this point, she didn't think it was possible to continue to keep his identity secret. In the end, it wouldn't matter anyway if Maddy killed Fournier.

She looked at Curtis. "Can whoever has the standalone machine activate the soldiers' nanoneurons?"

With warning in his tone, Fournier drawled, "Cur*tis*."

Dillo jammed the barrel of his gun into Fournier's cheek. "One more word."

Fournier wisely kept silent as Curtis said, "I can walk them through it."

Maddy waved a hand at Bryn. "Call him."

Bryn reluctantly nodded, but she wasn't about to set the shotgun down. "Mia?"

Peripherally, she saw Mia pull her cellphone from her purse and dial. After two rings, Scott's anxious face appeared. Bryn glanced at Fournier, who didn't show any surprise that the xeno he knew as Cougar was in fact an XIA agent.

"About time!" Scott said. "Is Bryn with you?"

"She's here." Mia held the holophone up. A small silence fell as Scott assessed the situation, followed by the deadly calm words, "What do you want, Maddy?"

Bryn jumped in. "It's not what you think. Long story short, Mia and I went to one of Fournier's dens by accident and he brought us to his new bioengineering facility. Maddy showed up and now we're all trapped inside the control room with his soldiers outside."

Before she could continue, Scott asked, "Where are you?"

"Mia can send you the coordinates, but we're at least half an hour outside the city. There's no time for you to get here. Do you have the nanoneuron program?"

Bryn wasn't sure at first if Scott was even at XIA headquarters because his surroundings were dark. Then she heard Shasta's stern voice. "We will not negotiate turning over that program."

"No one asked you to," Maddy retorted.

Bryn met Maddy's eyes and thought, *Yet*, but said, "Shasta, we might be able to escape if you use the program to disable Fournier's soldiers. The ones who have nanoneurons."

Shasta stayed in the shadows, but Bryn detected more than a spark of interest in her voice. "You have the password?"

"Yeah, and we're in kind of a hurry."

Shasta hadn't admitted to having the program, but after a short pause, she said, "The printer's interface is ready and waiting."

"Password is 8kl94mp002z*byf6," Curtis said, slowly enunciating the string of letters, symbols and numbers.

"Got it," Shasta said. Then, "It's asking for an authorized palm holoscan."

"What?" Curtis exclaimed.

Everyone in the control room looked at Fournier. The gun against his cheek distorted his smile. "I believe the ball is back in my court."

Bryn couldn't help but think she'd revealed Scott's identity for nothing. "Whose palm does it want?"

Fournier lifted his eyebrows. "Mine."

"Good to know," Maddy said. "I'll be sure to cut it from your cold, dead body once this is all over."

Another voice on Scott's end joined the conversation. "One other person can access it."

"Nicola, don't!" Fournier shouted angrily.

A young woman's face appeared in the bluish light of Scott's holophone. Bryn stared in shock at a younger version of her mother.

"I'm sorry, Daddy," Nicola said, "but I can't let them kill you."

Chapter Thirty

Nicola turned to Scott. "Savvy can access the program. I know where he went. If Maddy Singh swears not to kill my father, I'll take you to him."

Scott glanced away from her earnest face, thinking it would be easy to get Maddy to make that promise, but impossible to hold her to it.

"Maddy?" he asked.

"Cross my heart and hope to die," Maddy replied. Her holoimage practically radiated insincerity, but the words alone seemed to appease Nicola.

Scott looked at Bryn. She held the shotgun confidently, but her eyes were huge.

"Hurry," she said.

"I'll call you back." Scott shut his holophone and pinned Nicola with a hard stare. "Where is he?"

"Third floor."

Alton, standing next to Shasta, asked, "What's on the third floor?"

"A branch office for the National Library of Medicine." Shasta handed the printer to Scott. "Do *not* lose this. Alton, go with them."

Scott led the way to the stairwell on the other side of the building, keeping a cautious lookout for any lingering hostiles. Power to the building was out, so this stairwell, too, was dark. With Scott's flashlight illuminating the way, they went up past the destroyed door on the second-floor platform, and then stopped in front of the holoscanner near the door to the third floor. The backup generator ensured that essential systems were working, so Alton was able to gain them access to the floor.

Scott had never been on the third floor, but from what little he could see, the office space was configured similarly to that of XIA headquarters. He didn't know much about this branch of the National Library of Medicine except that it was obscure, and its employees kept to themselves.

He thought they'd have to hunt Savvy down, but Nicola called, "Felson! I need you," and within seconds the savant appeared within the circle of Scott's flashlight beam.

"What's wrong?" he asked.

"Daddy needs you to activate the program."

Savvy turned his head away and appeared to be studying the carpet. "He never said that."

"I know what he said, and you've done a great job, but things aren't working out the way they were supposed to. Maddy Singh showed up at the farm and one of her soldiers has a gun to Daddy's head." Nicola's voice broke.

"How do you know?"

"I just talked to him!"

"But if I activate the program, it will only affect your father's soldiers." Savvy began to rock a little, as if arguing with Nicola upset him.

"And Maddy is surrounded by them. If she can't escape, she'll kill him."

"Why doesn't he call them off?"

Nicola released a short, frustrated breath. "Because he doesn't trust her! But at least this way, there's a chance she won't kill him. If his soldiers attack, Daddy's dead for sure."

Savvy's mouth tightened. "No. I won't do it unless he tells me to."

Alton lifted his gun arm and pointed it at Savvy's head. "How 'bout if *I* tell you to?"

"You won't shoot me."

"That one?" Nicola said, glancing at Alton. "Yes, he will."

"Yeah, Felson," Alton said. "You don't want her to see your brains splattered all over the wall, do you?"

"How do I know this isn't a trick?"

Nicola put a hand on Savvy's arm. "This is coming from *me*, Felson. No one's pressuring me. Please just do it. I don't want Daddy to die."

Scott opened the printer and held it out.

Savvy looked so conflicted he seemed like he was about to implode upon himself, but he finally reached out and took it. He set it on a nearby surface and activated the holoscanner. Moments later, a holoscreen popped up.

"Wait," Scott said, as something occurred to him. "How does it work?"

"I send a signal through the nearest cell tower," Savvy said.

"Will everyone with nanoneurons be affected?"

"Unless I deselect their name."

"Then do it," Scott said. "Deselect Bryn Vega's name."

"Why is *she* there?" Savvy asked.

"Never mind," Nicola said. "Just hurry, okay?"

Scott watched over Savvy's shoulder as he scrolled through a long list of names. He found Bryn's and did something. When he gestured with his hand, every name but hers turned red and began to blink.

Scott took out his holophone and called Mia again. She answered immediately.

"You're good to go," he said.

Chapter Thirty-one

Dillo glanced out the door and muttered, "What are they *doing*?" After a moment, he added, "Oh, they're definitely freaking out."

There was a loud *pop*, and Dillo guffawed and exclaimed, "Guy just shot another guy! Looks like it's affecting three or four of them, at least. Now's the time."

Bryn's heart started beating faster. She had the shotgun, but barely knew how to use it. She didn't even know whether she had another shot left or if she'd already expended her one and only bullet. Even if she had more ammunition, she didn't know how to load it. It seemed a poor choice to go out into a gunfight under the circumstances. She hated to admit her lack of knowledge to Maddy, but she had no choice.

Before she could say anything, however, the Mad Eye queen bent over the dead xeno, unclipped an ammo belt from his waist and tugged it out from under him. She then strapped it around her hips, pulled Fournier's pistol from her inside jacket pocket and held it out to Bryn.

"Trade you. I'm more of a shotgun gal."

After they swapped weapons, Maddy swung the barrel of the short shotgun towards Curtis.

Bryn didn't know why she felt compelled to keep Maddy from killing the squirrelly man, but she said, "Don't shoot him."

"I wasn't going to," Maddy replied, but she fired the shotgun anyway, right past Curtis' head. She must have been aiming for the control room's circuit breaker panel, because the room went dark. Now Curtis wouldn't be able to monitor them after they left. Bryn's ears were ringing, but she heard Maddy's voice come out of the darkness. "Dillo?"

"Ready."

Diffuse light filled the room as he opened the door and yelled, "Hold your fire or the boss gets it!" He forced Fournier ahead of him out onto the platform. Maddy went next, and then it was Bryn's turn. She held her arms out in front of her like she'd seen on holovision, elbows locked, gun swinging from side to side. She knew Mia was very close behind her because she could hear her breathing.

The first thing she did after stepping over the threshold was lift the gun towards the roof of the prefab in case the sniper had returned. The last thing she expected was to see him there, just extending his rifle out over the edge to take Dillo out from behind. Firing at him wasn't even a conscious decision. Her finger twitched on the trigger and the gun bucked in her hand, turning her locked elbows to noodles.

The sniper disappeared from view, but she knew she'd hit him because the oddly shaped rifle fell to her feet. Dillo glanced around and met her eyes.

Yeah, I just saved your sorry life, Bryn thought.

Mia quickly picked up the rifle and nudged Bryn. "Go!"

Bryn was vaguely aware her shot had set off a response. As they ran for the stairs, she looked out over the railing to see two soldiers sprinting for the nearest door. One of them began firing blindly over his shoulder at them, until one of his comrades stepped out from behind a steel column and fired back.

"Look at 'em shoot each other!" Maddy sounded elated.

One of the running soldiers fell, but the other made it to the door. As soon as he disappeared outside, Dillo stepped up the pace, forcing Fournier down the steps and across the floor. When they reached the nearest steel column, Bryn saw one of the soldiers curled up in a fetal position behind it, lost in the throes of fear his nanoneurons were producing. Not far away, another man lay clutching his bloody midsection and rolling in agony.

She almost felt sorry for them. She'd experienced that same flood of terror only a few days ago, courtesy of Padme. Even the memory of it made her shudder.

The soldier who'd shot one of his own turned to them and fired, but his clip was empty. He kept trying to fire, spasmodically pulling the trigger until he finally threw the gun at them. It fell far short and clattered across the floor. He sank into a squat and wrapped his arms around his head, screaming, "Make it *stop*!"

Behind him, Bryn saw the scientists inside the biodome crouching behind and under the furnishings. She couldn't tell if they were affected by the signal, too, or simply hiding from the crazed gunmen.

They made it to the door. The soldier who'd run out was nowhere in sight, but a saddled, riderless horse stood nearby, its reins tied to a rusty pole. She wondered if it belonged to the sniper she'd shot. Walking quickly and in close proximity to each other, they left along the same broken walkway they'd arrived. Dusk was falling and the temperature had dropped.

113

Bryn was glad for the warm coat Mrs. Padilla had given her. She thought about pulling the wide hood over her quills but didn't want it to obstruct her vision.

When they reached the road in front of the old manufacturing plant, they found Rose, the female xeno Maddy had left guarding Fournier's soldiers. She was lying face-down on the tarmac and her jacket had been partially pulled from her body; evidence of a struggle. Bryn saw the woman's xenograft on her lower back: the orangey scales of a reptile in the shape of a rose. Mia knelt down to see if she was still alive, but from the size of the puddle of blood under the body, Bryn didn't think it was necessary to check.

Maddy shot Fournier a malicious look that spoke volumes about who she blamed for Rose's death. He seemed not to notice. There were dark pink splotches across his cheekbones, and his eyelids were rimmed with red. He was the only one not wearing a coat. When Dillo urged him to continue, he stumbled along, every ragged exhale visible in the frigid air. It was obvious pain and blood loss had worn him down.

They continued on through the open gate and up the little hill. The animals were still running loose, but Bryn didn't see as many. They'd either left the area, or with night falling, had located someplace to hide. The domesticated ones might have even gone back into the barn. As they made their way down the hill towards the farmhouse, Mia's holophone rang. It was Scott.

"Are you safe?"

"For now," Mia replied.

"Well, get out of there as soon as you can. Apparently, Padme built a failsafe into the new version of the program. The nanoneuron bursts are self-limiting to prevent killing anyone. You've got one minute until it shuts off."

Chapter Thirty-two

The moment the program shut off the signal, Alton took the printer from Savvy and Scott took him back into custody. As he was fastening the zip tie around Savvy's wrists, Nicola said, "That's how you thank him?"

"Oh, I won't be doing the thanking," Scott replied. "That's up to a jury of his peers."

"I'm peerless," Savvy muttered.

Scott assumed he meant he was too unique or intelligent to have peers. He shook his head, took Savvy's arm and said, "Move."

Back in the stairwell, he thought about what would happen next. Shasta would want to do *something* about Fournier, but with the lack of staff and the condition of the building, he didn't know what. He began to mentally compose an argument for her to send him in. If Maddy got away, chances were good Fournier would be dead when he got there. He tried not to think about Bryn's chances. He'd been worried about her *before* he saw her holding a shotgun in the company of Fournier and Maddy Singh, but now that he knew what she'd gotten herself into, his anxiety had reached panic proportions.

Halfway down the stairs, Alton asked Savvy, "What were you doing on the third floor?"

Nicola put a hand on Savvy's arm. "Is it done?"

"Yes," he said.

"Then go ahead and tell them."

"I hacked the database."

"For the National Library of Medicine?" Scott asked. "Why?"

"Because he told me to."

Scott sighed at the non-answer and swiveled his head in Nicola's direction.

"My father asked Felson to locate certain documents and release them to the media."

"Like what?"

115

"Medical articles that were withheld from the public."

They reached the bottom of the stairs and Scott opened the door. Bright headlights from a pair of large vehicles parked in front of the building were now illuminating the lobby. "Is that what this was all about?" He gestured to indicate the destruction.

"No." She shook her head adamantly. "Felson and I weren't supposed to be part of that. Daddy just wanted to get Lupus back. Everything I told you about running away was true, except...I did call him from the roadblock. He was really mad when he found out you were an agent and that you caught us...until he thought of a way to turn it to his advantage. He's good at that."

"Psychopaths generally are," Alton said.

"He's not a psycho! He's a brilliant surgeon who-"

"Yeah, yeah." Alton's voice drowned her out. "He's a misunderstood genius. Now go."

Nicola huffed out of the stairwell and stomped away, Alton on her heels. Scott had several more questions for her, not the least of which was how Savvy got access to the third floor, but now was not the time to interrogate anyone. He took Savvy's arm again and headed for Shasta.

The vehicles were military IMVs, which made sense, since National Guardsmen in tactical gear and surgical masks were now prowling the floor. Scott remembered what Carla had told him about the National Guard rounding up xenos, so he holstered his weapon and let go of Savvy's arm, shoving his hands into his jacket pockets to hide his alterations.

One of the guardsmen challenged Alton, but Shasta called out, "They're mine." She was standing near the destroyed stairwell talking with a dark-skinned man with short white hair dressed in fatigues. Scott didn't need to see his insignia to know he was in command.

His men had gathered up the dead and laid them side-by-side on a cleared space of floor near the far-left wall. They'd also corralled and were guarding the living; the men Alton had taken out in the stairwell.

From the commanding officer's insignia, Scott identified him as a colonel. He heard the tail end of what he was telling Shasta, "...are working on restoring power here and in several adjacent neighborhoods."

Shasta held her hand out for the printer well before they reached her, an indication of its value to her. When Alton handed it over, she asked, "Did it work?"

"Yes, ma'am."

"Excellent. I want all of you out at Fournier's facility ASAP. Bring him in alive if at all possible. Lo and Boardman are geared up and waiting in the UAAV. Alton, if the opportunity happens to present, work on Maddy Singh."

Scott knew Alton's recent assignment had something to do with getting Maddy to cooperate with the XIA, but he didn't know the specifics and didn't dwell on it. Shasta had given him the go-ahead to ensure Bryn's safety and he was determined that this time nothing would prevent him from doing just that.

He spun on his heel to hurry off, but Nicola stopped him with a plaintive, "What about me?"

Scott would have ignored her, but the question was valid. Shasta had just ordered every one of her available agents back into the field. The building security staff were either dead or en route to the hospital, and the building itself had been breached and was on backup power. The other XIA handlers and their agents were MIA in the city's chaos. Deputy Director Unger was also missing. Essentially, XIA headquarters was crippled. There was nowhere to keep the prisoners.

"I'm afraid you'll have to come with me, young lady," the colonel said.

"No." Shasta shook her head. "They're witnesses in an investigation and will remain in my custody."

"My orders are to detain *all* xenos – for their safety." He stared at Nicola's face, eyes lingering on her feather eyebrows. "We'll be taking them to a location called Poppy's Pier as soon as we're done here."

Scott jerked his head towards the four prisoners under guard. "What about them? You just letting them loose on the pier with everyone else?"

"Of course not, but the jails won't take them, so we're using prisoner transport vehicles to hold xenofreak offenders for the time being. Marshals are sending a bus."

"I understand you've got a job to do," Shasta said. "But I'm a senior agent with the XIA. You don't have jurisdiction here."

From the look on the colonel's face, Scott knew what he was going to say before he said it. "During martial law I do. All xenos. No exceptions. Those are my orders."

Shasta's eyes flashed, but she acquiesced with a grudging, "Fine." The colonel not only outgunned her, but he hadn't yet realized she and her agents were also xenos. If she pressed the issue, she might find herself with a one-way ticket to Poppy's Pier. For a moment, Scott was afraid Nicola or Savvy would point it out, but they didn't. Nicola had heard Shasta's request that they bring Fournier in alive, so it was unlikely she'd do anything to jeopardize that.

Nicola did protest vociferously when the colonel refused to let her keep the birdcage. Shasta took it from her, prying her fingers gently off the handle. "I'll take care of Perky. I promise."

When the commanding officer left, escorting Savvy and a still-protesting Nicola to a waiting vehicle, Shasta glanced at Scott's midsection, where his hands were securely hidden.

"How did you know?" she asked.

"Bryn's godmother told me they were rounding everyone up."

"Nothing good will come of that."

He nodded. "What are you going to do?"

"I can use the agency's mobile surveillance unit and keep an eye on your op from there. Now go rescue your girlfriend."

Chapter Thirty-three

At the bottom of the hill, a narrow dirt path split off from the gravel road. It went around the field between the house and the river and disappeared in the unkempt vegetation along the shore.

When Maddy turned onto the path, Bryn balked. She'd seen the yacht's outboard and knew it wouldn't hold them all. Maddy would most likely kill Fournier and dump his body in the Hudson River, and being witnesses to the crime, Bryn and Mia would be expendable.

She summoned her courage and lifted the gun. "This is where we part company."

Maddy's eyebrows rose. "How are you planning on getting out of here?"

"Dundee's truck. The keys are in his pocket."

To Bryn's surprise, Maddy didn't argue. She just nodded and said, "Alright. Good luck. And…thank you."

It felt like a trick, but as Bryn and Mia got closer to the farmhouse, it seemed more and more likely they would escape. When they reached Dundee's truck, Bryn was almost giddy with relief, even though she wasn't looking forward to rooting around in a dead man's pockets. She rounded the big vehicle and stopped in her tracks.

Dundee's body was gone.

"I was wondering if he was the sniper back there," Mia said.

"He wasn't. I saw the guy before I shot him! What are we going to do now? Can you hotwire it?"

Mia made a face. "No. They didn't teach us that in med school."

"Well, we can't go back." Bryn glanced over her shoulder at the gravel road, expecting a horde of angry men to appear at the top of the hill any second now.

Mia took her holophone out and pulled up their location, putting her finger in the center of the holomap. "We're here. There aren't any other roads out, but if we cross the field, we can follow the river to this park."

Bryn spotted Maddy and the others in the distance. They'd almost reached the tall grass, bushes, and trees along the riverbank. If Bryn and Mia cut across the field at a sharp angle, they wouldn't run into them. "Let's get going, then. It's almost dark."

Whatever crop had been grown in the field had been harvested close to the ground in wide rows. The dry winter stubble crunched under their boots as they hurried along. Bryn felt horribly exposed and was glad for the near darkness until they reached the field's far corner. There, the wild vegetation was almost as thick and tall as that along the river. They beat their way through the undergrowth until they were stopped by a chain link fence the same height as the main gate.

"I can't climb that." Mia sounded miserable.

"Let's head for the river. Worst case scenario, we have to get our feet wet."

After they followed the fence ten yards or so towards the water, Bryn realized she'd spoken too soon when she heard a growl that definitely came from a living thing. Her quills responded by puffing up around her head. With a flash of trepidation, she recalled the loose animals.

"What was that?" Mia asked.

As if in answer, the creature let out another growl that escalated into an eerie, moaning yowl. The vocalizations reminded Bryn of two tom cats threatening each other in an alley. She strained her eyes, but in the low light, couldn't see anything.

"Back away slowly and we'll try to go around," she whispered.

The animal continued making warning sounds as they retraced their steps through the underbrush. Whatever it was, it didn't attack, which was good, because Bryn didn't want to shoot it – not only because it didn't deserve to die, but because a gunshot would attract attention.

Although her plan had been to circle around it, the terrain in that direction sloped sharply downward towards the river. Mia was in no shape to attempt the treacherous footing, especially not in her high-heeled boots. They were forced to walk parallel to the river, each step bringing them closer to where Maddy had gone. Bryn was about to suggest they stop and wait awhile, when she heard raised voices up ahead.

The last thing she wanted to do was involve herself in whatever scenario was playing out, so she grabbed Mia's arm and pulled her down behind a bush to listen.

"Let her go." It was Maddy.

Dundee, with his distinctive Australian accent, said, "Trade you. Him for the girl."

Bryn didn't need to see who he was talking about to know it was Padme. Dundee, despite the horrific-looking head wound, must have regained consciousness and somehow gotten to Maddy's yacht. Probably, he'd planned to lie in wait for her, but instead he'd found Padme and taken her. That's why Padme hadn't answered her holophone the second time Maddy called.

"No," Maddy said. "He dies today."

"Then so does she."

"I don't think so." Maddy sounded confident. "Ask him. The baby is too important."

Bryn barely made out Fournier's response. "Don't kill her."

"See?" Maddy said.

"He dies, she dies, no matter what he says."

"Well, then," Maddy said. "I guess we're at an impasse."

"For now," Dundee replied, "but once it's full dark, I'll have the advantage."

"How so?"

"I'll still be able to see."

Maddy said something Bryn couldn't make out. The words were followed by a mocking chuckle from Dillo.

"Bryn," Mia whispered, pointing towards the water. "Look."

Through a break in the foliage, Bryn saw lights from the far shore reflecting off the water of the Hudson. Her gaze dropped to the near bank and she made out the silhouette of a dock. She couldn't see Maddy's outboard from this angle, but it had to be tied there.

They really didn't have much of a choice; they had to try for the boat. Bryn was about to suggest it when Mia's holophone rang.

"Oh, *crap!*" Mia fumbled in her purse to silence the phone, but it was too late.

"I recognize that ring-tone!" Maddy called. "Show yourselves, ladies."

Chapter Thirty-four

"Come *on*…pick up." Alton drummed his fingers on the arm of his seat, staring intently at Scott's holophone.

They were on the water now, traveling north up the Hudson River towards the coordinates Mia had sent them. They'd started out on the highway but ran into a traffic jam as people left the beleaguered city in droves. Lo had exited at the next available off-ramp and taken side roads to the river. At the first opportunity, she'd driven into the water and switched to amphibious mode. They were camouflaged and headed upstream at maximum speed, but to Scott, it felt like they were dogpaddling.

He fidgeted with the straps of his bullet-proof vest. Underneath it, his shirt was damp, and his wounds itched like crazy, but he didn't want to take it off in case things suddenly started happening. When Mia's holophone went to message, he disconnected, irritated and apprehensive. It didn't help that Alton kept drumming his fingers. Then he asked no one in particular, "Why didn't she answer?" which got on Scott's already frayed nerves. Before he could stop himself, he snapped, "What are *you* so worried about?"

"Huh?"

"You do know that whatever happened between you and Bryn wasn't real, right? She couldn't help it."

Alton gave him a look filled with derision. "Back off, kid. I'm not into her."

"Good." Scott was relieved but gave Alton a warning look anyway.

Lo expelled a loud sigh. "If you boys are done marking your territory, you should see this."

Ever since they'd entered the water, she and Boardman had been flipping through news channels on the holoprojector embedded in the UAAV's dash. The city was still under siege by its own residents. Despite the presence of the National Guard, day three of the riots showed no sign of abating. The violence, initially directed at xenofreaks, had inflamed existing antagonisms between inner city ethnic groups. Looting, assault and arson were rampant.

Lo turned up the volume. A male reporter was saying, "…and the backlash has flooded the interweb with government conspiracy messages. A spokesperson for the National Library of Medicine confirms the hack but refutes the validity of the leaked information."

The holo changed to a shot of a man in a business suit standing in front of a tall brick building. The words, "Alain Mehta, National Library of Medicine," scrolled across the bottom of the holo.

"What the public needs to understand," Mehta said in a thick Indian accent, "is that we only accept biomedical research that has been thoroughly investigated and evaluated by professional medical journals. We have stringent guidelines, and not all information submitted for inclusion in our database is acceptable for release to the public. From what I understand, the studies in question were all completed by rogue bioengineers and surgeons."

Scott met Alton's eyes. "Savvy," they said in unison.

"What about him?" Boardman asked.

"He's the one who hacked the Library of Medicine, on Fournier's orders," Scott said. "Whatever those studies were about, Fournier really wanted them out there."

"You missed the first part," Lo said. "The studies allegedly proved xenos are immune to stuff."

Scott noticed she said 'allegedly' with some sarcasm. Among the xenofreak community, it was common knowledge they rarely got sick.

"You know, that's why I got my graft." Lo had never talked about it before, but he'd heard her graft was a simple porcine strip across her chest to cover the scars of a double mastectomy.

"I had breast cancer." Her voice was matter of fact. "It was pretty aggressive, and I wasn't given much hope, but I fought it anyway. Then I met a woman in therapy who told me there were a whole bunch of survivors who swore their cancer didn't come back because they'd gotten grafted. My doctor was furious when I asked him about it. Said there were a lot of unethical people out there who made a living preying on desperate cancer patients. But I did it anyway, a few weeks after the mastectomy."

She lifted a hand. "And here I am, two years later, cancer free."

Mia would call Lo's story a 'testimonial,' something that didn't hold a lot of weight with doctors. Just the other day, Mia had been scanning through research abstracts and told Scott she'd been unable to corroborate what he and Shasta told her about xeno immunity. She'd called him paranoid when he'd commented that the research she was looking at had all been funded by pharmaceutical companies that profited from the sale of drugs to sick people. When he'd asked her how many studies on xenos the government had funded, she'd replied, "Medical research funding isn't allocated on a whim. What reason would the government have to study xenos?"

He'd been distracted from answering, but at the time, she wouldn't have taken him seriously anyway. It wasn't until she spent a night in vigil over the sickbeds of several people infected with the super typhoid – all of whom died, while not one xeno in the community even got sick – that she'd accepted the truth.

Not that Scott had ever heard xenografts protected against *cancer*. He thought it was limited to things like the flu – human illnesses that didn't occur in animals. He had a simplistic understanding of how xenografting worked, but knew it was more than just the merging of animal flesh with human. The donor animals were bioengineered so the human immune system wouldn't recognize the implant or graft as foreign, but clearly something else had happened, something the bioengineers hadn't intended. He flexed his cougar claws, thinking his donor had given him more than just the ability to blend in as an undercover officer.

As if she hadn't just revealed something very personal about herself, Lo switched the holo to a topography map of the Hudson River. "This is our destination, but the bank is too steep for the UAAV to make land." She switched the map to satellite view. "There's a small dock, or was last year when these photos were taken. I think we should head for it.

"And look at this." A wave of her hand and the UAAV's radar holo was displayed. "That vessel up ahead appears to be anchored right offshore. Boardman thinks it's Maddy Singh's yacht."

"If the yacht's still there, Maddy's not on it," Scott said.

"No, she definitely wouldn't stick around if she got the upper hand," Lo agreed. "It might be a good idea to pay the yacht a little visit."

"Disable it?" Scott grinned. "I like the way you think."

Alton started drumming his fingers again. "How long 'til we get there?"

Boardman made a fist and scratched his chin with the alligator hide covering his knuckles. "ETA ten minutes."

Ten minutes.

Scott and Alton loaded their guns, restocked on ammunition, and inserted earbugs to stay in contact with Lo and Boardman. They wouldn't have the same level of tech support for this op, but Lo pointed out the UAAV had some useful gizmos they hadn't had a chance to use last time. They'd already discussed the possible scenarios that might greet them when they arrived. Scott fingered the smooth casing on his last grenade, thinking if Bryn was dead, he'd take great pleasure stuffing it in the mouth of her killer.

He sat back in his seat, and then leaned forward when his back started itching again. He saw her in his mind's eye, standing in the doorway of the bathroom with the light behind her, wearing only a towel and a shy smile. She'd been so relaxed and content, a far cry from the girl who'd gotten her first good look at Nicola today. What a shock that must have been, to see her dead mother's face.

He knew how she felt. The first time he'd seen Nicola, it had been obvious she'd been created from the same genetic material as his adopted sister May. Fournier had cloned them both, but Scott didn't know how close in age they were. Fournier had made mistakes with May, though; mistakes that ultimately took her life at a young age.

A tone from the dash pulled him from his reverie. Lo brought up a holo of Shasta. She was in the surveillance van, gripping the steering wheel, a deep furrow between her brows.

With her customary brusqueness, she asked, "Where are you?"

"A few minutes out," Lo said. "Where are *you*?"

Shasta shook her head, lips thin with anger or impatience or both. "I got hold of Deputy Director Unger. He decided to drive up from D.C. with Congressman Abbott instead of getting on his flight. He and the congressman are stuck in the Holland Tunnel. That whole area around Poppy's Pier is overrun with rioters."

"You want us there?" Boardman asked.

Scott's breath caught in his throat until Shasta responded, "No, stay the course. I'm not going to be able monitor you, but you should know I checked local police scanners and there've been reports of exotic animals on the loose out there, so keep an eye out."

"Exotic how?" Boardman asked.

"Large and dangerous."

Lo flipped a switch and thrust the gearshift forward to slow the vehicle. "We're here."

"Good luck."

As Shasta's holo faded away, Lo said, "Pulling up to the dock's going to be tricky. The UAAV doesn't have bumpers and I don't want to damage the camouflage panels, so I'm going to get close and you guys are going to have to jump."

Chapter Thirty-five

Maddy had ordered them out of hiding, but Bryn had no intention of complying. It wasn't as if Maddy could walk away from the standoff she'd gotten herself into. In fact, as long as neither Maddy nor Dundee took action to end the stalemate, Bryn and Mia should be able to get to the dock. They didn't have keys to the outboard, but with any luck, they could untie it and simply float downstream until they'd gotten far enough away to call Scott back.

It was a theory that had a lot of potential holes in it, but it was all Bryn could come up with.

"We should try for the dock," she whispered.

"Okay," Mia whispered back.

They began to make their way towards the water. There was probably a path, but they definitely weren't on it. Bryn went first and tried to protect Mia from branches and help her past the roughest footing. After several yards, she heard something behind them that made her stop and drop into a crouch again, pulling Mia down into a thicket and hissing, *"Shhh!"*

Another sound, like that of a boot scraping on rock, alerted her to the fact that someone was coming. She knew it wasn't Maddy or Dundee, because they continued to threaten each other.

"There's two of us and one of you," Maddy said. "Shoot her, and I guarantee you'll hit the ground before she does."

"I won't need to shoot her," Dundee retorted. "You shoot *him* and she's my shield as I take you and your man out."

Bryn thought their verbal sparring would be almost comical if they weren't deadly serious. As it was, their conversation drew the newcomers away from Bryn and Mia. She saw them through the branches of the thicket, three figures moving stealthily towards Maddy. The lead man held a large weapon, like a machinegun, only with what looked like an oxygen tank attached to it. They had to be Fournier's men. Curtis would have told them his version of what happened, and Bryn's best guess was that they were extremely pissed off and looking for vengeance.

There was nothing for her to do but keep moving. She tugged on Mia's sleeve and headed down the slope toward the water again, probing the ground with each step to test her footing before shifting her weight. It was steep in places, and she was forced to walk sideways for traction, wincing each time a twig snapped, or dried leaves crunched underfoot. Despite the cold, she felt a trickle of sweat work its way down the middle of her back.

When she and Mia were maybe twenty feet from the dock, she saw there were two boats moored there, one on either side of it. The first she recognized as Maddy's outboard, but the second was a much-larger aluminum fishing boat that probably belonged to Fournier. Dundee wouldn't have had keys to Maddy's outboard either, so he must have used the fishing boat to get to the yacht. Maybe his goal had been to lie in wait for her. Instead, he'd found Padme.

Bryn paused behind the last of the bushes. The next stretch would bring them out in the open, where it was more than likely they'd be seen from the path. Dillo would still have a gun to Fournier's head, while Dundee presumably had one to Padme's. Maddy was the wildcard. If she saw Bryn and Mia about to take off in her outboard, there was a good chance she'd shoot.

Bryn tightened her cold fingers around the grip of Fournier's gun. If Maddy fired at her, she would sure as hell fire back, but she probably wouldn't need to – not with Fournier's men closing in.

"Ready?" she asked quietly.

"Yeah," Mia said, but then she gasped. "What's that?"

Bryn saw it, too. A vertical line of light had appeared out of nowhere at the end of the dock. It started out tall and narrow, but widened rapidly, like some kind of science fiction portal opening into another world. Two figures jumped out onto the dock. Even with the light behind them, Bryn recognized Scott and Jason. Of course it wasn't a portal; they'd arrived in the same nearly invisible vehicle they'd used to capture Lupus.

Before the relief of seeing Scott could take root in her heart, the light disappeared, and all hell broke loose.

Chapter Thirty-six

Of all the scenarios Scott and the others had anticipated, taking fire the instant they made land was the one he least expected, but here they were dodging bullets not three seconds after their boots hit the dock. They were exposed and vulnerable, but other than attempting to jump back into the moving UAAV or diving into the frigid river, their only choice was to drop flat against the rough wood planking of the dock. Scott's instinct was to return fire, but Bryn might be close, and he didn't want to shoot indiscriminately. Behind him, he heard the nearly silent engine of the UAAV whine as Lo maneuvered it away from the dock.

If things had begun smoothly, the plan had been for Lo and Boardman to check out Maddy's yacht while he and Alton scouted Fournier's property. Now, however, Lo would be forced to reveal the UAAV's presence in order to aid them.

Her voice sounded in his ear, "About to light the night."

She'd warned them the high-intensity spotlight installed in the roof of the UAAV would temporarily blind them if they looked at it, so he resolutely faced forward. When the light clicked on, its white shaft illuminated the wispy mist rising from the river like a laser beam, and the spot lit up a wide section of the vegetation as if it were noon on a cloudless summer day. Now he could see there were two boats tied to the dock. He recognized Maddy's outboard on one side, and on the other was a fishing boat like the one his grandfather used to have.

With the bright light, the shooting stopped, and he and Alton took advantage of their assailants' momentary disorientation to scramble to their feet and thunder down the dock.

In his ear, Boardman said, "To your right, behind the tree!" immediately followed by the *crack* of his rifle. From the corner of his eye, Scott saw someone fall, but then Lo said, "They're on the path – cut left! Cut left!"

128

Scott leapt off the end of the dock and switched direction, a stride ahead of Alton. Then with no warning whatsoever, a thick stream of orange fire blossomed over his right shoulder and the next thing he knew, Alton had tackled him to the ground. Instinctively, he rolled, the acrid scent of burnt hair filling his nose and Boardman's words, "*Flame thrower!*" in his ear.

His roll took him over the top of a boulder embedded in the soil, and he fell several feet down behind it, landing hard on his shoulder. Alton dropped next to him as another burst of flame scorched the ground above them. From this vantage point, they were maybe ten feet from the river's edge. He patted a smoking patch on his arm, thinking if the flame came any closer, they'd be forced to run for the water.

The stream of fire swung around towards the dock, singeing the tops of the reeds growing along the bank and sending black clouds rolling up into the sky. His eyes had adjusted to the UAAV's spotlight enough to see Boardman withdraw his rifle and shut the window before the flames hit.

"Oh, no you did *not*," Lo muttered in his ear as he and Alton hunkered down, catching their breath and waiting for her to pull something else from her bag of tricks. Sure enough, another trap door opened next to the one housing the spotlight on top of the UAAV and a thick spout raised up. A deep, rumbling hum alerted him just before the vessel's water cannon sent a high-pressure burst of river water arcing out over the dock.

"*Ha!*" Lo crowed. "Like that, fire man?"

Scott glanced around the boulder and grinned as the water swept the man off his feet. He attempted to stand, but Boardman shot him in the leg, saying, "Two down. Lost the third guy."

Lo used the water cannon to put out the flaming reeds near the shore, but its reach didn't extend far enough to extinguish the dry winter growth burning farther inland. Scott hadn't gotten a glimpse of the people she'd warned him about on the path, but something told him Bryn was among them.

He turned to Alton. "I have to find her."

Alton twisted his lips, checking his weapon. "For the record, I have a thing for the doc."

Scott blinked in surprise. "Oh. That's…"

"Yeah, whatever. Let's do this."

Scott looked over at the UAAV. Boardman had his rifle scope up to his eye, aiming for the path.

"I see them," he said. "One, two, three – five people. Fire's getting close, but they're just standing there."

"Recognize anyone?" Scott asked.

"Negative. Too much smoke."

Alton got to his feet. "Ready, kid?"

Scott nodded. This time Alton took the lead, running through the bushes along the edge of the path, skirting the areas that were burning. Ahead, a sound like the furious scream of a big cat brought Alton to an abrupt halt – and brought to mind Shasta's warning about 'large and dangerous' exotic animals on the loose. The fire must have flushed the animal out and would make it frightened and unpredictable.

Just as Alton began to move forward again – more cautiously this time – Scott heard the sudden *pop, pop, pop* of gunfire, which made them both duck into a crouch until they realized they weren't the targets. A blast from a larger gun was followed by an unmistakably female voice screaming in shrill hysteria.

For a heart-stopping moment, Scott thought it was Bryn, but the woman cried, "Maddy!" and he recognized Padme's voice. All caution forgotten, he and Alton beat their way through a copse of tall evergreen bushes. The bushes blocked most of the light from the UAAV, but the encroaching fire lit up the area well enough for him to assess the scene as they stepped onto the path.

Padme was kneeling over Maddy, who lay flat on her back gasping for breath, hand resting on a sawed-off shotgun. Nearby, Fournier sat slumped next to Dillo, who was face down in the dirt. Alton strode over to check Dillo, met Scott's eyes and shook his head.

Scott took the shotgun from Maddy's unresisting grasp and helped Padme to her feet. "Where's Bryn?"

"I don't know."

"What happened here?"

"The cheetah—it went after Dundee."

"Dundee?" The last Scott had heard of the Australian xeno, he'd been blinded by Bryn's quills. "Which way?"

She opened her mouth to respond, but behind her, a figure staggered through the smoke into the clearing, gun arm extended, barrel pointing right at her head. It was the third man, the one Boardman had lost sight of. His face was dirty, streaked with what looked like blood, and he smelled strongly of urine.

"Drop your weapons – all of you!"

It was the second time in one day someone had got the drop on Scott, only this time, Boardman and Lo weren't in a position to help. He kept hold of his gun but didn't risk lifting it and setting the obviously disturbed man off.

The man didn't seem to notice. He coughed a little from the smoke and then focused on Padme. "*You*," he spat. "You sent that fear, didn't you? I'm gonna cut those cow ears off and stuff them down your throat."

Behind him on either side, two more figures appeared, smoke swirling around them. One had a rifle and the other a handgun.

"No," Bryn said. "You're not."

Chapter Thirty-seven

She was prepared to kill the man if she had to, but thankfully, it turned out to be unnecessary. He hesitated for several tense seconds, sweat glistening on his brow, but then dropped his arm. The gun landed in the dirt with a thud that could barely be heard over the crackling of the burning bushes.

She raised her gaze. Scott held it for only a second, his blue eyes reflecting the light from the fire. Then he grabbed the man's arm, twisted it behind his back and efficiently secured him.

Out of the blue, he said, "Six incoming; two injured. Yes, they're both fine." He glanced at her again and she realized he must be talking to the rest of his team, the ones still on the water.

"Where's Dundee?" she asked. "He was here, I heard him!"

Scott glanced at Padme and said, "Something about a cheetah. We don't have time to hunt him down. We have to get out of here."

He and Alton quickly frisked and zip-tied Fournier, Padme, and Maddy. When Scott hauled Maddy to her feet, Padme exclaimed, "Be careful! She's shot."

"Stop fussing. I'm fine." Maddy looked at Scott. "Wearing your vest. Much obliged."

Bryn remembered Dillo had taken it from Scott at Edgemere, but instead of using it himself, he'd given it to his queen. Now he was lying in the dirt and they were out of time – the flames suddenly ignited the dry grass all around them in a whoosh of intense heat.

"*Run!*" Scott yelled, shoving Bryn from behind.

She didn't want to leave him, but the heat was overpowering, and thick, glowing sparks filled the clearing. In a running crouch, she sprinted along the path until she burst out into fresh air. She backed up into the winter field, horrified as she watched the conflagration, howling now like a live thing.

Mia appeared next, followed by the guy who'd tried to shoot Padme. He dropped to his knees, coughing and wheezing, as Maddy and Padme emerged behind him, holding hands. Scott and Jason arrived last, carrying Fournier between them.

"Where's Dillo?" Maddy cried, her face contorted with something that looked very much like grief. It wasn't the first time Bryn had witnessed the Mad Eye queen's intense emotions, but this time seemed different; underneath the shock and pain, Maddy seemed almost lost.

Scott, his face smudged with soot, looked away.

"You left him to burn? So you could save that piece of *shit*?" Maddy glared at Fournier with eyes that burned as intensely as the fire.

"He was too heavy, and we were out of time," Jason said. "For what it's worth, I'm sorry."

To avoid the smoke, they went upwind and circled back around to the river, where the strange vessel with the fire hose had kept the flames from spreading to the dock. The man who'd started the fire with the flame-thrower had dragged himself to the end of it and was sitting there, soaking wet and shivering as he nursed his gunshot leg.

Scott frowned when he saw him. "Just what we need: another injured prisoner."

He and Alton had a short conversation with the rest of their team. Even though Bryn only heard one side of it, she was able to determine that they'd accomplished their goal of capturing Fournier and didn't want to risk losing him again in the event any more of his men were lurking on the premises.

Or Dundee, she thought, staring into the darkness beyond the burning undergrowth.

Scott and the team agreed their only option was to take to the water, which was problematic, since the UAAV had a weight limit in amphibious mode. They decided to put Fournier's men on the UAAV and commandeer Maddy's yacht for everyone else. Getting the secured prisoners aboard the UAAV without tying it to the dock was easier said than done, but between them, Scott, Jason and Boardman managed it. Bryn and Mia happily relinquished their guns, which were put aboard the UAAV along with the prisoners' weapons.

They got to the yacht using Fournier's fishing boat, which still had the keys in the ignition from Dundee's trip. There was no one to take it back to the dock, so rather than set it loose on the river where it would be a potential hazard, they tied it to the back of the yacht, much to Maddy's irritation. When they got aboard, they found the captain was missing, and

Padme told them Dundee had thrown him overboard. Maddy offered to pilot the yacht, but Scott said, "No. Just tell me what to do."

She stood with him under the roof at the helm, obviously in pain from the gunshot Scott's vest had deflected. The rest of them had to sit under the open sky on the u-shaped seating of the cockpit; Fournier and Padme on one side where Jason could keep an eye on them, and Bryn and Mia on the other.

Scott followed Maddy's instructions, and as they got underway, a very subdued Padme asked for a blanket. Jason went below and came back with three of them, plus the ship's medical kit and several bottles of water. When he approached Padme with one of the blankets, she snatched it out of his hand and curled up on the seat as far from Fournier as possible.

Mia opened the medical kit, Jason hovering over her as she attended to Fournier's arm. After she'd bandaged it, she peeled off her rubber gloves and reached for her purse. Inside was the plastic bag with her post-op instructions. She removed a small bottle, opened it, and shook two white pills into her palm.

"Here," she said.

"What is it?" Fournier asked weakly.

"Pain meds from your den."

"Oh, right. Your graft." He obediently opened his mouth. She dropped the pills in, and then held a bottle of water to his lips.

"So you got the graft?" Jason asked.

She nodded. Bryn noticed she didn't take any of her own medication. Instead, she moved away from Fournier and perched on the edge of the seat near Bryn, back straight.

Jason sat next to her. "What'd you get?"

Bryn was interested to hear Mia explain her choice, but Mia only said, "Doesn't matter. He said it won't protect me for several weeks."

"That long?"

Jason waited for a response that never came. Mia just stared down at her clasped hands. He made a rueful face before pulling his gun from its holster and fiddling with it.

At the helm, Scott was keeping pace with the slower UAAV. The lights dotting the landscape seemed to abruptly disappear, even though the yacht was getting closer to the city. The orange glow that usually tinted the Manhattan skyline at night was absent. She could see the tops of the taller buildings, but there weren't nearly as many lights shining out of the windows as there should be. Closer to shore, other than car headlights and the occasional fire, everything was eerily black. *The power must be out*, she thought with a shiver. She didn't know much about the power grid but figured only a catastrophic failure would result in such widespread darkness.

"What are we going to do when we get ashore?" she asked.

"Meet up with Shasta," Jason said. "She's in one of the agency's surveillance vans."

"Shasta!" Mia gasped and put both hands to her face. "I should have called her the second you guys showed up."

Jason looked over at the UAAV. "Lo, can you get Shasta on the line?"

He listened to her reply and then shook his head. "She says she's been trying, but she isn't picking up."

Mia took her holophone out of her purse. "I'll send her a text. Hopefully she'll get it soon."

"What's so urgent?" Scott asked.

Mia tilted her head towards Fournier. "According to him, the typhoid carriers all have crocodilian grafts."

"Crocodilian?" Scott asked. "Not alligator?"

"Same difference." Mia didn't look up from her holophone, so she missed the concerned look Scott and Jason exchanged. Bryn saw it, though, and it took her a moment to realize what was bothering them: Boardman had an alligator graft – and he must have heard Scott's question through the earbug, because Scott said, "Fournier says the carriers all have croc or gator grafts. Sorry, man."

Maddy glanced sidelong at Mia. "Once you tell the CDC, they're going to round up everyone with those grafts and lock them up. Unless word gets out and the mobs kill them all first."

"Xenos are already being rounded up, regardless of their graft," Scott said.

"Rounded up? How?" Bryn asked.

"The National Guard's been conducting sweeps in xeno neighborhoods." He shrugged a little. "For their protection."

"Neighborhoods like – Carla's? Have you heard from her?"

He nodded. "Yeah. They took her."

"Where?"

"Poppy's Pier." He pointed downstream.

She looked at him uncomprehendingly. "Why there? That place is horrible."

"I don't know. She said she was safe, though."

Bryn still had a million questions, but Maddy scowled at Fournier and said, "See what you've done?"

"Give credit where it's due," he replied. "None of this would have happened if it weren't for your father."

She strode across the deck. "What does *that* mean, you miserable little cockroach?"

"It means," Jason said, leaning forward to rest his forearms on his thighs, gun hanging casually between his knees, "that your father's as dirty as they come. Remember that deal we made?"

"Null and void when my brother died." She turned back to Fournier and spat, "Because of *you*."

"I'm sorry for your loss," he said dully.

Maddy seemed like she was about to hurl herself across the table at him even though her hands were tied behind her back. Then she cocked her head to one side and narrowed her eyes at Jason. "Tell me, Dragila, was there an attack on the XIA building today? Did Lupus manage to escape?"

"He's dead," Alton said. "Your soldier shot him."

"Oh, no," she murmured, looking at Fournier with a falsely solicitous manner. "I'm so sorry for *your* loss."

Fournier turned his head away, face slack and eyes dull as the painkiller Mia had given him began to take effect.

Jason stood, moving to stand in front of Maddy. "You do realize you're going to prison, don't you? I might still be able to get you some leniency if you cooperate."

"I already told you I don't know anything about my father's business."

"You don't need to know anything," Jason said. "You just need to talk to him."

"You mean wear a wire?" She managed to appear offended and dumbfounded at the same time.

He didn't reply. His head went up, eyes getting that unfocused look that told Bryn he was listening to his earbug.

"Roger that," he said. Then to Bryn and Mia, "Lo says they're making land."

"We're going to split up?" Mia asked. "Is that wise?"

"It's necessary," Scott said shortly.

Bryn looked downstream, gaze picking out two lighted objects moving across the sky. Helicopters, circling something on the ground, spotlights flashing. Something told her the copters were directly above Poppy's Pier.

Chapter Thirty-eight

What Lo actually said was she was worried about Shasta and wanted to make land in order to head to the Holland Tunnel to see if she could locate her. That meant the UAAV would soon be out of range of their earbugs and they'd lose constant contact with the rest of the team.

Scott would have answered Mia's question about the wisdom of splitting up, but he didn't want Maddy and Fournier to know how tenuous their control of the situation really was. Without Shasta and the vehicle she was driving, they had no way to transport all the prisoners once they made land – although *where* to transport them was also up in the air. XIA headquarters was out, and the commanding officer of that National Guard unit said the jails weren't taking xenos. Not to mention, Fournier needed to get to a hospital.

Maddy was silently fuming after her confrontation with Fournier, but seemed triumphant at the same time, which Scott could only attribute to her finding out that the Mad Eye soldier she sent to take out Lupus had been successful. He was glad she'd shut up, though. Not that goading Fournier seemed to have much effect at the moment. He was hunched under his blanket, eyes closed. Padme hadn't moved.

Bryn had pulled the hood of her coat over her quills and tucked a blanket under her hips. It was bitterly cold, and he thought about sending her below, but didn't want to let her out of his sight. As he watched, she straightened and turned towards shore. "Did anyone hear that?"

The noise from the two circling helicopters almost obscured it, but he did hear something. It was faint but sounded like panicked screams and shouts. According to the radar they were just north of Poppy's Pier.

"Scott." Bryn's eyes were pleading. She didn't have to tell him she was thinking of Carla.

"Stay the course, Harding," Alton said.

Scott turned the ship's wheel. "It won't hurt to get a closer look."

The screams and shouts got louder as they approached the pier. It almost sounded like the roar of a crowd at a football stadium. There *was* an enormous athletics field at the center of the pier, but it was surrounded by a multi-story structure, and even with the helicopter spotlights, they couldn't see what was going on from the water.

On the radar, Scott noticed a slew of slowly moving green blips ahead of them and not far from the yacht's position. Some were at the surface, and others appeared to be slowly sinking. "What are these?"

Maddy shrugged. "Too small to be boats, too big to be fish, but you're headed right for them. Turn to starboard!"

As he veered away from the pier, he clearly heard someone call out, "Help!"

Bryn leapt to her feet and rushed to the rail. "There are *people* in the water!"

One of the helicopters was hovering in place, spotlight sweeping around in big circles. The light gave Scott his first good look at what Poppy had done to the pier that had been originally built as a passenger ship terminal almost a hundred years ago. The pylons holding it up all along the side facing the river had either given way or sunk into the river bottom. Whatever the cause, the pier was no longer level. The storm left the huge structure sagging precariously. In fact, at the southwestern corner of the pier, where an extension of the dock had once thrust out into the river, the thick concrete infrastructure was entirely submerged.

"Oh, my God, look!" Mia pointed to the top of the building, where dozens of buses were parked. The spotlight had settled on a group of people dragging someone to the edge. With no warning, they threw him over.

Scott halfway expected Alton to spout, "Stay the course" again, but he just shook his head and said, "We'll take on as many as we can."

"We can pick them up with the fishing boat," Scott said.

"No. Use the bathing platform at the stern." Maddy turned and lifted her bound hands. "I can maneuver close enough."

Scott exchanged a look with Alton.

"You don't have time to debate this." Maddy nodded to the blips on the radar. "Can't help the ones under the surface. You're going to need my finesse if you want to prevent any more from drowning."

"She's right." Scott pulled his knife from the sheath at his belt and cut her zip tie. He'd have to stay to keep an eye on her.

Alton gestured for Bryn to follow him. "It's you and me, kid."

Chapter Thirty-nine

The bathing platform was like a mini dock located at the very back of the boat. It was intended to make it easier for swimmers to get into and out of the water. Bryn imagined it would be a nice place to relax in a lounge chair on a sunny day, but at the moment it was treacherously slippery as the chop slapped against the bottom of the platform and kicked up an icy spray. Fournier's fishing boat was tied to one corner of it, but Maddy seemed to have taken it into consideration as she maneuvered the yacht around to the first victim.

Bryn clung to the stair railing as Jason hauled him aboard. The man crawled on his hands and knees until she reached out to help him to his feet. His hand was like ice. It seemed to take forever to get him up the steps into the salon. He was dressed in fatigues with no coat or shoes – he'd probably dumped them so they wouldn't weigh him down and drag him under. His lips were blue and his dark skin ashen. He didn't look much older than she was.

She cranked the thermostat on the wall of the salon to its maximum, saying, "You need to get out of those wet clothes. I'm going to find some blankets."

She hurried back out. In the smaller of the two cabins on the lowest level, there were two narrow beds, and from the clothes and items strewn about, she figured it had been occupied by the captain and Dillo. The larger cabin's lavish décor told her it was Maddy's bedroom. She went in and yanked all the linens from the bed, dragging them back to the salon.

The young man was still standing there attempting to unbutton his shirt. She helped him take it and his socks off but stopped short of reaching for the button on his pants.

"Bryn!" Jason called.

She draped the bedspread over the young man's shoulders and ran out.

They were closer to the pier now. One of the helicopters had moved out over the water directly above the yacht and aimed its spotlight at them. It was a news copter, and she didn't know whether they were trying to help with the light or just trying to film the best action, but the wind and noise were disorienting.

The light did reveal the yacht to the men in the water, though. Bryn saw some of them begin to swim sluggishly towards it. There were men standing on the unsubmerged portion of the pier who were gesticulating and appeared to be shouting. At first, she thought they were trying to help, but then she saw one of them brandishing what looked like a tire iron. With a sick sensation in her stomach, she realized why the men in the water hadn't simply climbed out onto the pier.

The next man to come aboard was older, also wearing a uniform, and must not have been in the water as long as the first man, because he was able to tell her what happened. In a dazed voice, he said, "We're National Guard. Just there to keep the peace. Had orders not to hurt anyone. Most of us had riot gear, shields and gasmasks, but no guns. We were outnumbered."

They pulled twelve men in all from the river, including the latest to have been flung into the frigid water, a stocky, middle-aged sergeant named Malone. According to him, there'd been quite a few more.

The survivors crowded into the salon as their soaked clothing piled up in the little kitchenette. Bryn ransacked the cabins and cupboards for all the blankets and towels she could find. Jason called Mia to come down to attend to the men with the worst hypothermia. Malone, who was the highest-ranking guardsman among them, asked if anyone on board could lend him some clothes. Bryn went back into Dillo's cabin but balked at rifling through the dead man's things. She brought his knapsack back with her and gave it to Malone.

When it looked like the situation was under control, Bryn, Mia and Jason went back up to the cockpit. The helicopters were gone. Padme was sitting up now and Maddy was at the helm, maintaining the yacht's position adjacent to the pier.

"How are they?" Scott asked.

"At a minimum, two need to get to a hospital," Mia replied. "It'd be best if they all got checked out."

"Did they say why they were thrown in?"

Jason snorted. "Their guests didn't like the accommodations."

"I'll bet," Maddy said.

From the stairway, another voice joined the conversation. "We were following orders."

"Sergeant Malone!" Mia exclaimed. "You should stay in the salon where it's warm."

"I'm fine. Wasn't in the water very long." He climbed the rest of the way onto the deck. "Whose boat is this?"

"Mine." Maddy scowled as she took in Malone's outfit: black pants rolled up at the cuff and a battered jean jacket at least two sizes too big. The only thing of Dillo's that seemed to fit were the boots on his feet.

"And you are?" His attitude suggested he was planning on taking over, but Jason quickly disabused him of that notion.

"*We're* XIA." He gestured to Scott and pulled his jacket open to flash the badge on his belt. Malone wouldn't fail to notice the gun in its shoulder holster.

"Thanks for the rescue," Malone said, "but if you're XIA, where were you when all that started?" He jerked his head towards the pier.

"That shouldn't have happened at all," Jason replied. "We wouldn't have detained them in the first place."

Even in the cockpit's low light, Bryn saw Malone's face go florid with anger. "That wasn't the detainees. Local jails cleared out all the xenofreaks from the general population. Put 'em in buses. Filled the pier's parking structure and just left' em there. Nowhere near enough of us to stop 'em when they broke out."

He ran his gaze over everyone present and then lingered on Bryn. "Don't I know you?"

The hood of her coat was still up; she'd kept it over her quills while helping him and his men, so all any of them had seen was her face. She was about to deny it, but he said, "You're that Bryn girl. The one from the news. What's going on here?"

"This is an active investigation, which we interrupted to pick you and your men up," Scott said firmly. "Happy to drop you off somewhere safe, but that's as far as we go."

Malone's jaw jutted forward as if he wasn't in agreement, but he said, "Whatever you say. I'll need to borrow a holophone to report to my superiors." As an apparent afterthought, he added, "Please."

Scott pulled his phone from his pocket, entered the passcode to activate it, and handed it to the sergeant. When Malone saw Scott's alterations, he recoiled slightly. "You a xenofreak, too?"

"XIA agents usually are. Tend to stay alive longer that way."

"Huh." Malone took the phone and lifted it. "Okay if I make this call down below?"

Scott nodded. After Malone had gone, he turned to Maddy. "Where's the nearest public dock?"

"Right there." She pointed to the radar holo. "And the sooner those grunts are off my ship, the better."

"Won't be your ship for long," Jason said.

"Mm." Maddy was still looking at the radar. Her face took on a greenish tinge as the holographic image of a large vessel floated through the air, on a course to pass very close by the yacht. "We'll see."

Chapter Forty

They were still lingering near the pier, but there hadn't been anyone thrown into the river in the last twenty minutes or so, either because the xenos had run out of guardsmen, or because there was no point tossing them in while someone was out here rescuing them.

According to the radar, the approaching vessel was several times larger than the yacht. Scott hoped it was the harbor patrol or navy coming to their aid, although it was more likely to be one of the many barges carrying cargo up and down the Hudson.

He was about to give the order that they head for the nearest dock to drop off their passengers when he heard Lo in his ear. "Alton? Harding? Is that you?"

"Lo?" Jason said. "Where are you?"

"On West Street between the Holland Tunnel and Poppy's Pier. Stuck behind a major blockade. We saw you guys on the news rescuing those men."

"Oh, yeah? You find Shasta?" Scott asked.

"No sign of *her*, but we can see her vehicle on the other side of the blockade."

"She inside?"

"Negative. Something's definitely wrong. She should have called by now. I have a bad feeling she's on the pier."

"Why would she go there?" Jason asked.

"To look for Nicola and Savvy. I'm pretty sure she feels responsible for them, doesn't want them to get hurt. Because things are crazy around here. Troops and tanks everywhere. Army's preparing for something big."

That would explain why the news helicopters had gone. The authorities would have ordered them to clear the air space, ostensibly for their safety. Scott was conscious that Bryn was watching and listening; he was glad she couldn't hear what Lo said. She was worried enough about Carla without knowing the army was converging on the pier. If they took action, there would be a lot of innocent xenos caught in the crossfire, including Nicola and Savvy.

He glanced over at Fournier, who appeared to have fallen asleep under his blanket with no knowledge that his 'daughter' was so close, or in such potential danger.

"Lo. Heads up." It was Boardman. "We got company."

The earbug picked up an unfamiliar man's voice. "You can't be here."

"We're XIA," Lo said.

"In an ice cream truck?"

"It's an Urban Amphibious Armored Vehicle with adaptive camouflage panels. See?"

She must have made the UAAV invisible or something, because the man said, "Jeez! Nice ride. You still can't be here."

They continued to argue, but Scott's attention was pulled away from the conversation by raised voices coming from below deck. There were thumps and crashing sounds and then Malone ordering someone to "Stand down, soldier!"

From the sound of it, he was having trouble convincing his men the fight was over.

Jason had been sitting next to Mia but stood to move closer to the stairs. He frowned at Maddy. "You don't have any weapons down there, do you?"

"What do you think?" From her expression, the answer was an unqualified yes.

Scott looked over at the pier. On the top level, someone had set fire to a bus. In the flickering light, he could make out the xenos who'd prevented the guardsmen from getting out of the river, still patrolling the pier. If the yacht moved a hundred yards or so closer, the guardsmen could get some payback.

Jason pulled his gun but didn't go below. Scott knew what he was thinking: the best place for him to be in the event the guardsmen rushed the cockpit was at the top of the stairs, where he could pick them off.

In his ear, Scott heard the man Lo was talking to say loudly, "Move out!"

Lo was unflappable. "I'd like to speak to your superior officer."

That was when Scott noticed the approaching vessel. Its running lights were bright enough that he could see it wasn't a barge. He wasn't terribly familiar with watercraft, but it didn't look utilitarian enough to be harbor patrol or navy. If anything, it appeared to be a much larger version of

Maddy's yacht. As it came alongside, he looked along its impressive length and saw the blades of a private helicopter near the stern.

A tone sounded from the helm and before Scott could ask Maddy what it was, she waved a hand through the radar holo and a face appeared. The man had smooth mahogany skin and black hair. Scott didn't immediately recognize him, but knew he'd seen him somewhere. It wasn't until Maddy said, "Hello, Father," that he realized he was looking at billionaire Philip Singh.

Chapter Forty-one

Bryn didn't connect Maddy's father with the huge boat that had come alongside them until Maddy glanced over at it and said, "I'm surprised you'd risk leaving international waters. How did you find me?"

"I saw you on the news. Where's Munnu?" His Indian accent was slightly heavier than Maddy's.

She hesitated, staring at her father's holo. "You already know, don't you?"

"Did you think you could keep it from me?"

"I-"

"Did you *really* think I wouldn't find out what you did? How far you've sunk into depravity? You are a vile degenerate, and I'm disgusted with-"

Maddy swept a hand through the holo and terminated the conversation before turning to everyone present with a strained smile. "Well, that was pleasant. I think perhaps we'd best leave as quickly as possible. My father's yacht is equipped with enough firepower to easily blow us out of the water."

"He wouldn't do that. Not here. He's too careful," Jason said.

"You said yourself he owns quite a few American politicians. You don't think he could make the official report read like a tragic accident?"

"Good point," Scott said. "Let's go."

Bryn gripped the edge of the seat as Maddy thrust the throttle forward and the yacht surged ahead. The other vessel was facing upstream in the opposite direction. It wouldn't be able to maneuver nearly as quickly, and as they left it behind, Bryn hoped that was the end of the confrontation. Unfortunately, Maddy's father had anticipated she might run.

Scott pointed to the radar. "We got incoming!"

Bryn saw two fast-moving blips just rounding the back end of the larger yacht. Maddy pulled the wheel to the left in a turn so sharp it caused

Fournier to slide several feet along the seat. He woke up and spluttered, "What…what?"

"Damn it!" Maddy cried. "That fishing boat is creating too much drag. If we don't cut it loose, they'll catch us for sure!"

Scott said, "I got it," and disappeared down the stairs.

Bryn couldn't see much more than the running lights of the speedboats chasing them, but the radar showed the distance between them rapidly narrowing.

"I suggest everyone hit the deck!" Maddy called out.

Bryn knew what that meant: they were about to get shot at again. She got down onto all fours between the seat and the table. Mia slid off next to her, ducked under the table, and wrapped her legs around the column supporting it. Bryn couldn't see Padme and Fournier, but she did catch sight of Jason by the stairs, squatting down behind the railing. Malone's voice echoed up the passageway, "What the hell's going on up there?"

"Brace yourselves!" Jason shouted back.

Over the noise of the yacht's straining engine, Bryn heard what sounded like a cat loudly purring. It was gunfire, of course. Scott would be totally exposed on the bathing platform.

Be safe, she thought, closing her eyes tightly and wishing her quills would allow her to put her hands over her ears.

"We're taking fire!" Jason stated the obvious, probably for Lo's benefit.

The next thing Bryn heard was more shouting rising from the lower deck, only this time, the guardsmen were yelling in unison. They *had* found Maddy's weapons stash, and from the sound of it, began enthusiastically returning fire. Louder, closer gunfire told her Jason, too, had begun shooting.

The yacht straightened out and Bryn opened her eyes. They were coming up on the pier again to their right, as Maddy headed back between it and her father's vessel. Then the Mad Eye queen suddenly dropped to her knees, the fingers of one hand still clenched around the steering wheel; it was immediately clear to Bryn she'd taken a bullet.

Bryn crawled towards her as the deck listed to the right. She craned her neck to look up at the looming pier and was just thinking if Maddy didn't straighten the wheel, the yacht would hit it, when the vessel jerked violently. Bryn was tossed several feet, and ended up face-down, hands clawing at the polished wooden deck for purchase as the underside of the yacht shuddered and scraped along the edge of the submerged pier with a screeching, grinding cacophony. Maddy made a heroic attempt to gain her footing, but before she could steer them to safety, the front of the vessel

147

thumped up against something that knocked her from her feet and sent Bryn rolling across the deck. Bryn had a flash of memory: the concrete dock surrounding the pier had only been partially submerged – it had risen from the river about halfway down the pier. She barely had time to realize they'd run aground before the yacht launched into the air and immediately slammed back down again. It skidded a short way before something unyielding brought its momentum to an abrupt stop.

Chapter Forty-two

After Scott cut the rope to the fishing boat, the driver of one of the outboards chasing them had to swerve to avoid hitting it. The driver lost control and sideswiped Singh's yacht. Scott had just laughed aloud when he was suddenly thrown head over heels into the Hudson River.

Hitting the frigid water was such a shock he barely managed to suppress the reflex to suck in a breath. His vest wasn't the inflatable kind this time, but it was waterproof and acted somewhat like a life vest as he struggled to the surface. Once there, he ineffectually thrashed about, lungs spasmodically taking in great gulps of air. He recognized that he was in danger of hyperventilating and tried to slow his breathing and take stock of his surroundings.

It was dark, but the light from the dying bus fire atop the pier revealed the second speed boat bearing down on him. To his left, he made out the silhouette of Maddy's yacht, listing to one side on top of the pier's dock. The occupants of the speed boat hung over the side, their guns ready to raze the crippled yacht's deck. Scott's cougar fingertips felt like frozen sausages, but he managed to wrap his hand around the remaining grenade on his belt and pull it free. He needed both hands to pull the pin, which meant he'd have to go under again, something he very much didn't want to do. But the thought of Bryn lying helpless and injured spurred him to take a deep breath before letting himself slide back beneath the cold, black water.

Once he'd resurfaced with the armed grenade in his right hand, he waited a couple more seconds for the speed boat to get close enough. They'd slowed significantly and were just about to pull even with the yacht when he scissor-kicked with as much strength as he could muster in order to lift himself a precious few inches from the water and hurl the grenade. As soon as he verified that it hit its target, he turned away so he wouldn't be blinded when the blast lit up the night.

It exploded with a satisfying boom that reverberated through the water. The dock ahead of him was illuminated just long enough for him to spot the most likely place to pull himself out of the river – about fifteen yards from the yacht. He began swimming in a weak breaststroke, and just before he reached his goal, he saw the slim beam of a flashlight appear like a beacon.

Someone called out, "Scott!"

It sounded like Alton's voice, although Alton had never used his first name before. When Scott finally made it to the pier and reached up with leaden arms, hands appeared and clasped his forearms. He wasn't much help hauling himself out and could only collapse in a shivering heap.

With chattering teeth, he ground out, "Bryn okay?"

"She's banged up," Alton replied. "We all were. Maddy took another bullet in the vest, but no casualties. That your grenade?"

Scott started to say, "Yeah," but the dock beneath them groaned alarmingly.

"Better get out of here." Alton ran the flashlight over him. "Can you walk?"

Scott wasn't about to admit he wasn't sure. His arms and legs felt both numb and cramped at the same time. It seemed like a major accomplishment just getting up onto all fours. Alton helped him to his feet and kept hold of his arm to guide him away from the yacht.

"Where we going?"

"Warm you up."

"Who's watching Maddy and Fournier?"

"Bryn. Gave her my backup piece."

Scott smiled to himself but couldn't tell if his frozen cheeks even moved.

"Here." Alton shone his flashlight on a broken section of wall. They went inside, stepping over and around the kind of decayed refuse that collects in abandoned buildings. Alton helped him up a flight of stairs, where he saw for himself how everyone had gotten off the yacht so quickly. It had crashed into the side of the building, ripping a hole in the stairwell wall. They'd only had to step from the deck onto the second-floor landing.

"Lucky, huh?" Alton asked.

"'Bout time we had a little luck," Scott replied.

They went up to the top level, where the door to the outside was missing. He looked out on what used to be a parking lot, and was being used for that purpose again; dozens of empty prisoner transport vehicles with the emblems of various law enforcement agencies were parked in neat rows. The buses he could see didn't look the worse for wear. The reinforced windows were all intact and there were no bodies or other evidence that whoever had been guarding the prisoners had been overpowered.

150

They began walking along the edge where the guardsmen had been thrown off, so Scott couldn't see the center of the pier, but he heard the constant roar rising from the crowd. It made him sick to think there were hardened criminals – criminals under the powerful influence of mob mentality – on the loose down there with the general xeno population.

He picked up a faint, annoying buzz from his earbug, like a bee had flown into his ear. Hooking a claw into the device, he pulled it out and flicked it over the edge. "Definitely not waterproof. What'd Lo say?"

"She's still trying to talk her way onto the pier to look for Shasta." Alton held an arm out to stop him, backing up against the front of a bus. "Careful."

Scott caught sight of several men sauntering between the rows of vehicles, bumping shoulders and laughing, a roving band of xenofreaks so brashly confident of their advantage they weren't paying attention to their surroundings.

Once they'd gone past, Alton led Scott directly to what remained of the burning bus. The lingering smoke was noxious, but Scott felt the heat from yards away. Suddenly, Bryn appeared, running full bore towards him. She threw herself silently into his arms, nearly knocking him off his numb feet. Her mouth felt hot against his cold lips. If her quills were poking him, he couldn't feel them and didn't care.

"Thank God you're alright," she whispered.

He pulled gently away. "You, too. But who's watching the prisoners?"

"We are."

Scott looked around. Malone was standing on the steps of an open bus door, holding a shotgun. The bus engine was idling, and it looked like everyone from the yacht was now sitting safely on board.

"Welcome to the xenofreak express," Malone said.

Chapter Forty-three

Bryn had been frantic with worry when Scott came up missing. No one had seen him get ejected from the yacht, but once the second speed boat blew up, Jason had immediately put two and two together.

Scott was in better condition than most of the guardsmen they'd rescued, but she could practically see the steam rising off him when he stepped onto the bus. One of the guardsmen was sitting in the driver's seat, speaking into an old-fashioned two-way radio. "Dispatch, do you read? This is Corporal Manuel Bastida of the Army National Guard. We are in need of assistance. Do you copy?"

The only response he seemed to be getting was static.

"Ah, it's warm," Scott said. "How'd you get it started?"

"Keys were in the ignition. That's why we picked it."

She hustled him down the center aisle to the back where he could strip in private. Once there, she helped peel off his jacket, vest, gun holster, utility belt and shirt. Unlike with the guardsmen, she didn't hesitate to reach for the button on his jeans. Once she'd dragged them down past his hips, she murmured, "Sit," and took off her coat to wrap around his shoulders.

The bus was softly lit inside by lights along the top and bottom of the windows, but it was dark near the floor when she knelt down in front of him. She had to untie his boots by feel, and after she'd tugged them and his socks off, she finished removing his jeans.

"Lucky me." She briskly rubbed her hands up and down the cold skin of his calves. "I finally got you almost naked."

He grabbed her upper arms and lifted. She didn't need an invitation to rise and place a knee on either side of his thighs. When she lowered herself onto his lap, his wet boxer shorts quickly soaked through the fabric on the inner thighs of her jeans. He slipped his hands under her shirt and she let out a squeal of shocked protest as the cold, damp fur of his fingers spanned her waist.

"Guys need any help back there?" Alton asked.

152

Bryn was about to say no, but Scott said, "Some dry clothes would be nice."

When one of Malone's men padded down the aisle, Bryn reluctantly slid off Scott's lap. Like most of the guardsmen, the approaching man was barefoot. Things had gotten tossed around on the yacht, and none of them had time to find and put on their wet boots before evacuating. They were all dressed in dry clothes, though, which they'd obtained helping themselves to what they could find in the cabins.

"Here." The man handed over a pair of grey slacks and matching suit jacket in a polished fabric. "We took up a collection."

"Uh, thanks." Scott accepted the offerings and looked them over with a dubious expression.

"You're not going to turn your nose up at vintage Gucci, are you?" Maddy called from six seats up.

Only Bryn heard him mutter, "I am never going to live this down, am I?"

"So what if it's a woman's suit?" She tried to sound practical, but inside she was valiantly fighting a smile. "Better than freezing, right?"

Scott looked like he was being forced to dry-swallow a bitter pill, but he yanked the slacks on. They were snug around his thighs, but he was able to zip and fasten them. He set Bryn's coat aside and picked up the jacket. It had thin shoulder pads and lapels that were wide at the top and tapering down to the one large black button at its midsection. He put it on and frowned down at the triangle of his naked chest. Bryn had to press her lips together and turn away to keep from laughing.

He grabbed up his soaked shirt and began wringing it out. Bryn helped him squeeze the water out of his leather jacket and jeans. They draped his clothes over the back of the seat in front of them. There was a heating vent nearby, but she figured it would take hours for everything to dry.

He'd just finished transferring the contents of his jean pockets to the slacks when Jason strode up the aisle. "You all thawed out? Lo says-" he made a choking sound when he caught sight of Scott but recovered brilliantly by coughing and continuing as if nothing had happened, "that she and Boardman are being allowed onto the pier."

"Really?" Scott hastily reached down to retrieve his bullet-proof vest and utility belt from the floor.

"Army thinks the UAAV might come in handy communicating with the xenos. It can broadcast a forty-foot holo just like drive-in holo theaters."

"Wow." Scott put the vest on, fastening it over the jacket with a satisfied little grunt before reaching for his holster. "We gonna drive out of here?"

"Try. Only thing is, Lo says the army's not letting anybody out."

Scott stood and placed his foot on the seat so he could tuck his pant leg into his boot. He lowered his voice. "She tell them we got the guardsmen?"

Jason nodded. "Not even them. Afraid they might be contagious now."

"It doesn't spread through non-xenos."

"You and I know that, but they don't," Jason said. "Um, Bryn, could you check on Dr. Padilla? She doesn't look so good."

She nodded and picked up her coat. Before she could shrug into it, Scott reached out and tilted her chin up. He'd never shown the slightest sign of affection towards her while on the job, so it surprised her when he planted a quick, hard kiss on her lips.

"Almost safe," he murmured.

She smiled, holding his gaze as he backed away. He turned to follow Jason to the front of the bus. When he passed Maddy's seat, she said, "You look fabulous, darling."

"Thanks," he replied.

Bryn found Mia's seat and slid in next to her.

"Jason asked me to check on you."

"I'm fine."

"Liar."

Mia turned to her with shadowed eyes. "I can deal with the pain. It's just...the whole world's gone crazy. Doesn't it bother you?"

Bryn shrugged. "The rest of the world can do what it wants. I plan on staying sane."

When Mia didn't respond, Bryn sighed and looked around. She saw the top of Padme's head in the seat next to Maddy. Across the aisle from them sat Fournier, his forehead resting against the window glass.

"Do you believe what Fournier said?" she asked. "That he's been trying to help people?"

"Fournier's a lunatic. All that talk of sacrifice for the greater good."

"But it's kind of obvious he was talking about Maddy's father, right?"

Bastida had begun backing the bus out of the parking spot. Mia stared out the window at the huge yacht still lurking off the pier. "I guess so. What difference does it make? Even if everything Fournier said was true – especially if what he said was true – we won't get very far trying to tell people. When he said the CDC sent me here because I would fail...? I thought the same thing when I got the assignment. It just didn't make sense that they'd choose me."

"Aren't you going to even try? To tell them?"

A spark of life appeared in Mia's eyes. "Of course I am. But you saw what Philip Singh is capable of. He just tried to kill his own daughter – or *son* – and everyone else on the yacht was just collateral damage to him."

"No one is untouchable, no matter how rich they are." Bryn had planned to say more, but she trailed off. Maddy had once commented that fathers were strange creatures. If Bryn's father hadn't forced the quills on her, she would have died soon after her first encounter with Junk. Then again, if he hadn't done it, she wouldn't have met Junk in the first place.

She shook her head to chase away the convoluted thoughts. If there was one thing she'd learned post-graft, it was never to speculate on the 'what ifs.' Still, she couldn't help but think no matter what had happened to her in the past, and no matter what her father or Fournier had done to set things in motion, the mutated typhoid would have eventually surfaced on its own.

Chapter Forty-four

Scott sat next to Jason behind the man who'd volunteered to drive the bus and checked his gun. It would fire wet, but he preferred not to take any chances, so he removed the clip and shook the water out of it.

Bastida had reached the end of the line of parked buses and turned left. The headlights showed that the parking lot exited onto a ramp leading down to a tunnel. To their left was the huge field at the center of the pier, filled with a veritable sea of xenos. There were dozens of bonfires and several areas where they'd gathered old fencing material and erected what Scott recognized as fighting rings. More than one fight appeared to be occurring as he watched.

As soon as the bus drove onto the ramp, xenos began gathering around it. After maybe fifty yards the crowd was so thick Bastida was forced to stop. From the light of the bonfires and the bus headlights, Scott saw the faces of the people surrounding them – men and women who were frightened and angry – justifiably so. They were shouting and screaming at the bus. He tried to make out individual voices to hear what they were saying, but it was impossible.

"Crap," Alton said. "I was afraid this was going to happen. Lo? Little help here?"

He listened for a moment and then stood to look out the front windshield. "Yeah, I see you."

Scott followed his gaze and made out the top of the UAAV. It, too, was surrounded by a crowd of xenos, but they were keeping their distance as it slowly moved towards the center of the field.

"Wish *we* had a force field," Alton muttered.

"Is that what it is?" Scott asked.

"Pretty much. Lo says anyone who touches the UAAV'll get a nasty zap."

Suddenly, the bus rocked a little on its shocks. Malone was seated across from them, looking out the window to the right. "Bastards are trying to push us over!"

"Can they do that?" Maddy asked. "Surely we're too heavy."

"You'd be surprised what an angry mob can do," Malone replied.

Now Scott heard a voice from outside – someone yelling, "One, two three, *push!*"

The bus rocked again, a little harder this time.

Alton had bound Maddy's hands behind her back again at some point, but she stood and wiped the condensation from the window with her shoulder so she could see out. "Stop! Stop it! Don't you know who I am?"

For the first time in hours, Fournier spoke. "Those aren't your people, Maddy. You don't want them to know who you are."

"Some of my people *are* out there. If they knew I was here, they could clear a path."

"Some of my people are out there, too," he replied. "I suspect they're too busy fighting each other to notice much of anything else."

The bus rocked again. Scott turned and saw Bryn gripping the top of the seat in front of her. She looked frightened but resolute.

"Lo," Alton said. "We could really use a distraction right about now."

The UAAV had stopped in an area bereft of bonfires. A forty-foot tall blue holosphere flickered into existence above it and a calm female voice blasted from the speakers, "May I have your attention, please?"

The men who'd been pushing the bus stopped and the crowd quieted down more rapidly than Scott might have expected – probably because they were desperate for information. Now their faces held had a mixed expression of doubt and hope.

The holosphere above the UAAV faded out and a man's face replaced it. Scott recognized him as the commanding officer of the National Guardsmen who'd helped secure XIA Headquarters.

"My name is Colonel Jeremy Carter. Due to the riots, Martial Law has been declared in New York and it's my job to restore order. I know you have a lot of questions and I'm not appearing before you now to offer platitudes. While it's true you've been detained for your safety, it's also true you've been removed from the populace because you present a potential danger to the rest of society. Until we know more about the disease that is being spread by people such as yourselves, we must continue to proceed with extreme caution. Let me assure you that food, water and supplies are on the way. Please be patient. These are tough times, but we are working diligently towards getting you back to your homes and families."

His face abruptly disappeared. Maddy rose from her seat, face twisted with outrage. "That's it? Are they kidding?"

Fournier smiled. "At least Martial Law has been declared."

"How is that better?" Maddy demanded.

"New people in charge."

"Less corrupt, you mean?" Bryn asked. "How do you know?"

"I don't. But sometimes you have to shake the tree to see what falls out."

"I suppose you're going to say this was part of your plan?" Mia snapped.

"It was one of many possibilities. Chaos begets change."

Scott frowned. "Chaos. Your man Savvy's favorite thing."

"He's here, you know," Alton said. "On the pier. Him and Nicola."

Maddy turned to Padme and made air quotes. "The daughter?"

When Padme nodded, Maddy crowed with laughter.

Fournier leaned his good arm against the seat to lever himself into a standing position. For some reason, he addressed Scott. "Please, Cougar. We have to find her. She's sick. She needs a transplant."

Maddy pointed to Padme's midsection. "Is *that* who it's for? You cloned a clone?"

"It's not what you think." Fournier turned to Padme. "If you care for her at all, you'll protect what you carry."

Padme looked like she was going to throw up. "I do care for her, but I won't let you kill this baby."

"It's not a baby," he said, just before the crowd outside the bus renewed their efforts to overturn it.

Chapter Forty-five

The people standing outside Bryn's side of the bus cleared out as it became more and more likely the vehicle would tip onto its side and crush them if they stayed.

Jason pulled his gun. "I don't want to shoot anyone, but we're going to have to stop them."

Scott nodded and turned to Bastida. "How do we open the windows?"

He peered at the dashboard and shrugged. "This is a prison bus. Do they even open?"

"We'll have to go out the door." Scott grabbed the pole by the front seat as the bus rocked again. This time it felt to Bryn as if the wheels left the tarmac. Padme let out a short shriek as it bounced back down.

"Hold on," Jason said. "Lo thinks she can appeal to them."

Bryn looked out the window, relieved to see the blue holosphere had appeared above Lo's strange vehicle again. "May I have your attention, please?"

Once again, the people outside the bus stopped what they were doing to listen.

"Those of you engaged in the attempt to overturn the bus on the exit ramp must cease and desist. You are in the process of committing a crime and will be prosecuted."

The blue holosphere winked out of existence and Maddy laughed. "That was an appeal? Dragila, I'm telling you, she should *appeal* to my people."

"Or mine," Fournier said.

"And what happens to us when your people show up?" Malone gestured around at the guardsmen. "We get tossed back in the water, that's what!"

The faces outside the bus looked angrier than ever to Bryn. She put her coat back on and pulled the hood up over her quills. She expected more rocking, but instead, there was a commotion at the edge of the crowd. Someone started screaming and she heard gunshots. Panic spread quickly and people began trampling each other to get away.

"What's going on?" Mia asked.

Before anyone could speculate on what was happening, the crowd magically parted. Out of the darkness, five men in ski masks made a beeline for the bus. It was hard to see them clearly, but they were definitely armed, and from the looks of it, the lead man was carrying an automatic weapon. Without warning, he opened fire on the bus, strafing all along one side of it. The rounds weren't explosive, but they pattered across the windows, leaving dozens of chinks in the reinforced glass. Padme shrieked again as she and everyone else aboard the bus dropped to the floor.

"Lo, we are under fire!" Jason shouted.

"Who the hell are they?" Malone asked.

"Who do you think?" Maddy was lying prone on the floor of the bus. She rolled to look up at Jason. "Did you really think my father would give up that easily? Tell 'Lo' to get my people over here!"

"Can the army help?" Jason was still talking to Lo. Bryn saw his lips thin as he looked at Scott and shook his head. "Lo says they *can*, but won't. We're on our own."

The guardsman who'd been driving climbed back into his seat and shifted the bus into gear, but before he could drive more than a few yards, the other gunmen surrounded the bus and shot out its tires.

One of them shouted, "We just want the transvestite!"

Maddy gasped in indignation at the slur, but said, "Don't believe it. You cannot negotiate with them. They will have orders to silence all of you."

"I tend to agree," Scott said.

Jason strode over and knelt by Maddy's head, holding out his holophone. "Lo says she can patch you in to the holoprojector. Better make it good, your Majesty."

"Am I on?" Maddy asked. Bryn heard her voice echo out over the pier.

"Yes!" Jason said. "Talk!"

Maddy licked her lips and lifted her chin, as if it was even possible to summon her dignity while lying bound on the floor of a prison transport bus.

"Mad Eyes, it is I, your queen."

Bryn remembered at Edgemere how Maddy loved posturing and theatrics, and 'her people' seemed to enjoy it just as much. But she'd essentially abdicated her throne when she told them to evacuate the underground community. She'd abandoned them. Would they come to her aid now?

Maddy said, "I am in the bus that is under siege and I require your assistance immediately. That is all."

From the light of the holophone, Bryn saw Jason's eyes briefly go wide as if he couldn't believe her arrogance. Before he could wave his hand to sever the connection, however, Fournier lurched out from behind his seat and cried, "XBestia soldiers! There is a truce between us and the Mad Eye. Honor it." His burning gaze dared Maddy to refute it.

Jason jerked the holophone away and disconnected as Fournier sagged against the edge of the seat. Maddy tilted her head at him. "Why did you say that?"

"If I hadn't shown myself, my soldiers would have attacked the bus to get to you."

"Lupus was your enforcer. Now that he's dead, will they listen to you?"

"They'd better," Fournier replied. "Otherwise we aren't getting out of here."

"How are you enjoying your chaos now?"

He chuckled weakly. "I would have preferred to watch from the sidelines, but that's chaos for you, isn't it?"

Chapter Forty-six

If Maddy planned a response to Fournier's quip, she wasn't able to deliver it because the assailants opened fire on the bus again, focusing on the windows on the right side, which quickly became so severely cracked, they were nearly opaque. Scott hoped the windows would last longer than their attackers' ammunition, but he'd gotten a good look at one of the men, and from the ammo belt slung over his shoulder it was apparent they'd brought plenty.

Every one of the guardsmen inside the bus was armed and waiting tensely to return fire as soon as it was breached. They weren't outmanned, but with that submachine gun out there, they were definitely outgunned.

The shooter wasn't able produce a constant stream of bullets without overheating the weapon, though, so in a momentary break in the gunfire, Alton told them, "Lo's bringing the UAAV closer. Hopefully Boardman can get a shot."

"Good." Scott lifted his head long enough to scan the vicinity out the front windshield for any Mad Eye or XBestia. The ramp was devoid of anyone but the masked men.

The shooter finally figured out he needed to choose one window and concentrate on it. He fired a short burst at a window midway down the bus, paused, and fired again. This time, several bullets penetrated, at least one of them ricocheting around inside. A guardsman yelped but immediately said, "I'm okay. Just nicked me!"

Malone was closest to the ruptured window. He popped up and thrust his gun into the hole, but before he could get off a shot, the shooter fired another burst. Malone's head jerked violently, and he toppled onto the seat without a sound. Scott could only see the top of his head, but Bryn and Mia were both facing him a few feet away. If Scott wasn't already sure the outspoken sergeant was dead, the abject horror on their faces confirmed it.

He stood and started to take off his vest to give it to Bryn when Maddy shouted, "Stop shooting! I give up!"

"What are you doing?" Padme cried.

"Stalling for time, what else?" Maddy said quietly. She struggled to her knees and then to her feet.

"They're going to kill you." Padme's voice cracked.

"No…it'll be alright." Maddy was staring out the front windshield.

Scott glanced in that direction and did a double take, his first thought: *hallelujah*.

Another crowd had formed and was marching out of the tunnel and up the ramp. Some were carrying torches, and he saw that the men and women at the forefront were wearing riot gear and holding clear curved riot shields. If Malone were alive, he'd no doubt point out that the xenos had gotten the gear from the guardsmen. As it was, the crowd may have looked formidable, but those shields weren't meant to deflect bullets. The masked man with the submachine gun seemed to know that, because he strode out confidently to meet them. Ten feet past the front of the bus, however, a faint '*crack*' sounded, and he stiffened and fell.

Alton laughed. "Boardman says, 'You're welcome.'"

Through the glass door of the bus, Scott heard the other masked gunmen engage in a short conversation. He couldn't make out their words, but if they were debating whether to check their fallen comrade – either to help him or take his weapon and ammo – they decided against it, turning instead and bolting back the way they'd come.

The crowd responded like a horde of barbarians, screaming and charging after them.

"Open the door!" Scott gestured urgently at Bastida. When the glass door folded in on itself, Scott said, "Tell Boardman it's me!" as he leapt over the steps. He landed hard on the tarmac and scrambled over to the dead man, snatching the weapon out of his hand. The crowd was only about ten yards away when he jumped back on the bus and the door closed behind him. The first wave of xenos, the ones with the riot gear, thundered past after the masked gunmen, but the majority stopped to surround the bus.

From his spot on the floor of the bus, Fournier looked up at Scott and Alton.

"Now what?" he asked.

Chapter Forty-seven

"I'll tell you what." Maddy walked up to Jason, turned her back to him and lifted her bound hands. "Cut me free and I won't tell them who you really are."

"Our cover was already blown today," Scott said. "There are xenos out there who know we're XIA."

"Well, you're with me now," she said. "If anyone dares to ask, I'll tell them you were my plant – just like Antonovich."

Bryn remembered Antonovich well. Jason had killed him, unaware at the time that he'd been an FBI agent on Maddy's payroll. Jason had shot him in the head, and Bryn shuddered at the memory as her gaze drifted to the spreading pool of blood under Malone's seat.

"We can't just let you go," Jason said.

Maddy twisted her torso to look over her shoulder at him. "I'm not asking for my freedom, Dragila, I'm simply offering to make a deal."

He bent and pulled his knife from his boot, but only examined the blade. "Deal's not on the table anymore. Your father's not going to talk to you now."

"Not true. I'm sure he's got a *lot* he wants to say to me."

"The XIA isn't interested in his opinion of you."

"Right. Well, anyway, that's not the deal I was referring to. You may have the guns, but that will only get you so far."

Someone outside the bus slapped his hands against the door and growled, "Open up!"

Along with everyone else, Bryn had risen from the floor, but she hadn't taken her seat because it was spattered with blood. Now she averted her eyes from Malone's body and stepped over the dark puddle in the aisle. Everyone around her looked shell-shocked. As she made her way to Scott's side, Fournier shuffled along behind her like a walking corpse.

"Maddy's right," Fournier said. "As soon as that door opens, every person on this bus will become a target in one way or another unless we all agree to cooperate. The Mad Eye want me; the XBestia want Maddy. If either of them find out you took us prisoner, you'll only last as long as your ammunition. And we all know what they think of the National Guardsmen. *No one* is going to step off this bus with the upper hand."

"Thank you, Nicolas, for so eloquently making my point for me." Maddy turned away and lifted her hands again. "Dragila?"

The man who'd banged on the door raised his voice. "Open this door now!" and began banging again.

Jason looked at Scott, who gave him an almost imperceptible shrug. Jason pointed the knife at Maddy and then Fournier. "We've got a sniper in that vehicle out there and I'm in constant contact with him. You will be in his sights at all times. The first hint either of you is going back on your word…"

Maddy nodded. "Understood."

"Agreed," Fournier said.

Jason slit their zip ties.

"Don't forget Padme." Maddy rubbed her wrists. "And if this is going to work, you and Cougar here are going to have to obey us…or pretend to."

Jason smiled thinly as he cut Padme's zip tie. "Shouldn't be a stretch."

"Yes, I suppose you've had a lot of practice faking it. The rest of you," she glanced around at the guardsmen, "should probably keep your mouths shut."

"I'm not going out there," Bastida said. "I'd rather take a bullet than get that disease."

The other guardsmen chimed in with their agreement.

"I don't blame you." Jason looked over at Mia, and Bryn saw his head go back a little as he realized she would have to stay with the guardsmen. He shoved his knife back into its sheath and said, "You guys take care of the doc, okay?"

"No." Mia made her way to the front of the bus. "I'm going with you."

Jason shook his head. "Too big a risk. There are probably carriers out there. You said it yourself, your graft won't protect you yet."

Mia had somehow kept hold of her purse through everything that had happened. She reached inside and pulled out a blue paper face mask. "This will."

Jason looked like he was going to argue with her, but Scott said, "It's her choice. Let's just get to the UAAV."

He nodded to Bastida, who opened the door. Maddy smoothed her hair, pushed past Jason and descended the steps regally, Padme on her heels. Jason went next, gun drawn, but Bryn noticed he was careful to point it away from Maddy. Fournier took the steps slowly, leaning heavily on the rail. Scott followed, the submachine gun pointed at the ground. Bryn and Mia came last and stayed close behind him.

The bus door shut with a '*shush,*' and the waiting xenos backed away to create a semicircle lit by torchlight. Bryn peered out at them from under her hood. It wasn't a consolidated group. There was a clear, grumbling line of division between the people of Edgemere and the denizens of the Warehouse. Bryn didn't recognize anyone from her short time at either place.

At the edge of the crowd, the men in riot gear had returned. One of them pushed his way through to the front and gingerly removed his helmet. White gauze had been wound around his forehead to hold the bandage on the back of his head in place. *Dundee.* Bryn curled her fingers under the bottom of Scott's vest, glad she still had Jason's backup gun in her pocket. Next to her, Mia reached up to the mask on her face, pushing down against the metal strip across her nose to secure it more tightly.

Maddy hooked an arm through Fournier's uninjured one and beamed at everyone around her. "It's so good to see you again. I'm sure you all have a lot of questions."

The pupils of Dundee's crocodile eyes glowed eerily as he stared her down. "Just one. Who the bloody hell do you think you're fooling?"

Chapter Forty-eight

Scott tensed and shifted to stand in front of Bryn. He didn't know how Dundee had gotten here, whether he'd been stopped on the highway by the army and rounded up, or if he'd followed Maddy's yacht with her outboard, but if things went south and Scott was forced to fire, that psycho would eat the first bullet.

"The truce is real." Fournier's quiet voice carried in the silence. "Maddy Singh and I have come to an agreement."

"After she-"

"You will *not* speak of what happened earlier."

"But Mad Eye scum killed Lupus!" Dundee's accusation was followed by angry muttering from several XBestia standing near him.

"Leaving you as my new lieutenant," Fournier snapped. "Congratulations on your promotion."

"It's true Lupus is gone," Maddy's words were ice cold, but calm. "And you returned the favor by killing Dillo. No one's denying there's plenty of bad blood between us, but we're telling you now is not the time."

She kept on speaking, something about dire circumstances and mutual trust winning out over vengeance, words that were probably wasted on most of her audience. Scott tuned her out and leaned closer to Alton.

"See Shasta anywhere?" he asked quietly. "She couldn't miss that broadcast."

"I was thinking the same thing," Alton said, "but this place is a zoo. Maybe she's holed up somewhere."

Scott's attention was drawn back to Dundee when the xeno pointed at him and demanded, "What about them?"

Fournier summoned the strength to stand taller. "There are factors involved that you are not aware of. For the time being, these men and women are protecting me, and in turn are under XBestia protection. Unless you'd like to continue questioning my orders?"

167

It was a testament to Fournier's control that Dundee said quickly, "No, sir."

"How about the rest of you?" Maddy asked, sweeping the crowd with her gaze. "I spy with my one mad eye…"

Several people in the crowd, including Alton, shouted, "*All the queen's men!*"

Scott looked sidelong at Alton, who quirked the corner of his mouth. If Scott didn't know better, he'd swear Alton secretly liked Maddy's outlandish ways.

As they began walking towards the tunnel, Scott stopped to take the ammo off the fallen man. The crowd stayed a respectful distance away from Maddy, Fournier and the rest of their group. The Mad Eye led the way, with Dundee and the other XBestia lurking at the rear.

Maddy was still holding Fournier's arm, giving him support as Padme shadowed her. She looked out beyond the edge of the ramp onto the field, eyes skimming over the sea of people and settling on the UAAV. Then she turned towards the water, where the top of her father's yacht was just visible.

"You know, Dragila," she said. "There may be a way to accomplish both our goals. The XIA wants my father, and I'd like to deliver him to you before he gets another chance to kill me."

"I'm listening."

Maddy lowered her voice. "Take the invisible vehicle for a little ride."

"Out to his yacht? Remember that part where you said he had enough firepower to blow us out of the water, and then he *did*?"

"I'm not talking about launching a big offensive, just force him to come to us here on the pier."

"How?"

"Sink it."

Alton's eyes narrowed as his interest intensified. Scott knew Alton had the same level of immunity he'd been given with Fournier. They were authorized to do almost anything necessary to complete their missions.

Alton didn't have a chance to respond to her proposal, though, because they'd entered the tunnel and the noise from all the xenos camped out in front of the army's blockade was deafening. Their group went left into a smaller passageway that eventually led onto the field. Once they emerged, a wave of xenos surrounded them, shouting questions none of them had answers to.

"There's no water! No bathrooms! When are we getting out of here?"

"Where's the food? How long will it take for the supplies?"

"We're freezing out here!"

The fear radiating off the detainees was almost palpable. Had they been here all day without food or water? Technically, there was shelter, if the broken-down structure surrounding the pier were taken into account, but there was no electricity and no heat except from the bonfires. From the thousands of people milling about on the field, it was clear what shelter could be found wasn't nearly enough. And what would happen when the combustibles they'd scrounged for the bonfires ran out?

The Mad Eye and XBestia were forced into forming a tight circle around their group as they inched their way to the UAAV. The commotion was overwhelming. Bryn stayed glued to Scott's side and Alton hovered over Mia.

They finally reached the vehicle, but by then the crowd had lost control. Pressure from the outer edges forced those closest to the center to surge inward. The Mad Eye and XBestia were no longer able to hold them back, and everyone was suddenly crushed up against the sides of the UAAV. Scott saw several people stiffen and go down before Lo must have switched off the protective electric barrier.

Alton got his boot up against the UAAV's door and shoved backwards, forming a small pocket of space for Mia. Scott's arms were trapped; he struggled to lift the submachine gun with the idea in mind that if he sent a burst upward, the crowd might stop crushing them.

Then Lo's voice blasted out of the UAAV. "Back away from the vehicle. Back away from the vehicle." Scott knew this was no ordinary PA system. Lo was deploying the vehicle's short-range acoustic device, a sonic weapon that delivered a targeted, painful warning to anyone within twenty yards or so. She repeated the message several more times, rotating the device to get full coverage of the crowd, but avoiding the sector occupied by Scott and the others. Within a surprisingly short amount of time, the crush had eased.

The door opened to Boardman's grinning face. "Come on in."

The injured prisoners Lo had taken aboard earlier were gone, but the inside of the UAAV still wasn't big enough to accommodate them all. Boardman grabbed his crutches and volunteered to stay outside with Bryn, Mia and Padme. Mia eyed the alligator graft on his knuckles and put a hand to the mask on her face.

"They checked me out," he said. "I haven't been exposed."

"I'll keep my distance all the same," she replied.

Scott ushered Maddy and Fournier inside. Once the door shut behind them, Fournier sank into the passenger seat, leaned his head back and closed his eyes. Maddy looked around the interior admiringly. "I have *got* to get one of these."

"Yeah, that's gonna happen," Lo said. She lifted an eyebrow at Scott. "What are you *wearing*?"

Scott sighed. "Can we focus, please?"

"Right. I heard something about sinking the old man's yacht...?"

"Might be my only chance of getting to him," Alton said.

"We can do it," Lo said slowly, "but there's lot that could go wrong."

She activated the holoprojector on the dash. The glowing green lines of a building schematic appeared. "This is the structure surrounding Poppy's Pier. Survey was conducted three months ago, so it should be accurate enough. See this area above the sunken portion? Side of the building's collapsed and there's a big hole. If there's not too much debris, we should be able to drive the UAAV right though and into the water."

"Stealth mode won't hide us from their radar," Alton said.

Lo pointed to something on the dash. "Jamming system will."

"Once we sneak up on him, what's the plan?" Scott asked.

"First and foremost, we don't want to *kill* him." Lo waved a hand and brought up another schematic. "This is Singh's yacht – the basic model anyway – we can assume he's had modifications done, but the engine room'll be in the same location. We blow the hull here, the explosion shouldn't reach the living areas."

Scott pointed. "Landing pad. Once the hull is breached, what's to stop him flying off in his helicopter?"

Alton shrugged. "I can go aboard beforehand. Take the copter out."

"No," Maddy said. "He's even more security-conscious than I am. You wouldn't get ten meters."

"She's right. Stealth will only get us so far." Lo flipped a switch on the dash and pointed to the floor of the UAAV where a compartment had opened up. "We had to give up our guns for the army to agree to let us in." It was an ironic statement given that stashed inside the compartment was an arsenal.

Alton's eyes gleamed. "We got a zook? Sweet."

"But not subtle," Lo said. "And explosives make shrapnel."

"We'll have to take that chance." Alton was getting worked up, which made Scott wary. Too much enthusiasm for any plan, much less a hastily cobbled together one, could get them all killed.

"That takes care of the copter and the hull, but he's got at least one working outboard." Scott turned to Maddy. "Does he have more than that?"

"No idea. I've never been invited."

Lo shifted in her seat. "We'll just have to lurk in stealth mode to make sure Singh is forced into the water."

Scott shivered a little. "He'll definitely head for the pier if he gets wet, but he won't be alone, and his men are armed."

"Leave that to us." Fournier spoke up without opening his eyes, so he didn't see Maddy nod in agreement.

Lo eyed the two of them and then turned to Scott and Alton. "Who's staying behind to monitor *that*?"

"Me." Scott was the logical choice. Lo was the UAAV pilot. Singh was Alton's op. Boardman was on crutches. Scott would stay behind to keep an eye on Maddy and make sure Singh was captured once he got ashore.

Before the UAAV left, Lo gave him another earbug. "Keep an eye out for Shasta, would you?"

"I'm not sure she's even here."

Lo looked thoughtful for a moment. "Me neither. But what about Nicola? She's here, right? Why hasn't she come for her father?"

Scott had thought the same thing. "Yeah, something's wrong. Let's hope whatever it is doesn't bite us in the butt."

Chapter Forty-nine

After the UAAV left the field, Scott had a discussion with Maddy and Fournier. Bryn was standing nearby and heard some of what he said; enough to realize the agents had concocted a plan to follow through with Maddy's suggestion to sink her father's yacht. When Scott was done speaking, he backed off a bit and settled into the role of bodyguard. Maddy called some of her men over and gave them quiet instructions, while at the same time, Fournier spoke with Dundee.

Not long afterward, everyone on the pier turned their attention to the sky to track the approach of a massive helicopter. It flew over the pier, its rotors churning out a throbbing sound that seemed to vibrate deep in Bryn's skull. It was one of those army cargo transport copters, and suspended below it was a net full of wooden crates. When the detainees realized Colonel Carter's promised supplies had arrived, they cheered.

Maddy held her arms up to get the attention of her people, shouting over the noise, her braid flying in the wind. "I fear there will be unequal distribution of the supplies if we don't intervene. Those who are weak will only get weaker if forced to go without. Can I count on you to help?"

A contingent of Mad Eyes volunteered for the job. Since the bulk of the detainees had rushed off to surround the supply drop, Maddy took advantage and moved their group to one of the bonfires, occupying a spot that had been abandoned.

Bryn sat cross-legged on a patch of dead grass next to Mia, and not far from Padme. Before the heat from the dying bonfire had a chance to take the chill off, she spotted a familiar face. It was the old woman who'd passed her the earbug message for Jason at Edgemere. Bryn had learned later that 'Esmie' was Shasta's informant.

"Scott!" Bryn jumped to her feet.

He came over. "You alright?"

She didn't need to say anything because Esmie made a beeline for them.

"Found you!" The old woman cried, like a child playing hide-and-seek. Her dirty white hair was still in two mussed braids, quite possibly the same braids she'd been wearing when Bryn first met her.

"You know where Shasta is, don't you?" he asked.

Esmie flashed her toothless grin. "Yes! She sent Esmie to find you."

"Why didn't she come herself?"

The old woman shrugged her narrow shoulders. "She's a little tied up."

"Well, unfortunately, I'm tied up, too." He glanced around at Maddy and Fournier and made a frustrated growling sound. "I can't leave right now."

Bryn straightened her shoulders. "I can."

"No. Too dangerous."

"How is it any more dangerous than anything else that's happened to me today?"

He put a hand on her arm and said softly, "I just don't want you out of my sight."

She bit her lip, gazing into his eyes. "I don't want to leave you either, but can you promise me that if I sit here and do nothing, I won't get kidnapped or shot at or…chased by cheetahs?"

He laughed a little. "I think I can guarantee the cheetah part won't happen."

"Really?!" She treated him to a deliberate stare, then said, "Remember what Shasta told me yesterday? She asked if the XIA could count on my cooperation. I'm offering to help, and I think you need it."

He got that look that told her Lo was talking to him. She must have encouraged him to let Bryn go, because he exhaled in an exasperated sigh. "Fine, but take this."

He pulled an oddly shaped flashlight from his belt. "See here?" He pointed to two small metal prongs sticking out at the end.

"Is that a stun gun?" she asked.

"Disguised as a flashlight." He turned the light on and off again.

"I'm not going to need that. I still have Jason's gun."

"Take it anyway. It's quieter. Pull the trigger here, and zap." He patted the pockets of his slacks. "Damn. Malone didn't give my holophone back."

Mia reached into her purse. "Take mine."

Bryn tucked the phone into her pocket next to the stun gun.

"Give it to Shasta," Scott said. "She can contact Lo, who can contact me."

Bryn smiled and put a hand to his face, rubbing the stubble on his jaw with her thumb. "It'll be fine."

"It better."

"It will."

"It better."

She laughed and turned to Esmie. "Remember me?"

"Porcupine and pretty face. How could Esmie forget?" Without another word, she walked away. Bryn tossed a quick wave to Mia before hurrying after the old woman.

They cut across the field at an angle, headed for the far corner of the pier, the one that wasn't submerged. The farther from the center of the field, the darker it got. The xenos they passed here on the outskirts seemed far less wholesome than those she'd seen thus far; they reminded her of the worst of the xenofreaks at the Warehouse: filthy, homeless, lawless. About a third of them were dressed in prison-orange jumpsuits. She kept her hood low over her forehead and avoided eye contact.

Some of the exterior walls of the dilapidated structure surrounding the field had collapsed. Esmie led her through one such section to the interior. There were more people here, huddled together around fires. The scent of smoke, urine and body odor was overpowering. In places, the second floor had fallen in, opening up black, cavernous spaces above them. The xenos camping here watched with predatory eyes as she followed Esmie through a frame that looked as if its door had recently been torn from its hinges.

Bryn curled her hand around the flashlight slash stun gun, glad Scott had insisted she take it. It was hard to believe Shasta was somewhere in this forsaken place. Esmie went farther in than Bryn would ever have ventured on her own. She was about to ask if she actually knew where they were going, but a chilling sound from up ahead echoed off the discolored walls; a ferocious clamor of voices, avid howling and shrieking that instantly reminded her of the Warehouse and its brutal grease fights.

They approached a chamber lit by a large central fire. In one corner, from the looks of the people gathered there, a fight *was* occurring. Esmie seemed more cautious now. She scuttled inside and melted into the shadows near the wall, hugging it as she crept to another doorway. Then she stopped and turned, a gnarled finger to her lips. Bryn heard heavy footsteps and followed Esmie's lead, dropping into a crouch and ducking to hide her face. All she saw of the man coming from the room up ahead was a dirty pair of men's work boots. He stomped off, headed for the fight, and Esmie waved for Bryn to follow her.

Inside the room, it was black as night, so Bryn took a chance and switched on the flashlight.

"Turn it off!" Esmie whispered, flapping her hands.

Bryn instantly complied. She'd seen all she needed to see.

Chapter Fifty

Scott had watched Bryn until she disappeared into the building. Her absence left him with a sinking feeling in his stomach, but he was too distracted to dwell on it for long. Between the constant chatter from the earbug and keeping an eye on Maddy and Fournier, he was multitasking in a big way. If Maddy was disturbed about what was coming, she gave no indication. She was in her element, dealing with her people as they came to her with their issues; problem-solving like a feudal lord conducting an informal audience with her serfs. Fournier, who sat in a daze by the bonfire, wasn't demanding much of Scott's attention, but Dundee skulked nearby, always watching.

Scott had made it very clear to the two of them that he was in charge, and so far, they'd seemed amenable. On his orders, they'd dispatched some of their people to scout a quick way through the building to the water, and the rest were waiting for word to move in.

In his ear, he heard Lo. "What's that? Over there, on shore."

Boardman said, "Looks like divers."

"Probably a search and rescue team for the drowned guardsmen." Alton said.

"Okay, let's stay on task." Lo's voice was strained. "You ready?"

"Target acquired," Alton replied.

"Scott?"

"Moving in." Scott nodded to Maddy, who immediately threw an arm up. Two dozen xenos dropped what they were doing and surrounded her.

Scott reached a hand out to help Fournier to his feet, but the XBestia leader shook his head wearily. "I can't."

Fournier was forcing Scott to make a split decision: drag the injured man along with them, creating a burden they could really do without, or leave him here. After finally catching the Bestia Butcher, the last thing he wanted to do was lose sight of him. Then again, trapped here on Poppy's

Pier, in Fournier's weakened state, he wouldn't get far if he tried to run. Scott looked around for Dundee, but at some point, Fournier's new lieutenant had slunk away.

The deep *boom* of an explosion made his decision for him. He pointed in Fournier's face. "Stay here."

Maddy and her people had already started running. Scott gripped the submachine gun in both hands and set off after them. He'd sprinted maybe fifty yards when the second *boom* sounded. He caught up just before they entered the structure surrounding the pier. Those in the lead met up with some of the scouts and were directed to a hole in the wall – the same one Alton had led him through earlier.

Scott was the only one with a gun, so Maddy and her men waited inside as he stole out onto the dock. With no cover to be had, he dropped flat and crawled to the edge where he could hold the barrel of the submachine gun out over the river. At some point, Maddy's yacht had slipped off the dock and was low in the water not far downstream. On Singh's yacht, the helicopter was burning, providing enough light for him to see that the bow of his vessel had already dipped towards the water. It would be interesting to see whether Singh had enough power to summon a rescue from the overwhelmed authorities before it sank to the bottom of the Hudson. Scott and the others were banking on his SOS being ignored just like everyone else's.

The helicopter lost traction and with a groan of protesting metal, slid into the back of the yacht's cockpit. With a wicked grin, Scott watched two men leap overboard.

"Inflatable being lowered," Lo said.

Scott didn't see anything, so he assumed it was on the other side of the yacht. After a few more tense minutes, Alton said, "Target confirmed. Repeat, Singh is aboard the inflatable."

"Should we take it out?" Boardman asked.

"Wait to see if they head for the pier," Scott said.

A moment later, he heard, "That's a negative on the pier. Looks like they're making a break for the Jersey side. Too bad they're about to spring a leak."

The *crack* of a rifle rang out and Alton chuckled. "Target has changed course. Be advised he is headed your way."

"Copy that," Scott said.

He released the trigger and held his hand to his mouth, breathing warmth onto his frozen fingers while he waited. The inflatable rounded the sinking yacht, its orange skin sagging as it struggled to stay afloat. From the sound of it, the pilot had opened up the little outboard motor, but it began to sputter as water flooded it. Some seconds later, it stopped altogether. Scott watched impassively as the three passengers took to the water about a hundred yards from the dock and began swimming, unaware of what awaited them.

The two men who'd jumped overboard were also swimming in, but they didn't have the benefit of life jackets like the men from the inflatable. Scott waited impatiently, trying not to sympathize with any of them.

It was quieter now. With food and water to pacify the detainees, they weren't as unruly. The gentle sound of water lapping against the underside of the pier was almost hypnotic. On the yacht, the helicopter fire had spread to the cockpit and was quickly becoming a conflagration. A bright streak of orange light reflected off the surface of the water. Scott's attention was caught by a trail of bubbles and he suddenly remembered there were divers in the water.

Chapter Fifty-one

"*A little tied up?*" Bryn hissed at Esmie.

"Okay. A *lot* tied up," Esmie replied.

Bryn stood indecisively near the door, eyes slowly adjusting to the sparse light coming in from the exterior chamber. There were exactly five people laid out on the floor of the little room. Bryn had a gun and a stun gun, but no knife to cut their bindings. Something told her Shasta wouldn't be lying there bound and gagged if the ropes around her wrists and ankles could have been untied.

A sound from outside warned her just in time; she flattened herself against the wall as the big man returned. Esmie hadn't moved though, and the man saw her instantly.

"What are you doing here, hag?"

The old woman squinted up at him. "Esmie is distracting you."

"What?" he snapped.

With a jolt, Bryn realized she was sending her a message. Bryn licked her lips and fit her finger to the trigger of the stun gun. It activated with a crackle that alerted the man. He twisted around and she thrust it against his chest, wincing away as the electrical charge overwhelmed his nervous system. He made a choking sound before crumpling to the ground. Esmie immediately bent over him, patting his pockets and pulling things out. "No knife."

Of course he didn't have a knife, Bryn thought. The National Guard would have ensured none of the detainees arrived armed, and the men from the prison buses would have nothing on them.

Shasta started making noises, so Bryn hurried over and worked the rag out of her mouth. There wasn't enough light to see her face clearly, but just from feel, Bryn could tell it was battered and bloody. Shasta nodded towards the back wall. "Picture."

Bryn looked over her shoulder. A framed photograph hung low on the wall at an odd angle. She stepped over the other captives and took it

179

down. The frame was black plastic, and it had been hung with string. The glass over the undistinguishable photo had a big crack running from top to bottom. She went back and knelt next to Shasta, who'd rolled onto her side. Bryn turned the picture over, and after twisting the clips to remove the backing, carefully removed a sliver of glass. She began sawing at Shasta's bindings. It wasn't rope; whoever had done this must have torn up an item of clothing and used the strips to tie her up.

"Where're my agents?" Shasta's voice was hoarse.

Bryn had a feeling Shasta wasn't going to like the truth, but she told her anyway. "Um, right about now they're attacking Philip Singh's yacht."

Shasta surprised her by laughing softly. "Of course they are."

A few slices at the material around Shasta's wrists, and Bryn was able to tear the rest away. After the material parted, Shasta sat up and reached for another shard of glass to start in on her ankles. "Get the others."

The gag on the first man was too tight to pull down; Bryn had to cut it. When it came free and he spoke, she recognized him as Deputy Director Unger.

"Help Congressman Abbott."

There were two other men. Bryn had never seen the congressman, but figured it was the white-haired man whose black suit didn't disguise the huge belly underneath it, rather than the thin man dressed casually. The congressman was lying ominously still, his gag soaked with what smelled like vomit. She was afraid he'd choked to death on it, but then felt his breath blow faintly against her hand. The stench was overwhelming; she held her own breath as she sawed at the moist material. He didn't respond when she peeled it away from his face.

"He's unconscious," she whispered.

"Surprised he's not dead," Unger said. "Bastards."

He retrieved Abbott's discarded gag and stalked over to their guard, who was moaning and attempting to lever himself into a sitting position.

"You like to beat up on women and old men?" Unger punched the guard in the face, and then forcibly stuffed Abbott's stinking gag into his mouth. While Shasta helped tie him up with the remnants of their bindings, Bryn cut the thin man free. She'd never seen him before either, but the fifth and last person was very familiar to her. Even in the low light, she recognized her mother's pale face.

"Thank you," Nicola Fournier said quietly.

Unger returned to the congressman's side and shook him gently. "Darrell...come on man, wake up." He pointed to the man standing with Nicola. "You. Help me with him."

180

Between them, Unger and the other man managed to raise Abbott's torso off the ground, but he was so grossly overweight they couldn't lift him. Unger muttered, "*Damn* it. Set him down."

Shasta went to the doorway and peered out. She turned to Bryn, gesturing to the guard lying on the ground. "Stun gun?"

"Yeah," Bryn replied.

"How'd you get it past the army? They took my weapon, guns, keys…"

"We came by boat. I also have a gun."

"Thank God," Shasta breathed, holding her hand out.

Bryn passed it to her and watched as Shasta popped the cartridge out to examine it.

"Fully loaded," she murmured. "Don't suppose you have a phone?"

Bryn nodded. She entered Mia's passcode and handed the holophone over.

Shasta didn't have a chance to call anyone, however. Footsteps warned them that someone was coming. The man who entered stopped cold when a gun appeared at his temple.

"Thaaat's right," Shasta drawled. "It's payback time."

Chapter Fifty-two

Scott stared at the water as the trail of bubbles got closer and then ended directly below him.

"How many divers were there?" he asked.

"Four," Lo said. "Why?"

"I think one of them swam under me. Under the pier."

"Makes sense. Bodies would get caught under there."

Something about the divers bothered him, but he didn't reply because Singh and his men had almost made it to the pier, and he didn't want them to hear him. Of the other two men, the ones who'd been forced to leap overboard, one was maybe twenty feet out, but the other was floundering. Scott didn't want to watch him drown, but there was nothing he could do to help. The UAAV was nearby, but still in stealth mode, waiting to assist if Singh and his men resisted. It occurred to him that the divers might assist the men, but it was dark and the water no doubt murky. He didn't know if they were even aware of what was going on at the surface.

He got to his feet as Singh reached the dock and struggled to climb out about ten feet to the left of him. Scott couldn't see Maddy, but knew she was watching. Having been in the water himself, he didn't think Singh's men would give him any trouble, but he didn't relax his grip on the submachine gun as he approached them.

All three lay gasping on the dock like fish out of water. One of them caught sight of Scott and fumbled at his life vest.

"Don't," Scott said.

The man hesitated only briefly before holding his hands up in surrender. He couldn't sustain the pose, however, as cold-induced muscle spasms forced his fingers to curl into his palms and his forearms shook uncontrollably. It was clear he was no threat in his condition, so Scott bent to unfasten his vest and frisk him. He found a shoulder holster under the man's left arm and removed the pistol.

The man in the water closest to the pier called out a garbled, "Help!"

Scott yanked the life vest off the man he'd disarmed and hurled it out over the water before getting back to the business of securing the prisoners. The second man's holster was tucked into the back of his pants. Singh wasn't carrying.

Scott stepped back and waited impatiently for the last man to reach him; the one who'd been floundering was nowhere to be seen. The straggler had reached the life vest he'd tossed him and was kicking listlessly towards the pier.

Maddy tromped out onto the dock, followed by four of her men.

"Hello, Father," she said. "Have a nice swim?"

Between the heavy accent and the chattering of Singh's teeth, it was hard to understand his response, but Scott picked out a profanity or two. Maddy sighed and looked at Scott. "What are we waiting for?"

Scott lifted his chin towards the last man in the water.

"If you're not planning on shooting him, just leave him with the others," Maddy said. "He'll either make it or he won't."

"Just want to see if he's armed."

"Oh, right. Heaven forbid one of my people might get hold of a gun."

"Would you feel the same if one of Fournier's people got hold of it?"

She crossed her arms and made a '*humph*' sound.

The man did make it a few minutes later. One of Maddy's men hauled him out of the water and Scott checked him for weapons.

"All clear," he said, and then for Lo's benefit, "Targets secured."

"Roger that. We're coming in."

Maddy directed two of her men to lift her father.

"Where are we going to do this?" she asked.

Scott considered it for a moment. "Someplace warm and private."

They left Singh's men to fend for themselves and headed straight for the bus. Scott wasn't sure the guardsmen would even let them back in, but Bastida cautiously opened the door.

"Just you three," he said, indicating Scott, Maddy and Singh. Maddy's men deposited Singh in a seat and left, grumbling a bit among themselves as they exited the warm bus.

The first thing Scott noticed was the guardsmen had moved Malone's body to the back seat. They didn't have anything to mop the blood up with, however, and gravity had spread it in a long, thin rivulet to the front of the bus.

"Saw the supply drop," Bastida said. "Don't suppose you brought us anything to eat?"

"Nah, brought something better." Scott gestured to the pathetically shivering Singh. "Meet the man who tried to kill us."

Chapter Fifty-three

Shasta gestured for the other guard to come farther inside and ordered him to strip.

With obvious reluctance, the man took off his jacket. Esmie moved in and patted him down, finding a shiv made out of a rusty nail attached to a stick that she tucked into her pocket.

"Shirt," Shasta said.

The man pulled his shirt off and Unger yanked it out of his hand before tearing it into strips that they used to tie him up with.

"There are a lot of xenos out there," Bryn said. "We can't tie them up one by one."

Unger knelt next to the congressman. "And we can't leave without him. He needs medical attention."

Shasta lifted Mia's holophone. "Let's hope my agents are free."

Lo answered on the first ring. "Shasta! Thank goodness. Where are you?"

"Cornered in the Northwest section of the pier. Did you get Singh?"

"Uh, yeah. That okay?"

"What's done is done, but don't interrogate him. And for God's sake, don't release him, whatever you do."

"Yes, ma'am," Lo said. "You should know we were forced to make some unusual alliances. Maddy Singh and Nicolas Fournier were in our custody, but at the moment, we're all sort of...working together."

Shasta sighed, but said, "I hear you. It's desperate times. I'll debrief you later. Right now, I'm sending our exact coordinates. We could really use an extraction here."

"On our way, but it'll take at least ten minutes."

"Bring a stretcher, a sturdy one."

"Roger that."

Shasta disconnected. From the darkness, Nicola asked, "What are you going to do with Mr. Singh?"

"That's XIA business," Shasta replied shortly.

"No. It's everyone's business."

"She's actually got a point." Unger's voice was harsh. "Singh won't talk, and since our only witness is practically comatose, we won't be able to hold him. He'll crucify the entire Agency. We can't keep what we know close to the vest anymore."

"You mean go public?" Shasta sounded resigned.

"Daddy did," Nicola said. "He said it was the only way."

Shasta frowned. "Your father's a psychopath."

"He is *not*! Stop saying that!"

Bryn put a hand on Shasta's arm. "Did you get Mia's message?"

"No. They took my phone. Why?"

"Fournier...you know how my father told us he wanted xeno regulation enacted to pave the way for human cloning? Well, there's more to it than that. A lot more."

"You can't believe anything he told you," Unger said. "The man's got a pathological God complex."

Bryn nodded. "Yes, he does. And I didn't say I believed him, just that he told me some stuff you need to hear."

"Go on."

She told them what Fournier had said about one man owning not only all of the government mandated bioengineering labs, but the donor waste disposal company, too. When she got to the part about how that company was selling the leftover parts on the black market instead of incinerating them, Unger snorted.

"We don't care that he's got competition."

"That's what Mia – I mean Doctor Padilla – said. Then he told her this man's bioengineers figured out how xeno immunity works, and they fixed it so it doesn't anymore."

Shasta's chin lifted in understanding. "Is that man Philip Singh?"

"I think so."

"Of course it's Mr. Singh," Nicola said. "You think my *dad's* crazy? At least he doesn't keep people sick so he can make money off them."

"But he does kill innocent people," Shasta snapped.

A voice came from the doorway. "Not deliberately."

Shasta swung around with the gun, but Dundee's hands were already in the air. "I'm not armed."

"Stay where you are."

He kept his hands where Shasta could see them. "I want you to know Fournier didn't order any of it. He had nothing to do with those people I infected at the bank. We didn't know the typhoid would kill anyone at that point. He never asked me to infect anyone except other xenos, and he only did that because he wanted to figure out who would become carriers."

"What about Robert Cruise?" Shasta asked. "He infected all those people at the courthouse."

"Who?"

"Junk," Bryn said.

Dundee shrugged. "Junk was a moron. He was pissed because he got a traffic ticket. Went there on his own for some payback."

"He didn't go to Edgemere on his own," Shasta said.

"No. Fournier sent him, but he didn't know there were kids there."

Bryn laughed in disbelief. "He didn't *care*. He said something horrible about killing the children of his enemies before they grew up to become enemies themselves. Why are you trying to make him sound so…innocent?"

He didn't answer right away, just stood there as if he was searching for the right words. "He isn't innocent. None of us are. But he saved me, in more ways than one. I was blind, literally and figuratively."

Bryn opened her mouth to point out he'd attacked her first, but he said, "I know. I deserved it and I don't blame you. I'm not the man I was. I don't expect you to take my word for it, but I *see* things differently, and not just with my eyes."

She knew he was trying to tell her something profound, but his confession only creeped her out. She did *not* want to bond with him, whether he thought he'd changed in any intrinsic way or not.

"Who ordered the attack on the congressman?" Unger asked.

Dundee glanced at Abbott, but said, "I don't know anything about any congressman."

"Then how'd you get in here?" Shasta asked. From the sound of it, the xenos in the outer chamber were still enjoying the fight.

"I go where I want."

"These aren't your men?"

"No. I'm just here for the girl."

Bryn knew he meant Nicola. Fournier must have sent him to follow her.

"She's in my custody." Shasta didn't look away from him, nor did she relax her stance. "Sir, this man is patient zero. Does Abbott have a graft?"

"I doubt it," Unger replied.

"I'll keep my distance," Dundee said, "but if you want to find out who's behind that," he nodded towards the congressman, "then why don't you ask them?" he nodded down at the guards.

"We don't have time to interrogate anyone," Shasta said.

The corners of Dundee's mouth turned down in a thoughtful frown as he contemplated the trussed guards. "Gimme thirty seconds."

Shasta looked from Dundee to Unger and back again, then stepped back. "Do it."

Chapter Fifty-four

Singh needed something dry to wear, but this time, none of the guardsmen were willing to volunteer their garments. Scott went to the back of the bus, where Malone's body was laid out on the seat. Singh was responsible for his death, and it would be an ironic penance to force him to wear the dead man's bloody clothes, but Scott instantly discarded the idea. Malone deserved better than that.

Scott's own clothes were draped over the back of the seat where he'd left them. He changed back into them even though they were still damp. Then he gingerly patted Malone down, finding the holophone he'd lent him in the pocket of Dillo's jacket.

When he brought the suit back to Maddy, her father was curled up in one of the seats holding his hands out over a heating vent, still wearing his life vest. His first intelligible words were, "We have to get off the pier."

"Yes, well, tell that to the army," Maddy said.

He looked up at her. "I will. Take me to them and I'll get us all out of here."

She took a breath and let it out slowly. "I believe you could do just that. But you won't. If we took you, you'd have us arrested at the very least. You're nothing if not predictable."

"Then why not kill me?"

"Because my friends would like to talk to you."

"And who are these friends?"

"The ones who blew your sorry ass out of the water," Scott said.

Singh's bleary eyes took in the submachine gun before sliding back to Maddy. "I have nothing to say, except if you don't get off this pier, you'll die."

"You might be in danger, but I'm not." Maddy pointed to her one brown eye. "I've got this, remember?"

"I'm not referring to the typhoid. You think I don't have a graft?"

189

Maddy's face didn't betray her confusion, but her words did. "You're utterly against them."

Singh's lips twisted in scorn. "Only because I saw what it did to you."

"What does that mean? What did it do to me?"

"You were a young *man* before he put that bloody pig eye in your head. From a *female* pig."

Maddy laughed. "Are you serious? Oh, my dear father. All you had to do was ask and I would have told you I was born this way. I've always known."

Singh turned away, his face frozen in a look of abhorrence.

"But if you must know," Maddy continued, "the surgery did change me. You forced it on me not because you were concerned about my eyesight, but because you were ashamed of my albinism. You wanted me to *look* normal, as if that would help me *be* normal. It was then I realized you would never accept me. In a way, it gave me the confidence I lacked – the strength to defy you and be myself."

She straightened her spine and held the suit out. "Now take off those wet clothes."

"No! Haven't you been listening to me? We have less than two hours to get off this pier!"

Scott stepped closer, leaning over Singh menacingly. "Why?"

Singh clamped his lips shut, leaning forward to remove his life vest. "You have to take me to Colonel Carter. I give you my word I won't mention any of what happened before."

"You mean the part where you attacked us? Tried to kill me?" Maddy asked disdainfully. "You're such a hypocrite. Your word doesn't hold much weight here."

Singh took off his shirt and reached for the suit in Maddy's hand, but she just stared openmouthed at the xenograft on his upper arm. It was in the shape of a rearing lion but wasn't made out of fur.

Scott took one look at it and turned to Bastida. "Keep your men back."

"What?" Singh snatched the suit out of Maddy's hand. "I told you I had one."

"A lion." Her tone held mild admiration. "It's beautiful. My compliments to your surgeon."

He thrust his arms through the sleeves of the jacket. "He was an artisan. The lion is from our family crest, not that you would care to recall."

"And the donor?" she asked with a lift of her eyebrows. "Crocodile, is it?"

Chapter Fifty-five

The last thing Bryn wanted to do was watch Dundee terrorize the guards. Nicola obviously didn't want to witness it, either, because she turned her back and moved closer to where Bryn was standing, her lower lip trembling. Bryn fought off the urge to reach out with some kind of comforting word or gesture, not because she was confused about her feelings, but because she didn't know whether Nicola deserved her sympathy.

"Did it work?" Nicola asked.

It took Bryn a second to realize she was asking about whether the nanoneuron activation back at her father's facility had distracted his men enough for Bryn and the others to get away.

"Yes."

"How's my dad?"

"He's okay."

At Nicola's tremulous smile, Bryn had a sudden flash of memory: her mother, lying in her hospital bed, stroking Bryn's hair with a painfully thin hand.

"I'll always be with you, Brynnie," she'd said. Then she'd offered that exact same curve of the lips.

Bryn felt the sharp sting of tears and turned away so Nicola wouldn't see. The thin man came into her frame of view. He was gazing intently at the ground, but briefly glanced up at her face.

"Bryn Vega," he said. "Failed social experiment."

"What?" She glared at him, but he seemed to be avoiding eye contact. There was something not quite right about the guy.

"You could've had them eating out of your hand," he said.

It was easier to pretend she didn't know what he was talking about, but whoever this man was, he clearly knew about her father's and Fournier's plan to make her the 'xenofreak poster child.'

Then out of the blue, Nicola said, "Padme says you know my mother."

"Your...*mother*?" Bryn stared at her, appalled.

"She doesn't mean her donor," the thin man said.

"Donor?" Bryn repeated. The word came out as the barest whisper.

"The woman who donated her cells so I could be cloned from them," Nicola said. "Padme told me she died, but the woman who carried me is still alive and that you know her."

Bryn's brain still refused to comprehend. "Padme told you this."

"Uh-huh."

"When she told you about your, um, donor, did she mention my relationship to her?"

Nicola shook her head. "No, she just said you knew Mouse."

Bryn took a sharp intake of breath, but anything else Nicola was planning to say was drowned out by the guard, who cried out in pain and then yelled, "I don't *know*! He gave us the license number and a description of the car. Told us it was stuck in the Holland Tunnel and that we should bring the fat man and his friend here."

"Who told you?" Dundee growled. Whatever he was doing to encourage an answer brought another cry of pain from the guard.

"I don't know, I don't know, I don't know..." the guard sobbed.

"That's enough," Shasta said. "Whoever's behind this would have stayed anonymous. The question is: how did that person know the congressman was in the Holland Tunnel?"

"Abbott made a call to his office," Unger said. "Told them where he was."

"And you made one to me. Our phones are secure. I assume the congressman's are, as well."

"I'm not suggesting security's been breached. Not from the outside anyway. Abbott suspected someone in his office was leaking information – that's why he didn't want to get on the flight. He was afraid Singh knew he was cooperating with us."

From the outer chamber came a sudden series of bright flashes accompanied by what sounded like greatly amplified firecrackers going off. *Bang! Bang! Bang!*

Shasta winced and stuck a finger in her ear. "They're here."

Moments later, Jason and Lo appeared in the doorway. Lo kept a lookout while Jason entered the room, carrying a black pack with wheels. He glanced around, frowned at Dundee and said, "Hello, ma'am...sir," to Shasta and Unger.

"Over here," Unger said.

Between Jason, Unger and the thin man, they managed to get Abbott loaded onto the portable stretcher. By then the outer chamber had been completely abandoned. Their escape was much easier than Bryn had anticipated. No one impeded their progress, and they made it safely to the UAAV.

They loaded the unconscious congressman into the UAAV, and once Shasta and Unger got on board, Lo drove to the center of the field, while the rest of them walked. Bryn recognized the bonfire they'd occupied earlier and was almost surprised to see Fournier and Padme still sitting there with Mia. Even more surprising was the sight of Carla standing nearby, holding hands with a large, bearded man in an orange coverall.

Nicola broke away from the group to run to her father. Carla saw Bryn, grinned widely, and waved. Bryn was glad to see she was okay, but at the same time, was terribly conflicted. Had Carla really given birth to Nicola?

Carla must have correctly interpreted the look on her face, because she glanced at Nicola and her grin faded, to be replaced by a rueful frown. When Bryn reached her, she said, "I'm so sorry I didn't tell you."

"Why did you do it?"

"Your mother asked me to."

For the second time that day, Bryn was so shocked all she could do was stare. Then as Carla's meaning sank in, tears flooded her eyes. "You mean Mom *wanted* it...?"

Carla put a hand on her arm. "She believed in him."

Bryn looked over at Fournier. He and Nicola were having what looked like a touching reunion.

"Mom needed a new heart, but she would never agree to killing a clone to save her own life."

"Honey," Carla said softly, "your mom knew she was dying when she agreed to it. The company that paid for the first pig heart refused to pay for a second one after it failed, and she knew a human donor wouldn't be found in time. Her clone was never going to be sacrificed."

"That's not what Dad told me. If that wasn't the plan, then why clone her at all?"

"Your mom's heart...she had *genetic* Dilated Cardiomyopathy. It's hereditary."

Bryn blinked. "I don't understand."

"He promised her he would try to cure it. For you."

Bryn put a hand to her chest. "You mean I have it, too?"

"No, no, but your children might."

"How could he cure it by cloning her?"

"I don't know exactly. Something about disabling the genes that caused it." Carla dipped her head and sighed. "There's something else. Nicola had a twin. I gave birth to two of them."

"Oh, my God. *May*…Scott's adopted sister."

This time it was Carla's turn to look shocked. "Are you kidding me?"

"No. Seriously. It's the reason Scott joined the XIA. May died because Fournier made mistakes in the cloning process. It devastated his parents."

Carla shook her head sadly. "I always wondered what happened to her. Did you tell your dad about Nicola?"

Bryn shook her head. When Fournier had been trapped in the tunnel and thought he was going to die, he'd given her a message that she'd never delivered. "Tell your father," he'd said, "Nicola is not for him. I made her for me. But she was never Miranda." It was why she'd believed her father when he told her Fournier had been in love with her mother.

She looked over just in time to catch Fournier's eye. He was watching her as if he knew what she and Carla were discussing. Why hadn't he told her any of this? He'd had plenty of opportunity. She didn't understand the man at all but didn't for a minute think she'd misjudged him. He was a monster pure and simple – which didn't make him incapable of doing seemingly selfless things.

The man standing next to Carla must not have been paying attention to their conversation, because he shoved a hand out as if they hadn't been discussing such an intense subject. "I'm Bluto."

Bryn tore her gaze away from Fournier.

"Nice to meet you." She took his hand absently because she'd noticed Mia coming towards her – and she looked terrible. Bryn excused herself and went to take her arm. Instead of shaking her off, Mia leaned on her.

"You okay?" Bryn asked.

"Just dizzy."

Carla appeared on her other side. "Why are you wearing a mask? Are you a carrier?"

"No. I'm not a xeno…or…I *am* a xeno, but—but–" she broke off with an exasperated exhale.

Carla pulled something from her pocket and held it up. "When's the last time you ate?"

Bryn flashed Carla a grateful smile and split the protein bar with Mia. While they scarfed it down, Shasta jumped out of the UAAV and stood by the open door. She seemed to be sucking in great gulps of the cold night air. Her battered face was expressionless, but Bryn suspected something was wrong.

She left Mia's side and walked over. "What is it?"

Shasta sighed. "The congressman is dead."

Chapter Fifty-six

With the constant stream of information coming through the earbug, Scott followed the events leading up to the rescue of Shasta and the others. When he heard of Congressman Abbott's passing, he went to the back of the bus to talk to Lo in private.

"Lo," he said. "You get any of what's going on here?"

"Sorry, no. Busy. What's up?"

"I've got good news and bad," he said.

"Bad news first."

"Singh's flipping out about being on the pier. Says we have less than two hours before we all die."

"Really. Die how?"

"Wouldn't say."

"Okay. The good news?"

"He's got a croc graft."

After a brief silence, Lo burst out laughing. "Are you serious?" Then she said, "No offense," and Boardman said, "None taken."

"*Philip Singh* has a crocodile graft?" Alton asked. "Did you see it?"

"Yeah," Scott replied. "Plain as day."

He heard Alton repeat the news to someone else and then heard Shasta in the background. "Why does that matter?"

Scott caught bits and pieces of the conversation that followed; the gist of which was that no one had told her what Fournier had said about the carriers. He caught Bryn's voice, "Ask him. He's right there."

Several minutes later, he heard, "Agent Harding?" It was Shasta loud and clear; she must have gotten an earbug.

"Yes, Ma'am."

"Bring Singh to me. *Now*."

"On my way."

He thought Maddy would protest when he told her they were leaving, but she looked around at the watchful guardsmen and said, "Yes, I think we've worn out our welcome."

Maddy's four soldiers escorted them down the ramp and through the detainees milling about in the tunnel. When Singh saw the barrier the army had constructed to keep the detainees on the pier, he lunged towards it, shouting, "Help me! I don't belong here!"

Maddy's men restrained him as he fought to get away. He began ranting and raving, spitting out obscenities and threats, and her men were forced to drag him along. Finally, as they were about to enter the corridor leading to the field, he appealed to Maddy directly, face apoplectic.

"If you don't listen to me, *we're all going to die!*"

"Yes, father, we know. Would you care to be more specific...?"

That shuttered look appeared again, but when Maddy turned to walk away, he shouted, "They're going to blow up the pier!"

Scott flashed on the divers, and with deep dread in his heart knew Singh was telling the truth.

"Lo, you get that?"

"Yeah."

"Oh, jeez," Alton said. "The divers."

Scott heard him explain what they'd seen to Shasta. She barked, "Agent Harding, I want you to bring Singh to me *now!*"

"Yes, Ma'am." Scott pointed the barrel of the submachine gun at Singh and told Maddy's soldiers, "Carry him."

They glanced at her for confirmation before lifting the struggling man by his arms and legs. Just like the last time they'd entered the corridor, they began to collect a crowd of detainees in their wake.

"What did he mean, 'They're going to blow up the pier?'" one of them shouted.

Like a flash fire, the news spread. This time, before the detainees could mob him, Scott pointed the submachine gun to the ceiling and fired a quick burst. Those closest to him scattered, and it bought Scott and the others enough time to get out onto the field. Unfortunately, they were surrounded again within thirty seconds.

"Lo? I could really use some of your magic right about now."

For the second time that night, Lo employed the short-range acoustic device, forcing the crowd back and allowing Scott and the others to get to the UAAV. Shasta grimly took custody of Philip Singh and slammed the door. The crowd lingered, but at a distance, grumbling.

Scott stayed outside with Alton to guard those gathered around the bonfire, but his earbug allowed him to hear everything going on inside. He leaned against the door as a strange kind of detachment came over him. His mind sifted through the events of the last few days, gaze drifting from face to face.

Fournier looked like hell, but he'd perked up some, probably because Nicola was with him. He'd said she needed a transplant, but she looked fine. He wondered if Nicola had the same kidney cancer that had killed his little sister. The doctors hadn't discovered May's cancer early enough to attempt a xeno transplant, but if Nicola had the same thing, why didn't Fournier do so? He thought back over the conversation in the bus. Fournier had said, "It's not a baby." What else could it possibly be?

He shifted his gaze to Maddy, seemingly in her element as she dealt with whatever issues her people brought her – and yet a veil of sorrow lay over her features. She'd not only lost Dillo, her best friend and protector, but her father had substantiated every bad thing she'd ever thought about him, and then some.

Carla was standing next to a prisoner Scott had never seen, but who reminded him of the wooden sign outside of Bluto's, the cut-out cartoon character with the full black beard that had greeted him the first time he'd gone there with Padme.

Padme herself was sitting alone staring into the dying fire, and if he didn't know better, he could swear she'd been crying.

Bryn was standing with Mia and Carla, but she turned and caught his eye. He gestured her over, and she nodded. He'd wanted to speak with her alone, but Mia and Carla came with her, along with the big bearded man. Somewhat to his irritation, Maddy wandered over, too. When he saw Fournier getting to his feet with the help of Dundee and Nicola, he sighed.

"Is it true?" Carla crossed her arms. "Is the army really going to blow up the pier?"

Before Scott could reply, Maddy said, "My father certainly seems to think so."

"Why would they do that?" Mia asked.

"To get rid of us once and for all," Carla said.

Mia shook her head. "That's ridiculous. The government doesn't just wipe people out because they're inconvenient."

"Tell that to the native Americans." Fournier spoke from several feet away, attracting the attention of the detainees lingering on the fringe.

"This is hardly the same set of circumstances. There would be nothing to gain from it."

"On the contrary." Fournier had joined them, but he didn't lower his voice. "Do you think it's a coincidence that Philip Singh just happened to know what the army planned to do?"

198

"The *army* is not going to blow up the pier!" Mia was getting agitated.

"Undoubtedly, the *entire* army is unaware of what a small faction is planning. If it were me, I'd go after the pylons supporting the structure. Everyone knows they're unstable. It'll be one of history's biggest tragedies, a horrible accident, like the Hindenburg or Titanic."

Scott glanced at Alton. Fournier was putting into words exactly what they'd suspected. They needed to shut him up, though, because the last thing they wanted was for him to give the already unsettled crowd the provocation it needed to spiral into complete anarchy.

In his ear, he heard Shasta tell Singh if he didn't want to die with the rest of them, he'd have to call off whoever it was that had ordered the destruction of the pier.

Singh laughed bitterly. "If he knew I was here, he'd probably blow it up that much faster."

"That's what happens when you blackmail people into doing your dirty work for you," Unger said. "Who is it? Colonel Carter? Lo, get him on the com."

"Um…I can't seem to get a signal anymore."

Singh's voice was full of despair. "No witnesses. No survivors."

"What the hell does that mean?" Unger snapped.

"It means," Lo said, "that the cell towers are down. We can't call for help. No one can."

Chapter Fifty-seven

Bryn wanted to agree with Mia that the army wouldn't do something so heinous, but Mia had a history of denying things that later turned out to be true. She also wanted to believe that the army was here to protect them and that even a 'small faction' wouldn't be so corrupt as to follow such a horrendous order. It was terrifying to think that any minute the ground beneath her feet might crumble into the Hudson River.

The crowd surrounding them had moved subtly closer. A fresh buzz of interest seemed to have sprouted up out of nowhere as more and more faces turned towards the group around the UAAV. Bryn caught a glimpse of the thin man walking among the detainees, which was puzzling, since he seemed so averse to making eye contact, she'd assumed he was autistic or something.

Fournier looked as if he was about to continue his rant, but Scott shifted the gun so it was pointed in his direction and said, "Shut it."

"What are you going to do? Shoot him?" Nicola cried. "Maybe he's just saying what you won't admit – that we're screwed!"

She burst out crying, and Fournier put his good arm around her. Then it seemed like everyone began talking at once.

Bryn stood next to Scott in a bubble of silence. She snuck a hand into his damp back pocket, noticing for the first time that he'd put his own clothes back on. It seemed like this might be a good opportunity, if not her last opportunity, to tell him how she felt. She shifted her weight until their hips were touching and said, "I heard you last night."

He looked down at her, eyebrows raised. "You did?"

She nodded.

"Oh. Why didn't you say anything?"

She lifted a shoulder. "I just figured if you wanted me to hear it, you would have told me when I was awake."

He let out a little laugh. "It *was* kinda chickenshit, wasn't it?"

"Kinda."

"I meant it, though."

She smiled. "Good."

He put a hand to her cheek and bent his head. The instant their lips touched, her quills went flat to her head and she leaned in, desperate to make it last. When he pulled away, he murmured, "We'll get out of this."

"I know we will," she whispered.

Behind him, the door to the UAAV opened. Shasta ducked out but stood on the running board looking down at them. "We need ideas and we need them fast. Singh says we've got a little over an hour."

"I say we fight our way out," Scott said. "Attack the barricade."

Several people raised their voices in support.

"There're only six of us," Shasta replied.

"Excuse me," Maddy said, "but we number in the thousands."

Shasta glanced down at Scott's submachine gun. "They've got all the firepower."

Scott pulled two guns out of the back of his jeans and handed one to Shasta. Then he deliberately turned to Maddy and gave her the second one. She accepted it with a dignified lift of her chin. "Thank you. For your trust."

Scott turned back to Shasta. "There's more where that came from in the bus, and the UAAV's stocked up, too."

"We've got the zook," Jason said.

"And they've got tear gas," Shasta replied. "Couple of canisters and it's game over."

"We've got four gas masks on board," Lo said.

Jason put a hand on Shasta's shoulder. "All we need is to create a hole big enough for one of us to get out. Tell the world what's going on here."

Shasta looked torn, but only briefly. "It really is the only way, isn't it? And at least this way, the Army can't keep ignoring us."

Everything happened quickly after that. The XIA agents mobilized in a matter of minutes, deciding where to hit the barrier, and distributing the weapons and what protective gear they had among the Mad Eye and XBestia. Scott ran off with Maddy and a group of men to the bus. Instead of impeding their progress, the crowd parted to let them through, cheering them on. The field swelled with detainees as the ones who'd been hanging out near the barricade vacated the area.

Jason came out of the UAAV with what looked like a portable rocket launcher slung across his back. He and the others were waiting for Scott to reach the bus, get the guns, and then give the signal from the ramp. Bryn stood with him and Mia, chewing nervously on a fingernail.

"So, Doc," he said casually. "You never did say what kind of graft you got."

"No, I didn't," Mia responded.

The disappointment that crossed Jason's face came and went so swiftly Bryn almost thought she imagined it. It occurred to her that he really liked Mia, who was as cool and distant as ever. Bryn didn't really know her that well; maybe she had a boyfriend – but then again, she couldn't imagine the germophobic doctor ever kissing Jason the way Bryn had just kissed Scott.

With a flash of comprehension, she turned to her. "*That's* why you got it!"

Bryn couldn't see Mia's expression behind the mask, but her eyes widened. "I'd rather not discuss it."

"Oh, really?" Bryn said. "What if you die without ever knowing what it's like?"

"What what's like?" Jason asked.

Bryn knew it wasn't her place to expose Mia's secret, but she couldn't let it go. "Tell him."

Mia closed her eyes. When she opened them again, she seemed resigned. "It's a Gila monster."

"What?" Jason exclaimed. "Why would you do that? Don't you know what it'll do to you?"

Mia's head went back. "I was *hoping* it would…help me."

He frowned and started to respond, but then the confusion cleared from his face as understanding dawned. "Ohhh," he breathed. "Yeah. Yeah, it'll definitely help with the—the germ thing."

"I just want to enjoy being touched," Mia's thick voice gave away her emotional state, and Bryn suddenly wished she were anywhere but witnessing this.

Someone shouted, "There they are!" and they all looked up at the ramp, where Scott and the others were holding the guns up in triumph.

Jason started backing away, but he pointed at Mia, eyebrows raised. "We'll discuss this later." Then he flashed an unabashed grin and joined Shasta and the ragtag team of xenos as they headed across the field.

Chapter Fifty-eight

Scott had only been a Marine for a day, but basic training had pounded home several fundamental rules, the most obvious being 'know your enemy.' As he approached the barricade and the soldiers patrolling it, he had to reconcile himself to the fact that he was about to turn on his own. The soldiers were only following orders, but it was the orders that made them the enemy.

The barricade was constructed mainly out of sandbags and barbed wire, built across the main entrance to the pier. Scott and the men and women with him on the ramp stopped just outside the tunnel entrance, while Jason and the others waited in the interior corridor. Shasta strode unarmed into the open and approached the nearest soldier.

"Stay back!" he called.

She stopped. "My name is Shasta Fox. I'm a senior agent with the XIA. Are you aware that this pier is going to be blown up in a little over an hour?"

"We have orders not to talk to any of you. Please back away from the barricade."

"There are thousands of innocent people here. I have reason to believe your commanding officer has been compromised."

The soldier's lips tightened. "Oh, yeah?"

"Yeah," Shasta said. "And I'd be happy to say that to his face."

The plan was for her to goad one of them into calling command, but Scott didn't think it would work. The detainees had no doubt spent the entire day unsuccessfully appealing to these same soldiers.

"Go on, *get!*" The soldier lifted his rifle and looked through his scope at her. It was meant to be a threat, but she didn't even blink. Then a lone shot rang out. For a moment, Scott thought the soldier jerked back from recoil when he'd fired at Shasta, but then he saw one of the xenos with Jason standing with arm outstretched, holding a smoking gun. He'd fired the first shot, hitting the soldier in the shoulder.

The other three soldiers raised their weapons as Shasta turned and ran, yelling, "Hold your fire! Hold your fire!"

The undisciplined Mad Eye and XBestia gang members ignored her. The soldiers took cover behind the barricade as bullets flew. Scott swore. They only had a limited amount of ammunition, and at this rate, the fight would be over before it began. When Shasta rounded the corner into the shelter of the corridor, Jason stepped out and knelt down, the zook resting on his shoulder. Their only chance was to blow the barricade and overwhelm the soldiers with sheer numbers.

"Fire in the hole!" Jason shouted.

Chapter Fifty-nine

Bryn stood by the UAAV with Mia, hands shoved deep in her pockets, fingers clenched so tightly her nails dug painfully into her palms. Word of the breakout attempt had spread. The detainees who'd camped out inside the structure abandoned their sites and wandered out onto the field. She'd never seen so many people in one place.

A huge contingent of men in orange jumpsuits had gathered outside the corridor leading to the barricade. For some reason, the prisoners had nominated themselves as the second wave, behind the agents and armed xenos. She didn't know why they were willing to risk their lives on what amounted to a rumor, but maybe their choice wasn't about the possibility of the pier blowing up. Maybe they just saw this as an opportunity to *really* break out of jail instead of just being 'free' on the pier. Either way, she was grateful for them – their jumpsuits would make bright targets. As soon as the thought occurred to her, she was ashamed of herself, but in her desperation, she couldn't help it; anything that might attract a bullet otherwise intended for Scott got her approval.

She wasn't able to see much of the action to begin with, but after the explosion sent a cloud of dust rolling out onto the field, all she could do was listen in fear and dread.

Gunfire and screams.

Somehow, she knew those sounds would occupy her dreams for weeks – assuming she survived this.

Mia was staring at her holophone, obsessively watching the clock tick down. The cloud of dust cleared, only to be replaced by another cloud, a greenish one. Just as Shasta predicted, the army used tear gas grenades that sent hundreds of xenos running away from the action. In no time at all it became obvious the agents' gambit had failed. The question remained whether anyone had managed to escape.

The injured began trickling back onto the field, and the detainees once again turned towards the UAAV looking for answers.

Bryn noticed the thin man talking to Fournier moments before he approached her. He raised his eyes to her face briefly before looking back at the ground. "Tell them who you are."

"What?"

She flinched away when he reached out, but all he did was push the hood of her coat off her quills. As if he'd flipped some kind of switch, people began murmuring and crowding even closer.

"It *is* her!" Someone said.

"Savvy was right! Bryn's here!"

Bryn knew that pretty much everyone had heard of her, but their reaction was odd, especially under the circumstances. What did it matter if she were here? On the pier, she was just another xeno. And Savvy? What did they mean when they said he was right? Then with a flash of insight, she realized who the thin man must be. She looked around, but he'd ducked his head inside the UAAV and was talking with Lo. Then, somewhat to Bryn's surprise, Lo invited him inside.

Bryn didn't want to turn back around; she practically felt the crowd staring at the back of her head in expectation. But expectation of what?

A few minutes later, Lo scrambled out of the UAAV, face tense with excitement. Above her, the holosphere had appeared like a huge blue bubble over the vehicle.

"We've got a plan. See that building?" She pointed to a nearby skyscraper, one of the few in Lower Manhattan with lights shining out of some of its windows. "It's obviously got a backup generator, right? Savvy located their wifi signal and rigged the UAAV's antenna to piggyback on it. We can send a live stream!"

"Will anyone see it?" Bryn asked.

"Right now, Savvy's jacking into a broadcast channel with millions of viewers."

Bryn and Mia exchanged a hopeful look. When Bryn turned back to Lo, the older woman was holding a holophone out. "Here. You're on, kiddo."

"What? No! Have Savvy do it."

"We need to appeal for help, and he spent the last two days riling everyone up against xenos. They're not going to listen to him if he does an about-face. Besides, he's autistic, he *can't* do it."

"But why me?"

"Who else?" Lo said earnestly. "They *know* you. Talk to them, Bryn!"

Chapter Sixty

They'd never even had a chance. If the soldiers hadn't for the most part been avoiding kill shots, it would have been a massacre.

Scott staggered back onto the field, one arm around Shasta and other around Alton. He wasn't sure who was helping whom; they'd all been hit. Both Scott and Alton had taken rounds in the chest – stopped by their vests – but Shasta had been hit in the lower leg.

The zook shell had taken out the sandbag barricade as planned, but before any of them had a chance to test the breach, tanks had moved in, forming a barrier of their own. The soldiers hadn't bothered to fire the big guns, though – didn't need to. Just as Shasta predicted, they'd simply launched a tear gas canister or two and began picking off the coughing, gagging xenos at their leisure. Scott had fit his gas mask over his face in time, but it hadn't made any difference.

He'd like to think things might have gone differently if the xenos hadn't panicked and started shooting, but the truth was: the army had swatted them like flies. It was a miracle they were still alive. The aftermath left the tunnel and corridor in chaos. Men in orange jumpsuits lay everywhere. He'd only found Alton and Shasta by talking to them through the earbugs. He hadn't seen Maddy fall but had no idea where she'd gone.

He expected to see the detainees on the field running around like someone had stuck a firecracker in their anthill, but most of them were standing still, gazing towards the center of the pier. When Scott saw what they were looking at, he stumbled and nearly fell, pulling Alton and Shasta to an abrupt stop with him. Lo had activated the holosphere again and Bryn's face stared out at the crowd. She looked terrified, but then she swallowed visibly and began to talk.

"Hi. Um, I'm Bryn Vega, and I don't have a lot of time. *We* don't have a lot of time. They tell me this broadcast is streaming live on the interweb, and it's pretty much our last hope, so that's who I'm talking to now. The people out there who aren't stuck here on Poppy's Pier with me and just about every other xeno in New York City. If you saw the news helicopter footage, then you know the army rounded us up and dumped us here. Anyway, I need to tell you two things. First off, and I know this is gonna sound crazy, but," she stopped and took a deep breath, "they're going to blow up the pier and kill everyone on it in about an hour. Um, I guess we have a—a clip that'll prove how we know it's true."

Bryn's face disappeared, to be replaced by Unger in the UAAV.

"This is Deputy Director Mark Unger of the XIA. With me is Senior Agent Shasta Fox. Behind me is the body of Congressman Darrell Abbott, who was kidnapped along with me from his car in the Holland Tunnel and brought to Poppy's Pier, where we are recording this message. Unknown conspirators allowed our attackers to bring us onto the pier, and Congressman Abbott was subsequently beaten to death. This holo is date and time stamped and what follows is the taped statement of Philip Singh."

The holo changed to Singh's face. He was sitting in the UAAV, still dressed in Maddy's ridiculous suit.

"State your name and occupation, and acknowledge that you've been read your rights," Unger said.

"My name is Philip Singh, CEO of Novusimha International. I've been read my rights, but I'm offering this statement under extreme duress," he looked off camera insolently. "It's not a confession."

"Duress?" Unger sounded incensed. "Of your own creation. Go on."

"I happen to be privy to a plan to destroy the infrastructure of the pier where the xenos are being detained."

Scott noticed he worded his statement very carefully. He'd only admitted to knowing about the plan, when it was very likely he'd had a lot more to do with it than that. He also made it sound like he wasn't even on the pier.

"What kind of explosives and detonation?" Unger asked.

"I wasn't informed about the explosives, but they're on timers. Can't be stopped now. Key supporting pylons will be destroyed, and the pier is expected to collapse into the river in a little over an hour."

Scott had to give it to Fournier, he'd predicted the method exactly.

"Who gave the order?" Unger asked.

Singh lifted his head but refused to answer.

"Why is the pier being targeted?" It was Shasta's voice.

Again, Singh didn't respond.

Bryn's face reappeared and she looked startled for a moment before composing herself.

"The second thing you need to know is about the super typhoid. It's true it's spread through the air by xenos, but only those with—" she turned, and Mia's face appeared in the background. Mia said quietly, "Crocodilian, which includes alligator, but that's unsubstantiated."

"Right," Bryn continued. "We've been told that any xeno with a crocodile or alligator graft might be a carrier. It doesn't mean they are, just that they might be if they were exposed. Xenos with other grafts don't appear to spread it. So please…stop the violence."

Scott urged Shasta and Alton to keep walking. He thought Bryn would end the transmission now that she'd delivered the message, but she seemed to have gathered her courage, and kept on talking.

"I think a lot of you know who I am. The girl whose own father…well…" she gestured to her head and a sprinkling of xenos in the crowd laughed. "But knowing my story doesn't mean you know *me*. And seeing someone with a xenograft doesn't mean you know what kind of person they are. I'm not going to lecture you on tolerance. You either have it, or you don't. I grew up with the most intolerant parent ever, and yet, somehow I—I try not to judge. Maybe I never would have chosen this life, and for sure my donor didn't give its life willingly or knowingly, but my graft has given me a—a gift.

"Xenografts aren't just an extreme form of body art. That's how it started out; as a fad or a statement, but it turns out there's more to it, and us being immune to the typhoid is only the beginning.

"Thing is…there are people who didn't want me to know that. People I should have been able to trust. But I'm no scientist – I have to rely on experts to explain the complicated stuff. And I have no way of knowing if they're keeping information from me or lying for their own benefit. The only thing I can do to protect myself from misinformation is to question what I'm told and keep an open mind. Because if there's one thing I've learned, it's that I have to find my own truth."

The crowd nearest Bryn was thick, but they'd left a big open space around her. Scott, Shasta and Alton pushed their way through to the front. Bryn saw him and her eyes shone with unshed tears.

"Anyway," she said. "In case we don't get out of this, at least you know what really happened here. Thanks for listening…"

The holosphere disappeared, the crowd burst into applause, and Bryn ran into Scott's arms.

Chapter Sixty-one

The first indication that the broadcast had been seen was the news helicopters. This time there were five of them, maneuvering for space above the pier.

Fifteen minutes later, the first boat showed up. It was a privately-owned tugboat, and the captain and his two crewmen wore blue face masks. They took as many xenos as they could carry, with the exception of anyone wearing an orange jumpsuit. After that, boat after boat appeared; barges, tour boats, ferries and trawlers. The evacuation of the detainees was unscripted and unauthorized, but the army did nothing to stop them.

Half an hour after the broadcast, special units had been mobilized and soldiers swarmed onto the pier. The prisoners, including Bluto, were rapidly and efficiently shuttled into the prison transport buses and driven away, while the remaining detainees were herded off the pier and onto the Hudson River Greenway.

The UAAV, driven by Lo as usual, with Boardman in the passenger seat, took Shasta, whose gun-shot leg had been field-dressed by Mia, as well as Fournier, Singh, Dundee, and Congressman Abbott's body. The rest walked behind as it drove off the field and onto the street beyond the pier.

Bryn laced her fingers with Scott's, Jason stayed close to Mia's side, Nicola walked between Carla and Savvy, and Unger took up the rear with Padme.

Maddy had disappeared.

Lo pulled up next to the surveillance vehicle Shasta had been driving. The keys had been taken from Shasta, but luckily the vehicle had keyless entry and start capability. Unger got into the driver's seat, Jason sat shotgun, and everyone else piled in. There weren't enough seats for everyone, but they made do by doubling up or sitting on the floor. Nicola cried out happily when she saw Perky's birdcage. Scott lifted a black box from one of the seats and set it on the floor to make room for Bryn.

Soldiers directed them north along West Street, but they'd only gone a couple hundred yards when a series of muted *booms* resonated through the ground and shook the vehicle. No sooner had the tremors subsided when a throbbing roar began to build, shuddering through the air and the street like an earthquake.

The surveillance van was solid along its sides, but Bryn was seated to the rear of the vehicle with a clear view out the back windows. She gaped at the pier, lit quite dramatically by spotlights from the news helicopters.

The remaining windows in the structure surrounding the pier shattered as the infrastructure collapsed. The walls crumbled and the roof of the building – the parking lot – caved in. Billowing dust rose into the air, mingled with steam from the bonfires, rapidly extinguished by rushing water. The side of the pier parallel to the river sank rapidly, and displaced water created a mini tsunami that radiated out from the epicenter. Waves crashed into the seawall and flooded the road.

"My God." Mia sounded awestruck and humbled. "It really happened."

Soldiers they'd driven by moments before caught up to them on foot. As one of them ran past, he waved his arms wildly and shouted, "The road's collapsing! Move it, move it, *move it*!"

The UAAV took off, and Unger pushed his foot down on the electrigas pedal, squealing the van's tires and driving down the street until they encountered another roadblock. He pulled up next to the UAAV and they just sat there, stunned, as the dusty aftermath of the pier's collapse drifted through the air and blanketed the vehicles.

After a few minutes, a man in fatigues appeared out of the haze, cut across the front of the vehicle through the headlight beams, and made his way to Unger's window. He rapped his knuckles on the window, and Unger rolled it down. Bryn didn't recognize him at first because of his face mask, but when he spoke, his voice gave him away as the colonel who'd addressed the detainees through the holosphere.

"You are Deputy Director Unger of the XIA, is that correct?"

"Yes."

"I'm Colonel Jeremy Carter. Sir, on behalf of the United States Army, I'd like to thank you for your warning. This would have been a terrible tragedy if you hadn't gotten word out. Is Philip Singh in your custody?"

"I'm not releasing him to you."

Colonel Carter's white eyebrows shot up. "I'm afraid that's not your call. And…need I remind you that members of your team attacked a

211

National Guard unit this evening? Some of my men were injured. I'd be well within my rights to arrest all of you."

Mia stood and made her way to the front of the van, pulling her face mask down to hang around her neck. She reached across Unger to stick her hand out the window. Colonel Carter shook it as she introduced herself. "Doctor Mia Padilla with the CDC. My team was dispatched to identify the pathogen and verify its mode of transmission, which we've done. Patient zero is in that vehicle." She jerked her thumb at the UAAV. "Philip Singh is sitting next to him, which normally wouldn't be a problem, because Singh is protected by a xenograft. However, if you listened to the broadcast, you'll know that we strongly believe the carriers of this disease are xenos with crocodile or alligator grafts. Unfortunately, Singh has one such graft. Being as how he's definitely been exposed to the bacterium, the CDC will be quarantining him for an indefinite period of time."

The colonel didn't look convinced, but Unger jumped in before he could respond. "We have several injured agents and witnesses who need to get to a hospital. I respectfully request that you back the hell down."

Bryn wasn't sure swearing at the man was the best tack for Unger to take, but Colonel Carter surprised her.

"Look. I don't like to admit this, but I've been second-guessing orders all day. My superior officer told me specifically that your warning was a hoax. If my men hadn't seen a SEAL dive team enter the water several hours ago, I would have followed his orders and ignored it. But nothing that's happened today was sitting right with me, and I couldn't do it. Damned glad I didn't, either, because I probably would have blown my brains out if I'd been responsible for all those deaths.

"I don't know what the deal is with Singh. I'm supposed to take him into custody, but I'm not going to. The piss is going to trickle down all over me no matter what I do at this point, so I'm just going to keep doing what I think is right."

He stepped back and signaled to his soldiers to let them pass. Unger offered a jaunty little salute and then accelerated past him. Bryn heard his sigh of relief all the way at the rear of the van.

As soon as Mia sat back down, she rummaged through her purse for the hand sanitizer. Then she asked Jason to use the van's equipment to contact her team. However, it wasn't until they'd driven within the sphere of a working cell tower that he was able to get through. Mia directed her people to assemble at Middleborough Hospital, advising them to initiate quarantine protocol. After that, she contacted the coroner's office about Abbott's body.

Unger spent the rest of the ride on the phone conducting agency business. Bryn tuned him out while Scott dozed next to her, snoring lightly.

Nicola was sitting cross-legged on the floor with the birdcage on her lap. She had a hand stuck through the door and the grey bird sat on her hand while she rubbed the feathers on its head with her thumb. She looked up at Carla.

"You seem familiar."

"She should," Padme said.

Carla shot Padme a warning look, but Nicola had already latched onto the hint and come to the correct conclusion. "Arc you Mouse?"

"My name is Carla, but yes, they call me Mouse."

Nicola beamed. "Hi."

Carla smiled back, shaking her head fondly. "You look so much like her."

Nicola set the bird on its perch, took her hand out of the cage, and deliberately shut and latched the little door. "I know her name was Miranda McKim…but who was she?"

Carla made a regretful face like she wasn't going to tell her, but Bryn spoke up. "She was Carla's best friend. And my mother."

Nicola swung her head around, eyes wide. "Really?"

"Really."

"That's…" Nicola stopped and considered it. "What does that make us?"

Bryn laughed a little. "I have no idea."

"But family, though, right?" Nicola asked. "I've never had a family. It was always just Dad and me."

Bryn still didn't know how she felt about the situation, but she didn't want to be responsible for crushing the hope in Nicola's eyes. She reached out and put a hand on the girl's shoulder.

"Definitely family."

Chapter Sixty-two

When they arrived at the hospital emergency bay, Mia's team met them decked out in hazmat suits. Mia got out of the van first, and one of her team members helped her into a suit of her own. Only then did she direct them to let the passengers out of the vehicles – all but Boardman, Dundee and Singh.

Fournier and Shasta were taken away in wheelchairs. Scott and the others were escorted into a large room marked 'Quarantine.' Against one wall, there was an empty hospital bed with a blue curtain hanging from the ceiling on a pull-track. The rest of the room was just an open space with plastic chairs, except for a small table in one corner with bottled water and snacks on it, and a holovision mounted on the wall. A line quickly formed to use the one attached bathroom.

Nicola set Perky's cage down on the snack table and refilled the bird's water dish.

"Well, this is nice," Lo said, looking around at the sterile white walls. "Homey."

Carla opened a packet of crackers and stuffed one into her mouth, speaking around it. "Better than the pier."

"Let's can the chit-chat," Unger said brusquely. "I've got some pretty big gaps in my knowledge of what went down today."

He grabbed the back of two chairs and dragged them to the far corner of the room near the bathroom door, then went back to get two more. He switched the holovision on and said, "You four." He indicated Carla, Nicola, Savvy and Padme. "Sit over here so I can talk to my agents in private. You can watch holovision."

Bryn obviously wasn't an agent, but Unger seemed to want to include her. Scott sat wearily next to her with the 3D printer in his lap. He'd taken it from the UAAV because Shasta wouldn't want him to let it out of his sight.

They spent the next half hour filling the deputy director in on their eventful day. In the background, the holovision had been tuned to a news channel. Every once in a while, they stopped talking to watch coverage of the disaster at Poppy's Pier.

It was during one such break that Scott caught a glimpse of someone familiar standing on the deck of a tugboat. He jumped up and strode over to the holo, sweeping his hand to reverse it.

"Well, what do you know," Lo said. "Maddy Singh, on the run."

Scott looked at Padme. She seemed neither surprised nor betrayed that Maddy had left her behind. Padme glanced at Nicola and answered Scott's unspoken question. "It was my decision not to go. Just in case Fournier was telling the truth."

Not long after that, Mia arrived with two women in white lab coats and a man in blue scrubs. She was no longer dressed in the Hazmat suit, but they all wore face masks and gloves. The man pushed a portable device on wheels over to the hospital bed.

Nicola stood. "How's my Dad?"

"He and Agent Fox are in surgery," Mia replied. "This is Doctor Bales and Doctor Knox." She indicated the two women. Then she walked over to Nicola.

"Your father said you were sick. What can you tell me about that?"

Nicola's brows came together in uncertainty. She turned to Padme, who shook her head and said, "I didn't know until he told us on the bus."

"Felson?" Nicola asked.

Savvy stared down at his clenched hands, rocking back and forth slightly. "He told me not to tell."

"What's wrong with me?" she asked tearfully.

"The woman you were cloned from wasn't healthy," he replied. "So neither are you."

Nicola looked across the room at Bryn. "What was wrong with her?"

"It was her heart," Bryn said.

Scott shifted in his seat. He and Bryn had wondered how Fournier managed to raise Nicola down in the facility under the Warehouse. He must have kept her from watching the news, or she would know Bryn's story – and what happened to Miranda Vega.

Nicola blinked a few times. "Well, that's not too big a deal, right? I mean, major surgery sucks, but I can get a—a pig heart."

Mia nodded. "Yes, if it turns out to be necessary, that's definitely an option. The thing is, your father made a comment earlier that we would like to investigate." She turned to Padme. "Would you agree to a holosound?"

Padme practically leapt up out of the chair. "Yes…please!"

215

The doctors directed her to lie down on the hospital bed, and then they pulled the curtain. Scott and the others could hear everything they said, up to the point when their voices were replaced by the sound of a beating heart. They spoke in hushed whispers after that. One of the doctors rushed out and came back several minutes later with a man whose lab coat covered a business suit. They disappeared behind the curtain and he heard her introduce the man to Padme. "This is our chief of surgery, Doctor Gellar."

After a few minutes of silence, a man's deep voice said, "Extraordinary. I went to medical school with Nicolas Fournier. He was a brilliant man, but disturbed. This is…if it's a *human* heart, it's absolutely ground-breaking. Look at the umbilical cord and the stunted circulatory system. It's so…graceful…I've never seen anything like it."

Scott caught Bryn exchanging a look with Carla, who smiled and held both thumbs up.

"What's going on?" he asked quietly.

"He did it," Bryn said, voice laced with admiration. "Remember what my dad said in jail? That cloned organs would eventually be grown in host bodies? Fournier grew Nicola a new heart."

Chapter Sixty-three

Since it was late and no one was going to be released any time soon, hospital staff pushed cots into the quarantine room for them. Bryn didn't think she'd be able to sleep, but she passed out soon after her head hit the pillow.

By morning, nothing had been resolved, but Unger assured them things would happen quickly or he'd know the reason why. Shasta was reportedly up and about on crutches already, efficiently conducting agency business from a borrowed holophone.

The first thing to be decided was that Padme should be admitted to the hospital. Apparently, experts from all over the US were converging on the hospital to examine her. She was moved to a private room in order for them to determine what to do with the cloned heart growing in her uterus. When Doctor Gellar had asked her, she told him if the heart was viable, and as long as it didn't endanger her life, she would continue to be its incubator – for Nicola's sake.

Bryn didn't really know what to think about that. Padme had always been an enigma.

Fournier had come out of surgery but was still unconscious. He was in serious but stable condition and wouldn't be fit to answer any questions for another day at least.

He had a lot to answer for. There was no doubt he would spend a good portion of the rest of his life in prison, but among the doctors at Middleborough Hospital at least, he was a celebrity. Once word of his astonishing accomplishments got out, he would certainly be respected worldwide.

Bryn thought it ironic that the man widely known as the Bestia Butcher, a modern-day Doctor Frankenstein, could have taken a concept straight out of the pages of a science fiction novel into the realm of reality. Given the things he'd told her about government corruption, it struck her that maybe only someone as twisted and ruthless as Fournier could have done it.

"*Chaos begets change,*" he'd said, but despite the chaos he'd caused, she didn't think much *would* change. It seemed to her that even before any given problem was rooted out, another was waiting to take its place. The whole 'history is doomed to repeat itself' thing would always keep people scrambling.

Thinking of change brought Dundee to mind. He'd wanted her to believe he'd become a different person after getting his crocodile eyes. He'd vehemently defended Fournier; telling them his boss had unleashed the typhoid not to kill anyone, but with the express purpose of finding out how it spread. Perhaps that was partially true. Bryn figured with Fournier's fondness for chaos, he probably had more than one reason for doing the things he'd done. In the end, though, he'd been caught. But so had Singh.

She hoped Singh and Dundee would spend a good long time in quarantine. On the other hand, Boardman was stuck in there, too. She wondered what would happen if they had their grafts surgically removed. Would it reverse the process? If that was the answer to stopping the spread of the disease, she assumed Boardman and Singh, at least, would agree to it. But what about Dundee? It was very unlikely he'd consent to being made blind again.

Still, like Fournier, he faced a lifetime of incarceration for his crimes. Maybe they'd put him in solitary confinement, where he'd be able to see, but not see any*one*.

At least Mia was encouraged that her team seemed to be on the verge of proving Fournier right – something about the influence of a crocodilian graft on its human host created the perfect incubator and delivery system for the mutated typhoid. She'd consulted with local officials on how best to handle the rounding up of potential carriers, but area hospitals had already reported that dozens of xenos with crocodile and alligator grafts had turned themselves in.

At some point during the night, Singh must have been allowed a phone call, because his attorneys – three of them – arrived at the hospital, and from what Bryn heard, were lurking in the corridors like a trio of hungry vultures. They would no doubt begin harassing the hospital's legal advisors as soon as they arrived, which, given the state of the city, might not be any time soon.

The city did seem to be settling down, though. Experts had popped up all over the news, citing statistics that suggested this kind of unrest was self-limiting. The near tragedy of the collapse of Poppy's Pier appeared to be the event that turned the tide. Pro-xeno sentiment was on the rise, and stories supporting the notion that xenos were immune to more than just the typhoid abounded.

Unger was furious that they'd blown their chance of bringing Singh to justice. Abbott had been his only witness, and the congressman's death crippled the investigation. The DA would never agree to prosecute without his testimony. Even the attack on Maddy's yacht, or later, the attack on the bus that caused Malone's death, couldn't be linked to Singh with no physical evidence and none of his men in custody. All they had was the word of four 'rogue' agents – and that of Bryn and Mia. In fact, Unger seemed resigned to the high probability that once Singh realized he was in the clear, he would take action against the XIA for destroying his yacht. With the man's unlimited resources, his legal team would bury them.

"But he admitted he knew about the pier," Bryn said.

"So?" Unger snapped. "He can say anything. He overheard strangers talking about it. Whatever."

Even though Unger's terse response seemed to have been designed to shut her down, she plucked up her courage and said, "Remember what I told you on the pier, though? About the corporation that bought the xenofarms and the disposal company? Can't you link that back to him? I mean, why else would he want to kill all those xenos? Every one of them had an older graft, right? They were immune to stuff. Maybe that's why he wanted to wipe them all out."

Unger's forbidding expression eased as he gave it a moment's thought. "Maybe. Assuming what Fournier told you was true."

Savvy pointed to the printer in Scott's lap. "The proof is right there."

"In the printer?" Unger looked skeptical.

"On the hard drive," Savvy said. "I'll show you."

"But first," Nicola put in, "we talk about making a deal for my dad."

Chapter Sixty-four

Scott had slept a little but was still punchy from exhaustion by the time they were cleared to leave the hospital. Unger managed first thing to arrange an impromptu meeting with the DA. He took Savvy – and the printer – with him in the surveillance van. Hospital staff had contacted Children's Protective Services to deal with Nicola, and Carla opted to stay behind to talk to them.

"What can you do?" Bryn asked.

Carla shrugged. "I'm her birth mother. That's gotta count for something, right? Maybe I can keep her out of the system."

The sun was high in the sky when Scott, Bryn, Lo and Alton walked out to the UAAV. Lo had just started it when Mia knocked on the passenger side window. Alton hastily rolled it down.

"I, um, don't have any way to get back to my hotel," Mia said. "My rental car's still parked out in front of Fournier's den. I don't suppose I could catch a ride?"

"We're going to headquarters to pick up our cars," Alton replied. "I'd be glad to give you a ride from there."

Mia nodded and climbed aboard. Scott caught Bryn hiding a smile and asked quietly, "What's that all about?"

"I think she likes him," Bryn whispered.

"Oh, yeah? Well, I happen to know it's mutual."

She laughed and leaned her head on the back of the seat, rolling it languidly towards him until her lips were only inches away from his. Whether she intended it as an invitation or not, he took advantage. Her mouth tasted like coffee and something sweet, like honey. He wanted to savor the moment, but they weren't alone, so he reluctantly backed off.

"Later, okay?"

She smiled again and bit her lip, eyebrows raised in promise.

There was more traffic on the roads today, an indication that things were getting back to normal. When they arrived at XIA Headquarters, the building security company had dispatched a team of armed guards to supervise a construction crew as they began clean-up and repairs.

Scott got a glimpse of the destroyed stairwell and thought about Bob. The duty of notifying Bob's family of his death had fallen to Shasta. He hoped she told them he'd been brave in his final hour.

In the parking garage, Lo stopped for a moment to look at the burnt-out husk that had been assigned to her. She made a wry face at it. "Glad it wasn't my car. See you guys tomorrow."

She walked off with a little bounce in her step.

Bryn and Mia stared at each other for a long moment.

"Take care, okay?" Mia said.

"You, too."

"Lighten up," Alton said. "It's not like you'll never see each other again."

Mia looked up at him soberly. "I'm going back."

"To the CDC?" He seemed surprised. "Isn't that in Georgia or something?"

"Or something. My flight leaves tomorrow morning."

He flinched as if her bald statement stung him, but a businesslike mask slipped over his features. "Let's get going, then."

Scott took Bryn's hand to walk her over to his motorcycle, but she said, "Wait!"

Alton and Mia turned.

Bryn let go of Scott's hand and took a few steps towards Mia. "You're coming back, right?"

Mia hesitated. "I don't know."

Bryn nodded decisively and looked at Alton. "Don't let her push you away. It's a defense mechanism."

Mia frowned in indignation, but Alton only laughed.

"I'll take that under advisement." He reached out and chucked Bryn under the chin. "Maybe we can double-date."

Mia's cheeks turned bright pink, but she didn't protest. Bryn grinned and took Scott's hand again.

When Alton started up his ancient truck, exhaust filled the parking garage. Bryn waved goodbye as they drove past, but Scott coughed and waved his hand through the air sarcastically.

"Quit it!" she said, slapping at his hand and giggling. "He was undercover and needed a ride befitting a Mad Eye."

She lifted his helmet from the back of his bike and thumped him in the chest with it. Then she squinted and reached up to brush her fingers through his hair.

"You're missing a chunk right here."

"Am I? Probably the flame thrower."

"Ah. Of course."

He picked up her helmet. "I see you're missing a chunk yourself."

"That would be courtesy of the jerks who broke into your apartment."

He gently fit the helmet over her quills. "Maybe tomorrow will be a normal day."

"That would be nice for a change."

He drove a little faster than usual on the way back to his apartment. The door was still on its hinges, but the frame on the knob side was splintered. Someone had closed it for him, though, and it didn't look as if anything was missing.

Once he'd propped a chair up against it, he turned to Bryn. "I really need to get out of these clothes."

"Oh?" She looked interested.

"Yeah, they're dry now, but they chafed me something awful."

"Ouch." She moved in closer, reaching for the buttons on his shirt. "By the way," she said, looking up at him as the quills slowly went flat to her head. "I love you, too."

The end.